# THE
# FORTIETH
# DOOR

Mary Hastings Bradley

1st WORLD
LIBRARY
Literary Society

# The Fortieth Door

## Mary Hastings Bradley

© 1st World Library – Literary Society, 2004
PO Box 2211
Fairfield, IA 52556
www.1stworldlibrary.org
First Edition

LCCN: 2005901358

Softcover ISBN: 1-4218-1173-1
Hardcover ISBN: 1-4218-1073-5
eBook ISBN: 1-4218-1273-8

Purchase *"The Fortieth Door"*
as a traditional bound book at:
www.1stWorldLibrary.org/purchase.asp?ISBN=1-4218-1173-1

1st World Library Literary Society is a nonprofit organization dedicated to promoting literacy by:

- Creating a free internet library accessible from any computer worldwide.
- Hosting writing competitions and offering book publishing scholarships.

Readers interested in supporting literacy through sponsorship, donations or membership please contact:
literacy@1stworldlibrary.org
Check us out at: www.1stworldlibrary.ORG
and start downloading free ebooks today.

***The Fortieth Door***
*contributed by Tim, Ed & Rodney*
*in support of*
*1st World Library Literary Society*

TO
ARTHUR MILLS CORWIN

# CONTENTS

I. A RASH PROMISE ............................................................... 7

II. MASKS AND MASKERS ................................................. 15

III. IN THE PASHA'S PALACE .......................................... 36

IV. EXPLANATIONS ............................................................ 50

V. AT THE GARDEN GATE ............................................... 59

VI. A SECRET OF THE SANDS .......................................... 71

VII. TO McLEAN'S ASTONISHMENT .............................. 76

VIII. TEWFICK RECEIVES ................................................ 84

IX. A WEDDING PRESENT ............................................... 97

X. THE RECEPTION .......................................................... 107

XI. THE FORTY DOORS .................................................... 120

XII. THE UNINVITED GUEST .......................................... 129

XIII. THE BEY RETURNS .................................................. 140

XIV. WITHIN THE WALLS ............................................... 149

XV. UNDERGROUND ....................................................... 164

XVI. OUT OF THE DARKNESS ......................................... 174

XVII. AZIZA ....................................................................... 182

XVIII. AZIZA IS OFFENDED ............................................ 186

XIX. AN INTERRUPTION ................................................. 199

XX. BEYOND THE DOOR ................................................. 207

XXI. MISS JEFFRIES MAKES A CALL ............................... 221

XXII. FROM THE BAZAARS ............................................. 235

XXIII. IN THE DESERT ..................................................... 239

XXIV. THE TOMB OF A KING .......................................... 244

XXV. IN CAIRO ................................................................. 261

XXVI. THE PAINTED CASE .............................................. 271

# CHAPTER I

## A RASH PROMISE

He didn't want to go. He loathed the very thought of it. Every flinching nerve in him protested.

A masked ball - a masked ball at a Cairo hotel! Grimacing through peep-holes, self-conscious advances, flirtations ending in giggles! Tourists as nuns, tourists as Turks, tourists as God-knows-what, all preening and peacocking!

Unhappily he gazed upon the girl who was proposing this horror as a bright delight. She was a very engaging girl - that was the mischief of it. She stood smiling there in the bright, Egyptian sunshine, gay confidence in her gray eyes. He hated to shatter that confidence.

And he had done little enough for her during her stay in Cairo. One tea at the Gezireh Palace Hotel, one trip to the Sultan al Hassan Mosque, one excursion through the bazaars - not exactly an orgy of entertainment for a girl from home!

He had evaded climbing the Pyramids and fled from the ostrich farm. He had withheld from inviting her to the camp on the edge of the Libyan desert where he was excavating, although her party had shown unmistakable signs of a willingness to be diverted from the beaten path of its travel.

And he was not calling on her now. He had come to Cairo for supplies and she had encountered him by chance upon a corner of the crowded Mograby, and there promptly she had invited him to to-night's ball.

"But it's not my line, you know, Jinny," he was protesting. "I'm so fearfully out of dancing - "

"More reason to come, Jack. You need a change from digging up ruins all the time - it must be frightfully lonely out there on the desert. I can't think how you stand it."

Jack Ryder smiled. There was no mortal use in explaining to Jinny Jeffries that his life on the desert was the only life in the world, that his ruins held more thrills than all the fevers of her tourist crowds, and that he would rather gaze upon the mummied effigy of any lady of the dynasty of Amenhotep than upon the freshest and fairest of the damsels of the present day.

It would only tax Jinny's credulity and hurt her feelings. And he liked Jinny - though not as he liked Queen Hatasu or the little nameless creature he had dug out of a king's ante-room.

Jinny was an interfering modern. She was the incarnation of impossible demands.

But of course there was no real reason why he should not stop over and go to the dance.

\*   \*   \*   \*   \*

Ten minutes later, when she had extracted his promise and abandoned him to the costumers, he was scourging his weakness.

He had known better! Very well, then, let him take his medicine. Let him go as - here he disgustedly eyed the garment that the Greek was presenting - as Little Lord Fauntleroy! He deserved it.

Shudderingly he looked away from the pretty velvet suit; he scorned the monk's robes that were too redolent of former wearers; he rejected the hot livery of a Russian mujik; he flouted the banality of the Pierrot pantaloons.

Thankfully he remembered McLean. Kilts, that was the thing. Tartans, the real Scotch plaids. Some use, now, McLean's precious sporrans.... He'd look him up at once.

Out of the crowded Mograby he made his way on foot to the Esbekeyih quarters where the streets were wider and emptier of Cairene traffickers and shrill itinerates and laden camels and jostling donkeys.

It was a glorious day, a day of Egypt's blue and gold. The sky was a wash of water color; the streets a flood of molten amber. A little wind from the north rustled the acacias and blew in his bronzed face cool reminders of the widening Nile and dancing waves.

He remembered a chap he knew, who had a sailing canoe - but no, he was going to get a costume for a fool ball!

Disgustedly he turned into the very modern and official-looking residence that was the home of his friend, Andrew McLean, and the offices of that far-reaching institution, the Agricultural Bank.

A white-robed, red-sashed and red-fezed houseboy led him across the tiled entrance into the long room where McLean was concluding a conference with two men.

"Not the least trace," McLean was saying. "We've questioned all our native agents - "

Afterwards Ryder remembered that indefinite little pause. If the two men had not lingered - if McLean had not remembered that he was an excavator - if chance had not brushed the scales with lightning wings - !

"Ever hear of a chap called Delcasse, Paul Delcasse, a French excavator?" McLean suddenly asked of him. "Disappeared in the desert about fifteen years ago."

"He was reported, monsieur, to have died of the fever," one of the men explained.

McLean introduced him as a special agent from France. His companion was one of the secretaries of the French legation. They were trying every quarter for traces of this Delcasse.

Ryder's memory darted back to old library shelves. He saw a thin, brown volume, almost uncut....

"He wrote a book on the Tomb of Thi," he said suddenly. "Paul Delcasse - I remember it very well."

Now that he thought of it, the memory was clear. It was one of those books that had whetted his passion for the past, when his student mind was first kindling to buried cities and forgotten tombs and all the strange store and loot of time.

Paul Delcasse. He didn't remember a word of the book, but he remembered that he had read it with absorption. And now the special agent, delighted at the recognition, was talking eagerly of the writer.

"He was a brilliant young man, monsieur, but he was of no importance to his generation - and he becomes so now through the whim of a capricious woman to disinherit her other heirs. After all this time she has decided to make active inquiries."

"But you said that Delcasse had died - "

"He left a wife and child. Her letters of her husband's death reached his relatives in France, then nothing more. They feared that the same fever - but nothing, positively, was known.... A sad story, monsieur.... This Delcasse was young and adventurous and an ardent explorer. An ardent lover, too, for he brought a beautiful French wife to share the hazards of

MARY HASTINGS BRADLEY

his expedition - "

"An ardent idiot," thrust in McLean unfeelingly. "Knocking a woman about the desert.... Not much chance of a clue after all these years," he concluded with a very British air of dismissal.

But the French agent was not to be sundered from the American who remembered the book of Delcasse.

From his pocket he brought a leather case and from the case a large and ornate gold locket.

"His picture, monsieur." He pressed the spring and offered Ryder the miniature. "It was done in France before he returned on that last trip, and was left with the aunt. It is said to be a good likeness."

Ryder looked down upon the young face presented to his gaze with a feeling of sympathy for this unlucky searcher of the past who had left his own secret in the sands he had come to conquer - sympathy mingled with blank wonder at the insanity which had brought a woman with it....

McLean couldn't understand a man's doing it.

Jack Ryder couldn't understand a man's *wanting* to do it. Love to Ryder was incomprehensible idiocy. Woman, as far as he was concerned, had never been created. She was still a spectacle, an historical record, an uncomprehended motive.

"Nice looking chap," he commented briefly, fingering the curious old case as he handed it back.

"I'll keep up the inquiries," McLean assured them, "but, as I said, nothing will come of it.... It's been fifteen years. One more grain lost in the desert of sand.... By luck, you know, you might just stumble on something, some native who knew the story, but if fever carried them off and the Arabs rifled their camp, as I fancy, they'll jolly well keep their mouths shut. No white man will know.... I don't advise your people to spend much money on the search."

"Odd, the inquiries we get," he commented to Ryder when the Frenchmen had completed their courteous farewells. "You'd think the Bank was a Bureau of Information! Yesterday there was a stir about two crazy lads who are supposed to have joined the Mecca pilgrims in disguise.... Of course our clerks are Copts and *do* pick up a bit and the Copts will talk.... I say, Jack, what are you doing?" he broke off to demand in astonishment, for Jack Ryder had seated himself upon a divan and was absorbedly rolling up his trouser leg.

"The dear Egyptian flea?" he added.

"Not at all. I am looking at my knees," said Ryder glumly. "I just remembered that I have to show them to-night.... A ball - in masquerade. At a hotel. Tourist crowd.... How do you think they'll look with one of your Scotch plaidies atop?" he inquired feelingly.

"Fascinating, Jack, fascinating," said the promptly sardonic McLean. "You - at a masquerade!... So that's what brought you to town."

He cocked a taunting eye at him. "Well, well, she must be a most engaging young person - you'll be taking her out on the desert with you now, like our friend Delcasse - a pleasant, retired spot for a body to have his honeymoon ... no distractions of society ... undiluted companionship, you might say.... Now what made you think she'd like your knees?" he murmured contemplatively. "Aren't you just a bit - previous? Apt to startle and frighten the lady?"

"Oh, go on, go on," Ryder exhorted bitterly. "I like it. It's better than I can do myself. Go on.... But while you are talking trot out your tartans. Something clannish now - one of those ancestral rigs that you are always cherishing ... Rich and red, to set off my dark, handsome type."

"Set off you'll be, Jack dear," promised McLean, dragging out a huge chest. "Set off you'll be."

*   *   *   *   *

Set off he was.

And a fool he felt himself that night, as he confronted his brilliant image in the glass. A Scot of the Scots, kilted in vivid plaid, a rakish cap on his black hair, a tartan draped across his shoulder, short, heavy stockings clasping his legs and low shoes gay with big buckles.

"Oh, young Lochinvar has come out of the west," warbled McLean merrily, as he straightened the shoulder pin of silver and Scotch topaz.

"Out of Hades," said Ryder, rather pointlessly, for he felt it was Hades he was going into.

Chiefly he was concerned with his knees and the striking contrast between their sheltered whiteness and the desert brown of his face.... Milky pale they gleamed at him from the glass.... Bony hard, they flaunted their angles at every move.... He was grateful that he was not a centipede.

"Oh, 'twas all for my rightful king,
That I gaed o'er the border;
Twas all for -

"You didn't tell me her name, now, Jack."

"Where's my mask?" Ryder was muttering. "I say, aren't there any pockets in these confounded petticoats?"

"In the sporran, man.... There!" McLean at last withheld his hand from its handiwork. "Jock, you're a grand sight," he pronounced with a special Scottish burr. "If ye dinna win her now - 'Bonny Charley's now awa,'" he sung as Ryder , with a last darkling look at his vivid image, strode towards the door.

"He's awa' all right - and he'll be back again as soon as he can make it."

With this cheerless anticipation of the evening's promise, the departing one stalked, like an exiled Stuart, to his waiting carriage.

For a moment more McLean kept the ironic smile alive upon his lips, as he listened to the rattle of the wheels and the harsh gutturals of the driver, then the smile died as he turned back into the room.

"Eh, but wouldn't you like it, though, Andy," he said to himself, "if some girl now liked you enough to get you to go to one of those damned things.... The lucky dog!"

# CHAPTER II

## MASKS AND MASKERS

Moors and Juliets and Circassian slaves and Knights at Arms were fast emerging from lift or cloak room, and confronting each other through their masks in sheepish defiance and curiosity. Adventurous spirits were circulating. Voices, lowered and guarded, began to engage in nervous, tittering banter.... Laughter, belatedly smothered, flared to betrayals....

The orchestra was playing a Viennese waltz and couple after couple slipped out upon the floor.

Lounging against the wall, Ryder glowered mockingly through his mask holes at the motley. It was so exactly as he had foreseen. He was bored - and he was going to be more bored. He was jostled - and he was going to be more jostled. He was hot - and he was going to be hotter.

Where in the world was Jinny Jeffries? He deserved, he felt, exhilaratingly kind treatment to compensate him for this insanity. He gazed about, and encountering a plump shepherdess ogling him he stepped hastily behind a palm.

He fairly stepped upon a very small person in black. A phantom-like small person, with the black silk hubarah of the Mohammedan high-caste woman drawn down to her very brows, and over the entire face the black street veil. Not a feature visible. Not an eyebrow. Not an eyelash, not a hint of the small person herself, except a very small white, ringed hand, lifted as if in defense of his clumsiness.

"Sorry," said Ryder quickly, and driven by the instinct of reparation. "Won't you dance?"

A mute shake of the head.

Well, his duty was done. But something, the very lack of all invitation in the black phantom, made him linger. He repeated his request in French.

From behind the veil came a liquidly soft voice with a note of mirth. "I understand the English, monsieur," it informed him.

"Enough, then, to say yes in it?"

The black phantom shook its head. "My education, alas! has only proceeded to the N." Her speech was quaint, unhesitating, but oddly inflected. "I regret - but I am not acquainted with the yes."

A gay character for a masked ball! Indifference and pique swung Ryder towards a geisha girl, but a trace of irritation lingered and he found her, "You likee plink gleisha?" singularly witless.

He'd tell McLean just how darned captivating his outfit was, he promised himself.

And then he caught sight of a familiar pair of gray eyes smiling over the white veil of an odalisque. Jinny Jeffries was wearing one of the many costumes there that passed for Oriental, a glittering assemblage of Turkish trousers and Circassian veils, silver shawls and necklaces and wide bracelets banding bare arms.

As an effect it was distinctly successful.

"Ten thousand dinars could not pay for the chicken she has eaten," uttered Ryder appreciatively in the language of the old slave market, and stepped promptly ahead of a stout Pantalon.

"Jack! You did come!" There was a note in the girl's voice as if she had disbelieved in her good fortune. "Oh, and beautiful as Roderick Dhu! Didn't I tell you that you could find something in that shop?" she declared in triumph.

"Do you imagine that this came out of a costumer's?" Ryder swung her swiftly out in the fox trot before the crowd invaded the floor. "If Andy McLean could hear you! Why this, this is the real thing, the Scots-wha-hae-wi'-Wallace-bled stuff."

"Who is Andy McLean?"

"Andrew is Scotch, Single, and Skeptical. He is a great pal of mine and also an official of the Agricultural Bank which is by way of being a Government institution. These are the togs of his Hieland Grandsire - "

"Why didn't you bring him?"

"Too dead, unfortunately - grandsires often are - "

"I mean Andrew McLean."

"It would take you, my dear Jinny, to do that. You brought me - and I can believe in anything after the surprise of finding myself here."

Jinny Jeffries laughed. "If I could only believe what you say!"

"Oh, you can believe anything I say," Jack obligingly assured her. "I'm very careful what I *say* - "

"I wish I were."

"You'd have to be careful how you look, Jinny - and you can't help that. The Lord who gave you red hair must provide the way to elude its consequences.... I suppose the Orient isn't exactly a manless Sahara for you?"

She countered, her bright eyes intent, "Is it a girl-less Sahara for you, Jack?"

"The only woman I have laid a hand on, in kindness or unkindness, died before Ptolemy rebuilt Denderah."

"That's not right - "

"No? And I thought it such a virtuous record!"

"I mean," Jinny laughed, "that you really ought to be seeing more of life - like to-night - "

"To-night? Do you imagine this is a place for seeing life?"

"Why not?" she retorted to the irony in his voice. "It's real people - not just dead and gone things in cases with their lives all lived. I don't care if you are going to be a very famous person, Jack, you ought to see more of the world. You have just been buried out here for two years, ever since you left college - "

Beneath his mask the young man was smiling. A quaint feminine notion, that life was to be encountered at a masquerade! This motley of hot, over-dressed, wrought up idiots a human contact!

Life? Living?... Thank you, he preferred the sane young English officials ... the comradeship of his chief ... the glamor of his desert tombs.

Of course there was a loneliness in the desert. That was part of the big feeling of it, the still, stealing sense of immensity reaching out its shadowy hands for you.... Loneliness and restlessness.... These tropic nights, when the stars burned low and bright, and the hot sands seemed breathing.... Loneliness and restlessness - but they gave a man dreams.... And were those dreams to be realized here?

MARY HASTINGS BRADLEY

The music stopped and the ever-watchful Pantalon bore down upon them. Abandoning Jinny to her fate, Ryder sought refuge and a cigarette.

The hall was crowded now; the ball was a flash of color, a whirl of satins and spangles and tulle and gauze, gold and green and rose and sapphire, gyrating madly in vivid projection against the black and white stripes of the Moorish walls. The color and the music had sent their quickening reactions among the throng. Masks were lending audacity to mischief and high spirits.

Three little Pierrettes scampered through the crowd, pelting right and left with confetti and balloons, and two stalwart monks and a thin Hamlet pursued them, keeping up the bombardment amid a great combustion of balloons. A spangled Harlequin snatched his hands full of confetti and darted behind a palm.

It was the palm of the black phantom, the palm of Ryder's rebuff. Perhaps the Harlequin had met repulse here, too, and cherished resentment, not a very malicious resentment but a mocking feint of it, for when Ryder turned sharply after him - oddly, he himself was strolling toward that nook - he found Harlequin circling with mock entreaties about the stubbornly refusing black domino.

"Will you, won't you, will you, won't you, won't you join the dance?" chanted Harlequin, with a shower of confetti flung at the girl's averted face.

There was such a shrinking of genuine fright in her withdrawal that Ryder had a fine thrill of rescue.

"My dance," he declared, laying an intervening hand on her muffled arm.

His tartan-draped shoulder crowded the Harlequin from sight.

She raised her head. The black street veil was flung back, but a black yashmak was hiding all but her eyes. Great dark eyes they were, deep as night and soft as shadows, arched with exquisitely curved brows like the sweep of wild birds' wings.... The most lovely eyes that dreams could bring.

A flash of relief shone through their childish fright. With sudden confidence she turned to Ryder.

"Thank you.... My education, monsieur, has proceeded to the Ts," she told him with a nervous little laugh over her chagrin, drowned in a burst of louder laughter from the discomfited Harlequin, who turned on his heel and then bounded after fresh prey.

"Shall we dance or promenade?" asked Ryder.

Hesitatingly her gaze met his. Red and gold and green and blue flecks of confetti were glimmering like fishscales over her black wrap and were even entangled drolly in the absurd lengths of her eye-lashes.

"It is - if I have not forgotten how to dance," she murmured. "If it is a waltz, perhaps - "

It was a waltz. Ryder had an odd impression of her irresolution before, with strange eagerness, he swept her into the music. Within the clumsy bulk of her draperies his arm felt the slightness of her young form. She was no more than a child.... No child, either, at a masquerade, but a fairy, dancing in the moonlight.... She was a leaf blowing in the breeze.... She was the very breeze and the moonlight.

And then, to his astonishment, the dance was over. Those moments had seemed no more than one.

"We must have the next," he said quickly. "What made you think you had forgotten?"

"It is nearly four years, monsieur, since I danced with a man."

"With a man? You have been dancing with girls, then?"

She nodded.

"At a school?"

"At a - a sort of school." The black domino laughed with ruefulness. "At a very dull sort of school."

"To which, I hope, you are not to return?"

She made no answer to that - unless it was a sigh that slipped out.

"At any rate," he said cheerily, "you are dancing to-night."

"To-night - yes, to-night I am dancing!" There was triumph in her young voice, triumph and faint defiance, and gayety again in her changing eyes.

Extraordinary, those eyes. Innocent, audacious, bewildering.... To look down into them produced the oddest of excitement.

He took off his mask. Masks were hindering things - he could see so much better without.

She, too, could see better - could see him better. Shyly, yet intently, her gaze took note of him, of the clean, clear-cut young face, bronzed and rather thin, of the dark hair that looked darker against the scarlet cap, of the deep-set eyes, hazel-brown, that met hers so often and were so full of contradictory things ... life ... and humor ... and frank simplicity ... and subtle eagerness.

He looked so young and confident and handsome....

"You are - a Scotchman?" slipped out from her black yashmak.

"Only in costume. I am an American."

She repeated it a little musingly. "I do not think I ever met an American young man." She added, "I have met old ones - yes, and middle-aged ones and the women - but a young one, no."

"A retired spot, that school of yours," said Ryder appreciatively. "You are French?"

"That is for your imagination!" Teasingly, she laughed. "I am, monsieur, only a black domino!"

It was the loveliest laugh, Ryder was instantly aware, and the loveliest voice in the world. Yes, and the loveliest eyes.

He forgot the crowd. He forgot the heat. He forgot - alas! - Jinny Jeffries. He was aware of an intense exhilaration, a radiant sense of well-being, and - at the music's beginning - of a small palm pressed again to his, a light form within his arm ... of shy, enchanting eyes out from the shrouding black.

"Do put that veil away," he youthfully entreated. "It's quite time. The others are almost all unmasked."

Her glance about the room returned to him with mock plaintiveness. She shook her head as they spun lightly about a corner.

"Perhaps, monsieur, I have an unfortunate nose."

"My nerves are strong."

"But why afflict them?" Prankishly her eyes sparkled up at him over the black veil that made her a mystery. "Enjoy the present, monsieur!"

"Are you enjoying it?"

Her lashes dropped, like black butterflies. She was a changeling of a girl, veering from gayety to shyness.... Her gaze was now on her wrist watch, a slender blaze of platinum and diamonds.

"The present - yes," she said in a muffled little voice.

He bent his head to hear her through the veil.

A tormenting curiosity was assailing him. It had become not enough to know that she was young and slender, with enchanting eyes and a teasing spirit of wit.... Vaguely he had thought her to be French, one of the quaint _jeunes filles_ so rarely taken traveling.

But who was she? A child at her first ball? But what in the world was she doing, back in the palms, away from her chaperon?

He realized, even in the cloud of his fascination, that French *jeunes filles* are not wonted to lurk about palms at a ball.

Was she a little Cinderella, then, slipping among the guests? Some poor companion, stealing in for fun?... She was too young. And there was that watch, that glitter of diamonds upon her wrist.

"Have you just come to Cairo?"

She shook her head. "For some time - I have been here."

"Up the Nile yet?"

"The Nile - no, monsieur."

"But you are going?"

"That - that I do not know. Sometime, perhaps."

She sounded guarded.... He hurried into revelations.

"I am staying not far from Cairo, myself. I am an excavator - on an expedition from an American museum."

"Ah, you dig?"

"Well, not personally.... But the expedition digs.... We've had some bully finds."

"And you came from America - to dig in the sands?" The black domino laughed softly. "For how long, monsieur?"

"This is my second year."

Still laughing, she shook her shrouded little head at him. "But I cannot understand! What wonderful thing do you hope to find - what buried secret - ?"

"Nothing half as wonderful as to know who you are," he said boldly.

"That, too, is - is buried, monsieur!"

"But not beyond discovery," he told her very gayly and confidently, and danced the music out.

As the last strains died, they paused for an instant as if the spell still bound them, then his arms fell slowly away, and he heard the girl draw a quick, startled breath. Her eyes sped to that tiny, blazing watch; when she lifted them he thought he surprised a gleam of panic.

"How fast is an hour!" she said with an excited little laugh. "Time is a - a very sudden thing!"

Sudden, indeed! How long since he had been a badly bored, impatient young man, mocking the follies of the masquerade? How long since he had danced with Jinny, flouting her notion of this sort of thing as life? How long since he had looked into a pair of dark disquieting eyes ... listened to a gay little voice....

Many important things in life happen suddenly. Juliet happened very suddenly to Romeo. Romeo happened as suddenly to Juliet.

But Jack Ryder was not remembering anything about Romeo and Juliet. He was watching that glance steal to the wrist watch again.

Then, as if with a determination of the spirit, they smiled up at him.

"Monsieur the American," said the black domino, "you have been most kind to an - an incognita - of a masque. I hope that you dig out of your sands all the secrets that you most desire."

"You sound as if you were saying good-bye," said Jack Ryder with quick denial in his blood.

The smile in her eyes flickered.

"Perhaps I have kept you too long from the other guests."

He shook his head. "They don't exist."

"Ah! I will give you the chance to say such nice things to them."

"But I never say nice things - unless I mean them!"

"Never - monsieur?"

"Never. I am very careful what I say," he assured her, even as he had assured another girl, in what different meaning, hours or centuries before. "You can believe anything that I say."

"A young man of character! Perhaps that goes with the Scotch costume. I have read the Scots are a noble people."

"They haven't a thing on the Americans. You must know me

better and discover - "

But again her eyes had gone, almost guiltily, to that watch. And when she raised them again they were not smiling but very strangely resolved.

"Monsieur, it is so hot - if you would get me a glass of sherbet?"

"Certainly." Convention brought out the assent; convention turned him about and marched him dutifully toward the crowded table she indicated.

But something deeper than convention, some warning born of that too-often consulted watch and that strange look in her eyes, that uneasy fear and swift resolve, turned him quickly about again.

Other couples had strolled between them. He hurried through and stepped back among the palms.

The place was empty. The black domino was gone.

*   *   *   *   *

He wasted one minute in assuring himself that she was not hidden in some corner, not mingled with the crowd. But the niche was deserted as a rifled nest. Then his eyes spied the door that the green decorations had conspired to hide and he wrenched it open.

He found himself on a little balcony overlooking the hotel garden. He knew the place in daytime - palms and shrubs and a graveled walk and painted chairs where he had drunk tea with Jinny and watched a Russian tourist beautifully smoking cigarettes.

Now the place was strange. Night and a crescent moon had wrought their magic, and the garden was a mystery of velvet dusks and ivory pallors. The graveled path ran glimmering beneath the magnolias. Over the wall's blankness the eucalyptus defined its crooked lines against the blue Egyptian sky.

No living thing was there ... nothing ... or did that shadow stir? There, just at the path's end.

Ryder's lithe strength was swift. There was one breathless moment of pursuit, then his hand fell with gripping fierceness upon the huddled dark figure that had sped so frantically to the tiny door in the garden's end.... A moment more and she would have been through.

His hand on her shoulder turned her towards him. Her eyes met his with a dash of desperation.... He was unconscious how his own were blazing ... how queerly white his face had gone under its desert brown.

She was actually running away. She had meant never to see him again. He had frustrated her, but the blow she had meant to deal him was still felt.

His voice, when it came, sounded shaken.

"You were going to leave me?"

Strangely her eyes changed. The defiance, the panic fear, faded. A cloud of slow despair welled up in them.

"What else?" she said very softly.

He did not lose his hold on her. He drew her back into the shadows with involuntary caution, and he felt her slender body trembling in his grasp. The tremors seemed to pass into his own.

A sense of urgency was pressing upon him. He was not himself, not any self that he had known. He stood there, in the Egyptian night, in the motley of a Scotch chieftain, grasping this mysterious creature of the masquerade, and he heard a voice that he did not know ask of her again and again, "But why? Why? Why were you going?"

It was not, he was telling himself, and her eyes were telling him, as if she wanted to go. He knew what he knew.... Those had been enchanted hours.... Yet she had deceived and fled from him.

Her eyes looked darkly back at him through the dusk.

"Because I must return to my own life." Her voice was a whisper. "And I did not want you to know - "

"To know what? Who are you? Where were you going?" A confusion of conjecture, fantastic, horrible, impossible, was surging in him. Dim, vague, terrible things....

"Who are you, anyway?"

She looked away from him, to the door which she had tried to gain.

"No masker, monsieur.... For me, there is no unveiling."

Ryder's hand stiffened. He felt his blood stop a moment, as if his heart stood still.

And then it beat on again in a furious turmoil of contradiction of this impossible thing that she was telling him.

"That door, monsieur, is to the lane, and in the lane another door leads to another garden - the garden of a girl you can never know."

He was no novice to Egypt. Even while his credulity was still battling with belief, his mind had realized this thing that had happened ... the astounding, unbelievable thing.... He had heard something of those Turkish girls, daughters of rich officials, whose lives were such strange opposition of modernity and tradition.

Indulgence and luxury. French governesses and French frocks ... freedom, travel, often, - Paris, London, perhaps - and then, as the girl eclipses the child - the veil. Still indulgence and luxury, still books and governesses and frocks and motors and society - but a feminine society.

Not a man in it. Not a caller. Not a friend. Not a lover.... Not an interview, even, with the man who is to be the husband - until the bride is safe in the husband's home. Hidden women. Secret, secluded lives.... Extinguished by tradition - a tradition against which their earlier years only had won modern emancipation.

And she - this slim creature in the black domino - one of those invisibles?

Stark amazement looked out of his eyes into hers.

"You - a Turk?" he blurted.

"I - a Turk!" Her head went suddenly high; she stiffened with defensive pride. "I am ashamed - but for the thing I have done. That is a shameful thing. To steal out at night - to a hotel - to a ball - And to dance with a man! To tell him who I am - Oh, yes, I am much ashamed. I am as bold as a Christian!" she tossed at him suddenly, between mockery and malice.

Still his wonder and his trouble found no words and the shadow on his face was reflected swiftly in her own.

"I beg you to believe, monsieur, that never before - never have I done such a thing. My greatest fault was to be out in the garden after sunset - when all Moslem women should be within. But my nurse was indulgent."

Almost pleadingly she looked up at the young man. "Believe

this of me, monsieur. I would not have you think of me lightly. But to-night something possessed me. I had heard of the masque, and I remembered the balls of the Embassy where I danced when I was so young and so I slipped away - there was a garden key that I had stolen, long ago, and kept for another thing.... I did not mean to dance. Only to look on at the world again."

"Oh, my good Lord," said Jack Ryder.

And then suddenly he asked, "Are you - do you - whom do you live with?"

And when she answered in surprise, "But with whom but my father - he is Tewfick Pasha," he drew a long breath.

"I thought you'd tell me next you were married," he said limply.

The next moment they were laughing the sudden, incredibly absorbed laughter of youth.

"No husband. I am one of the young revoltees - the moderns - and I am the only daughter of a most indulgent father."

"Well, that's something to the good," was Ryder's comment upon that. He added, "But if that most indulgent father caught you - "

He looked down at her. The secret trouble of her answering look told him more than its assumption of courage.

This was no boarding school girl lingering beyond hours.... This was a high-born Moslem, risking more than he could well know.

The escapade was suddenly serious, tremendously menacing.

She answered faintly , " I have no idea - the thing is so

impossible! But of course," she rallied her spirit to protest, "I do not think they would sew me in a sack with a stone and drop me in the river, like the odalisques of yesterday!"

She added, her voice uncertain in spite of her, "I meant only to stay a moment."

"Which is the way?" said Jack briefly.

With caution he opened the gate into the black canyon of the lane. Silence and darkness. Not a loiterer, only one of the furtive starved dogs, slinking back from some rubbish....

The girl moved forward and keeping closely at her side he followed; they crossed to the other wall, and turned towards the right, stopping before the deeper shadow of a small, pointed door set into the heavy brick of the high wall. From her draperies the girl drew out a huge key.

She fitted it into the ancient lock and turned it; carefully she pressed open the gate and stared anxiously into the gloom of the shadowy garden that it disclosed.

Relief colored her voice as she turned to him.

"All is quiet.... I am safe, now.... And so - good-bye, monsieur."

"And this is where you live?" Ryder whispered.

"There - in that wing," she murmured, slipping within the gate, and he stole after her, and looked across the garden, through a fringe of date palms, to the outlines of the buildings.

Dim and dark showed the high walls, black as a prison, only here and there the pale orange oblong of a lighted window.

"Did you climb out the window?" he murmured.

From beneath the veil came a little sound of soft derision.

"But there are always bars, even in the garden windows of the haremlik!... No, I stole down by an old stair.... That wing, there, on the right."

Barred on the garden, and on the street the impregnable wooden screens of the mashrubiyeh, those were the rooms where this girl beside him was to spend her life - until that most indulgent father wearied of her modernity and transferred her to other rooms, as barred and screened, in the palace of some husband!... That thought was brushing Ryder ... with other thoughts of her present risk ... of her lovely eyes, visible again, above the veil, thoughts of the strangeness and unreality of it all ... there in the shrubbery of a pasha's garden, the pasha's daughter whispering at his side.

"What about your mother - ?" he asked her. "Is she - ?"

"She is dead," the girl told him, with a drop in her voice.

And after a long moment of silence, "When I was so little - but I remember her, oh, indeed I do ... She was French, monsieur."

"Oh! And so you - "

"I am French-Turk," she whispered back. "That is very often so - in the harems of Cairo.... She was so lovely," said the girl wistfully. "My father must have loved her very much ... he never brought another wife here. Always I lived alone with my old nurse and the governesses - "

"You had - lessons?"

"Oh, nothing but lessons - all of that world which was shut away so soon.... French and English and music and the philosophy - Oh, we Turks are what you call blue stockings, monsieur, shut away with our books and our dreams ... and our memories ... We are so young and already the real world is a memory.... Sometimes," she said, with a tremor of suppressed passion in her still little tones, "I could wish that I had died when I was very young and so happy when my father took me traveling in Europe.... I played games on the decks of the ships ... I had my tea with the English children.... I went down into the hold to play with their dogs..."

She broke off, between a laugh and a sigh, "Dogs are forbidden to Moslems - but of course you know, if you have been here two years.... And emancipated as we may be, there is no changing the customs. We must live as our grandmothers lived ... though we are not as our grandmothers are..."

"With a French mother, you must be very far from what some of your grandmothers were!"

"My poor French mother!" Whimsically the girl sighed. "Must I blame it on her - the spirit that took me to the ball?... To-morrow this will be a dream to me.... I shall not believe in my shamelessness.... And you, too, must forget - "

"Forget?" said Ryder under his breath.

"Forget - and go. Positively you must go now, monsieur. It is very dangerous here - "

"It is." There was a light dancing in his hazel eyes. "It is more dangerous every moment - "

"But I mean - " Her confusion betrayed itself.

"But I mean - that you are magic - black magic," he murmured bending over the black domino.

The crescent moon had found its way through a filigree of boughs. Faintly its exploring ray lighted the contour of that shrouded head, touched the lovely curves of her arched brows and the tender pallor of the skin about those great wells of dark eyes.... From his own eyes a flame seemed to pass into hers.... Breathlessly they gazed at each other ... like dim shadows in a garden of still enchantment.

And then, as from a palpable clasp, she tried to slip away. "Truly, I must go! It is so late - "

Ryder's heart was pounding within him. He did not recognize this state of affairs; it was utterly unrelated to anything that had gone before in his merry, humorous, rather clear-sighted and wary young life.... He felt dazed and wondering at himself ... and irresponsible ... and appalled ... but deeper than all else, he felt eager and exultant and strangely, furtively determined about something that he was not owning to himself ... something that leaped off his lips in the low murmur to her, "But to-morrow night - I shall see you again - "

She caught her breath. "Oh, never again! To-night has no to-morrow - "

"Outside this gate," he persisted. "I shall wait - and other nights after that. For I must know - if you are safe - "

"See, I am very safe now. For if I were missed there would be running and confusion - "

He only drew a little closer to her. "To-morrow night - or another - I shall come to this door - "

"It must not open to you.... It is a forbidden door - forbidden as that fortieth door in the old story.... There are thirty and nine doors in your life, monsieur, that you may open, but this is the forbidden - "

"I shall be waiting," he insisted. "To-morrow night - or another - "

She moved her head in denial.

MARY HASTINGS BRADLEY

"Neither to-morrow nor another night - "

Again their eyes met. He bent over her. He knew a gleam of sharpest wonder at himself as his arms went swiftly round that shrouding drapery, and then all duality of consciousness was blotted out in the rush of his young madness. For within that drapery was the soft, human sweetness of her; his arms tightened, his face bent close, and through the sheer gauze of her veil his lips pressed her lips....

Some one was coming down the walk: Footsteps crunched the gravel.

Like a wraith the girl was out of his arms ... in anger or alarm his whirling senses could not know, although it was their passionate concern. But his last gleam of prudence got him through the gate he heard her locking after.

And then, for her sake, he fled.

# CHAPTER III

## IN THE PASHA'S PALACE

Nearer sounded the footsteps on the graveled walk and in frightened haste the girl drew out the key from the gate and slipped away into the shrubbery, grateful for the blotting shadows.

At the foot of a rose bush she crouched to thrust the key into a hole in the loose earth, covering the top and drawing the low branches over it.

"Aimee," came a guarded call. "Aimee!"

Still stooping, she tried to steal through the bushes, but the thorns held her and she stood up, pulling at her robes.

"Yes? Miriam?" she said faintly, and desperately freeing herself, she hurried forward towards the dark, bulky figure of her old nurse, emerging now into the moonlight.

"*Alhamdolillah* - Glory to God!" ejaculated the old woman, but cautiously under her breath. "Come quickly - he is here - thy father! And thou in the garden, at this hour.... But come," and urgently she gripped the girl's wrist as if afraid that she would vanish again into the shadows of the shrubbery.

Aimee felt her knees quake under her. "My father!" she murmured, and her voice died in her throat.

Had he discovered ? Had some one seen her slip out? Or

MARY HASTINGS BRADLEY

recognized her at the ball?

The panic-stricken conjectures surged through her in dismaying confusion. She tried to beat down her fear, to think quickly, to rally her force, but her swimming senses were still invaded with the surprise of those last moments at the gate, her heart still beating with the touch of Ryder's arms about her ... of that long, deep look ... that kiss, beyond all else, that kiss....

Little rivers of fire were running through her veins. Shame and proud anger set up their swift reactions. Oh, what wings of wild, incredible folly had brought her to this! To be kissed like - like a dancing girl - by a man, an unknown, an American!

How could he, how could he! After all his kindness - to hold her so lightly.... And yet there had been no lightness in his eyes, those eager, shining young eyes, so gravely concerned....

But she could not stop to think of this thing. Her father was waiting.

"He came in like a fury," the old nurse was panting, as they scurried up the walk together, "and asked for you ... and your room empty, your bed not touched!... Oh, Allah's ruth upon me, I went trotting through the house, mad with fear.... Up to the roofs then down to the garden ... sending him word that you were dressing that he should not know the only child of his house was a shameless one, devoid of sense."

"But there is no harm in a garden," breathed the girl, her face hot with shame. "To-night was so hot - "

"Is there no coolth upon the roof?"

"But the roses - "

"Can roses not be brought you? Have you no maids to attend you?"

"I am tired of being attended! Can I never be alone - "

"Alone in the garden!... A pretty talk! Eh, I will tell thy father, I will have a stop put to this - *hush*, would you have him hear?" she admonished, in a sudden whisper, as they opened the little door at the foot of the dark well of spiral steps.

Like conspirators they fled up the staircase, and then with fumbling haste the old nurse dragged off the girl's mantle and veil, muttering at the pins that secured it. She shook out the pale-flowered chiffon of her rumpled frock and gathered back a strand of her dark, disordered hair.

"Say that you were on the roofs," she besought her.

For a moment the girl put the warm rose of her cheek against the old woman's dark, wrinkled one.

"But you are good, Dadi," she said softly, using the Turkish word for familiar old servants.

With a sound of mingled vexation and affection Miriam pushed her ahead of her into the drawing-room.

It was a long, dark room, on whose soft, buff carpet the little gilt chairs and sofas were set about with the empty expectancy of a stage scene in a French salon. French were the shirred, silk shades upon the electric lamps, French the music upon the chic rosewood piano.

And then, as if some careless property man had overlooked them in changing the act, two window balconies of closely carved old wood, of solidly screening mashrubiyeh wood, jutted out from one cream-tinted wall, and above a gilded sofa, upholstered in the delicate fabric of the Rue de la Paix, hung a green satin banner embroidered in silver with a phrase from the Koran.

Tewfick Pasha was at one side of the room, filling his match case. He was in evening dress, a ribbon of some order across a rather swelling shirt bosom, a red fez upon his dark head.

At his daughter's entrance he turned quickly, with so sharp a gleam from his full, somewhat protuberant black eyes that her guilty heart fairly turned over in her.

It made matters no more comforting to have Miriam packed from the room.

She would deny it all, she thought desperately ... No, she would admit it, and implore his indulgence.... She would admit nothing but the garden.... She would admit the ball.... She would *never* admit the young man....

With conscious eyes and flushing cheeks, woefully aware of dew-drenched satin slippers and an upsettingly hammering heart, Aimee presented the young image of irresolute confusion.

To her surprise there was no outburst. Her father was suddenly gay and smiling, with a flow of pleasant phrases that invited her affection. In his good humor - and Tewfick Pasha liked always to be kept in good humor - he had touches of that boyish charm that had made him the *enfant gate* of Paris and Vienna as well as Cairo and Constantinople. An *enfant* no more, in the robustly rotund forties, his cheerful self-indulgence demanded still of his environment that smiling acquiescence that kept life soft and comfortable.

And now it suddenly struck Aimee, through her tense alarm, that his smile was not a spontaneous smile, but was silently, uneasily asking his daughter not to make something too unpleasant for him ... that something that had brought him here, at an unprecedented midnight ... that had kept him waiting until she, supposedly, should rise and dress....

If it were not then a knowledge of her escapade - ?

The relief from that fear made everything else bearable. She was even able to entertain, with a certain welcome, the alternative alarm that he had decided to marry again - that nightmare from whose realization the unknown gods (or more truly, the unknown goddesses of the Cairene demi-monde!) had assisted to save her.

There was a furtive excitement about him that fanned the supposition.

Then, quite suddenly, the illuminating lightning cut the clouds.

"My dear child, I have news, really important news for you. If I have not been discussing your future," said Tewfick Pasha, staring with stern nonchalance ahead and determinedly unaware of her instant stiffening of attention, "I have by no means been neglectful of it.... To-day - indeed to-night - there has been a consummation of my plans.... It is not to every daughter that a father may hurry with such an announcement."

Her first feeling was a merciful relief. He knew nothing then of the ball! She could breathe again.... It was her marriage that had brought him.

No new danger, that, but the eternal menace that she had always to dread.... But how many times had he promised that she should have no unknown husband, imposed by tradition! How many times had she indulged dreams of Europe, of bright, free romance!

And now he was off on some tangent from which it would need all her coaxing wit to divert him. With wide eyes painfully intent, her little, jeweled fingers very still in their locked grip in her lap, the color draining from her cheeks, she sat waiting for the revelation.

What was it all? Had he really decided upon something? Upon

some one?

Tewfick Pasha appeared in no hurry to inform her. He wandered rather confusedly into a rambling speech about her age and her position and the responsibilities of life and his inabilities to prevent their reaching her, and about his very tender affection for her and his understanding of all those girlish reticences and reluctances which made innocent youth so exquisite, while silently his daughter hung her head and wondered what he would be saying if he knew that she had broken every canon of seclusion and convention, had talked and danced with a man....

His astonishment would be so horrific that she flinched even from the thought.

And if he knew, moreover, that this man had caught her and kissed her - !

She told herself that she was disgraced for life. She had a dreamy desire to close her eyes and lean back and dream on about that disgrace....

But she must listen to her father. He was talking now about the powers of wealth, not merely the nominal riches of his somewhat precarious political affiliations, but solid, sustaining, invested and invulnerable wealth.

Unexpectedly Aimee laughed. "He must be very plain," she declared, her face brightening with mockery, "if you take so long to tell me his name!"

Not, she added to herself under her breath, that any name would weigh a feather's difference!

"On the contrary," and the pasha's eyes met hers frankly for the first time and he seemed delighted to indulge a laugh, "he has the reputation of good looks. He is much *a la mode.*"

"Beautiful and golden - did you meet him just to-night, my father?" Aimee went on, in that light audacity which he had loved to indulge.

Now he smiled, but his glance went uneasily away from her.

"Not at all. This is a serious affair, you understand - the devil of a serious affair!" and for the first time she felt she heard the accents of his candor.

But again he was back to voluble protestation. This man was really an old friend. He boggled over the word, then got it out resonantly. A man he knew well. Not a young man, perhaps - certainly he was not going to hand his only daughter to any boy, a mere novice in life! - but a man who could give her the position she deserved. Not only a rich man, but an influential one.

His name, he brought out at last, was Hamdi Bey. He was a general in the armies of the sultan.

It was a long moment before she could piece any shreds of recollection together.

Hamdi Bey ... A general.... Why, that was a man her father had disliked ... more than once he had dropped resentful phrases of his airs, his arrogance ... had recounted certain clashes with malicious joy.

And now he was planning - no, seriously announcing -

A general ... He must be terribly old....

Not that it made any difference. Old or young, black or white, general or ghikar, would mean nothing in her life. She would have none of him ... none of him.... Never would she endure the humiliation of being handed over like a toy, an odalisque, a slave....

What had happened? She could only suppose that her father had been overcome by that wealth of the general's on which he had made her such a speech. Or perhaps his dislike of Hamdi had been founded on nothing but resentment of Hamdi's airs of superiority, and now that the bey was condescending to ask for her hand her father's flattered appeasement was rushing into genial acceptance.

Anything might be possible to Tewfick Pasha's eternally youthful enthusiasms.

She told her frightened heart that she was not afraid.... Her father would never really fail her.... And she would never surrender to this degradation; for all her fright and all her flinching from defiance she divined in herself some hidden stuff of resistance, tenacious to endure ... some strain of daring which had made her brave that wild escapade to-night.

Was it still the same night? Were the violins still playing, the people still dancing in their fairy land of freedom?... Was that young man in the Highland dress, that unknown American, was he back there dancing with some other girl?

What was it he had said? To-morrow night, and another night, he would be there in the lane.... If she would come! As if she would demean herself, after his rude affront, to steal again to the gate, like a gardener's daughter - !

Her thoughts were so full of him. And now she had this new horror to face, this marriage to Hamdi Bey. Did her father dream that she would not resist? It was against such a danger that she had long ago stolen a garden key, a key to the outer world in which she had neither a friend nor a piaster to save her....

"My dear father," she said entreatingly, "please do not tell me that you really mean - that you really think you would like to - that you would consider - this man - "

He turned on her a suddenly direct, confessing look.

"Aimee, I have *arranged* this matter."

He added heavily, "To-night. That is what I came to tell you."

In the silence that settled upon them he finally ceased his effort to ignore her shocked dismay. He abandoned his airy pretense that the affair could possibly evoke her enthusiasm. He sucked at his cigarette like a rather sullen little boy.

"I have always indulged you, Aimee," he said at last, without looking round at her. "I hope you are not going to make me infernally sorry."

"I think you are m-making me inf-fernally sorry," said an unsteady little voice.

He looked about. His daughter was sitting very still upon the gilded sofa beneath the banner of Mahomet; as he regarded her two great tears formed in her dark eyes and ran slowly down her cheeks.

With a sound of impatience he jumped to his feet and began to pace up and down the room.

This, he pointed out heatedly, to her, was what a man got who indulged his daughter. This is what came of French and English governesses and modern ideas.... After all he had done - more than any other father! To sit and weep! Weep - at such a marriage! What did she expect of life? Was she not as other women? Did she never look ahead? Had she no pride, no ambition - no hopes? Did she wish never to marry, then, to become an *old mees* like her English companion?

"I am but eighteen," she said quiveringly. "Oh, my father, do not give me to this unknown - "

"Unknown - unknown! Do I not know him?"

"But you promised - "

Angrily he gestured with his cigarette. "Do I know what is good for you or do I not? Have I your interest at heart - tell me! Am I a savage, a dolt - "

"But you do not know what it is to be unhappy. I beg of you, my father, - I should die with such a life before me, with such a man for my husband. I am too French, too like my mother - "

"Ah, your mother!... Too French, are you?... But what would you have in France?" he demanded with the bursting appearance of a man making every effort to restrain himself within unreasonable bounds. "Would not your parents there arrange your marriage? You might see the fiance," he caught the words out of her mouth, "but only for a time or two - after the arrangements - and what is that? What more would you know than what your father knows? Are you a thing to be exhibited - given to a man to gaze at and appraise? I tell you, no.... You are my daughter. You bear my name. And when you marry you marry in the sanctity of the custom of your father - and you go to your husband's house as his mother went to his father."

Timidly she protested, "But my mother - and you - "

"Do not speak of your mother! If she were here she would counsel gratitude and obedience." He turned his back on her. "This is what comes," he muttered, "of this modernity, this education...."

He pitched away his stub as if he were casting all that he hated away with it.

She had never seen him so angry. Helplessly she felt that his vanity and his word were engaged with the general more than she had dreamed. She felt a surge of panic at the immensity of the trouble before her.

"But, my father, if you love me - "

"No, my little one, if *you* love *me*!"

With a sudden assumption of good humor over the angry red mottling his olive cheeks, he came and sat beside her, putting his arm about her silently shrinking figure.

"I am a weak fool to stay and drink a woman's tears, as the saying goes," he told her, "but this is what a man gets for being good natured.... But, tears or not, I know what is best.... Come, Aimee, have I not ever been fond of you - ?"

He patted her hand with his own plump one where bright rings were sparkling deep in the encroaching flesh. Aimee looked down with a sudden wild dislike.... That soft, ingratiating hand, with its dimples and polished nails, which thought it could pat her so easily into submission....

It was nothing to him, she thought, chokingly, whether she was happy or unhappy. He had decided on the match - perhaps he had foreseen her protests and plunged into it, so as to be committed against her entreaties! - and he was not stopped by any thought of her feelings.

After all her hopes! After all he had promised!

But she told herself that she had never been secure. Beneath all her trust there had always been the silent fear, slipping through the shadows like a serpent.... Some instinct for character, more precocious than her years, had whispered through her fond blindness, and initiated her into foreboding.

"Come now, my dear," he said heartily, "this is a surprise, of course, but after all you will find it is for the best - much for the best - "

His voice died away. After a long pause, "You may make the arrangements," she told him in a still, tenacious little voice, "but you cannot make me marry him.... I will never put on the marriage dress.... Never wear the diadem.... Never stir one step within his house."

A complete silence succeeded this declaration. He got up violently from beside her. She did not dare look at him. He was going away, she thought.

It would be the beginning of war. She did not know what he would do but she knew that she would endure it.

And the gossip of the harems would be her protection. Her opposition, bruited through those feminine channels, would not be long in reaching Hamdi Bey.... And no man could to-day be so callous of his pride or the world's opinion that he would be willing to receive such a revolting bride.

Did her father think of that, that poor, pale power of hers? He stood irresolute, as if meditating a last exhortation, and then suddenly turned on her the haggard face of a violent despair.

"Would you see me ruined?" he said passionately.

Sharply he glanced about the room, at the far, closed doors where it was not inconceivable that old Miriam was lurking, and strode over to her and began talking very jerkily and huskily, over her bent head.

"I tell you that Hamdi is making this a condition - it is the price of silence, of those papers back.... He came to me to-night. I knew that hound of Satan had been smelling about, but I could not imagine - as if, between gentlemen - "

At that, she lifted her stupefied head.... Her father, with the face of a cornered fox!... She caught her breath with the shock of it. Her lips parted, but only her mute eyes asked their startled questions.

Hurriedly , shamefacedly , with angry resentments and

self-justifications, he was pouring a flood of broken phrases at her. She caught unintelligible references to narrow laws and the imbecile English, to impositions binding only upon the fools.... And then the word *hasheesh*.

Sharply then the truth took its outlines. Her father had been smuggling in hasheesh. Hamdi Bey had discovered this, and Hamdi Bey, unless silenced, had threatened betrayal.

The danger was real. English laws were stringent. Vaguely the horrors loomed - arrest, trial.... Even if he escaped the scandal was ruin....

Small wonder that her father had come flying upon the wings of his danger and its deliverance, small wonder that his brow was wet and his lips dry and his eyes hard with terror.

Thrown to the winds now his pretense of affection for Hamdi Bey! He hated and feared him. The old fox had done this, he declared, to get a hold upon him, for always there had been bad blood.

And the bey had heard, of course, of the beauty of the pasha's daughter. Some cousin had babbled.... And undoubtedly the rumor of that beauty - Tewfick Pasha received his inspiration upon the moment, but that was not gainsaying its truth - had determined the bey to find some vulnerable hold.

He was like that, a soft-voiced, sardonic devil! And this accursed business of the hasheesh had served his ends. To-night, he had come with his proofs....

"So you see," muttered Tewfick Pasha, "what the devil of a serious business this is. And how any talk of - of unreadiness - if you were not amiable, for example, to his cousin when she calls upon you - might serve to anger him.... And so - "

Significantly his glance met hers. Her eyes fell, stricken. The color flooded her trembling face. She quivered with confused pain, with shame for his shame, with terror and fright ... with a hot, protective compassion that tore at her pride....

She struggled against her dismay, trying for reassuring little words that would not come. Her heart seemed beating thickly in her throat.

She never knew just what she said, what little broken words of pity, of understanding, of promise, she achieved. But her father suddenly dropped beside her, with an abandon reminiscent of the *enfant gate* of his Paris days, and drew her hands to his lips, kissing their soft, quiescent palms.... She drew one away and placed it upon his dark head from which the fez had tumbled.

For the moment she was sorry, as one is sorry for a hurt child. And her sorriness held her heart warm, in the glow of giving comfort.

She had need of that warmth. For a cold tide was rising in her, a tide of chill, irresistible foreboding....

For all the years of her life.... For all the years....

# CHAPTER IV

## EXPLANATIONS

The remaining hours of Jack Ryder's night might be divided into three periods. There was an interval of astounding exhilaration coupled with complete mental vacancy, during which a figure in a Scots costume might have been observed by the astonished Egyptian moon striding obliviously along the silent road to the Nile, past sleeping camels and snoring *dhurra* merchants - a period during which his sole distinguishable sensation was the memory of enchanting eyes, of a voice, low and lovely ... of a slender figure in a muffling tcharchaf ... of the touch of soft lips beneath a gauzy veil....

This period was succeeded by hours of utter incredulity, in which he lay wide-eyed on the sleeping porch of McLean's domicile and stared into the white cloud of his fly net and questioned high heaven and himself.

Had he really done this? Had he actually caught and kissed this girl, this girl whose name he did not know, whose face he had never seen, of whom he knew nothing but that she was the daughter of a Turk and utterly forbidden by every canon of sanity and self-preservation?

In the name of wonder, what had possessed him? The night? The moon? The mystery of the unknown?... If he had never really kissed her he might have convinced himself that he had never really wanted to. But having kissed her - !

He looked upon himself as a stranger. A stranger of whom he

MARY HASTINGS BRADLEY

would be remarkably wary, in the days and nights to come ... but a stranger for whom he entertained a sort of secret, amazed respect. There had been an undeniable dash and daring to that stranger....

During the third period he slept.

When he awoke, late in the morning, and descended from a cold tub to a breakfast room from which McLean had long since departed, he brought yet another mood with him, a mood of dark, deep disgust and a shamed inclination to dismiss these events very speedily from memory. For that shadowy and rather shady affair he had abandoned the merry and delightful Jinny Jeffries and got himself involved now in the duty of explanations and peacemaking.

What in the world was he going to say?

He meditated a note - but he hated a lie on paper. It looked so thunderingly black and white. Besides, he could not think of any. "Dear Jinny - Awfully sorry I was called away."

No, that wouldn't do. He could take refuge in no such vagueness. Unfortunately, he and Jinny were on such terms of old intimacy that a certain explicitness of detail was expected.

"Dear Jinny - I had to leave last night and take a girl home - "

No, she would ask about the girl. Jinny had a propensity for locating people. It wouldn't do.

His masculine instinct for saying the least possible in a matter with a woman, and his ripening experience which taught him to leave no mystery to awaken suspicion, wrestled with the affair for some time and then retired from the field.

He compromised by telephoning Jinny briefly - and Jinny was equally as brief and twice as cool and cryptic - and promising to take her out to tea.

He reflected that if he took her to tea he would really have to stay over another night, for it would be too late to regain his desert camp. But the circumstances seemed to call for some social amend.... And no matter how many nights he stayed he certainly was not going to lurk about that lane, outside garden doors!

He must have been mad, stark, staring, March-hatter mad!

\*   \*   \*   \*   \*

That morning, during its remainder, he concluded his buying of supplies and saw to their shipment upon the boat that left upon the following morning. That noon he lunched with an assistant curator of the Cairo museum who found him a good listener.

That afternoon he escorted Jinny Jeffries and her uncle and aunt, the Josiah Pendletons, to tea upon the little island in the Cairo park, where white-robed Arabs brought them tea over the tiny bridge and violins played behind the shrubbery and white swans glided upon the blue lake, and then he carried them off in a victoria to view the sunset from the Citadel heights.

Not a word about the dance - except a general affirmative to Mrs. Pendleton's question if he had enjoyed himself. The Pendletons had not stayed to look on for long, and Jinny had apparently not worn her bleeding heart upon her sleeve.

But this immunity could not last. He could not hug the protecting Pendletons to him forever.

Nor did he want to. They waned upon him. Mrs. Pendleton's conversation was a perpetual, "Do look at - !" or dissertations from the guide books - already she had imparted a great deal of Flinders Petrie to him about his tombs. Mr. Pendleton was neither enthusiastic nor voluble, but he was attacking the objects of their travels in the same thorough-going spirit that he had attacked and surmounted the industrial obstacles of his career, and he went to a great deal of persistent trouble to ascertain the exact dates of passing mosques and the conformations of their arches.

The travelers had already "done" the Citadel. They had climbed its rocky hill, they had viewed the Mahomet Ali mosque and its columns and its carpets and had taken their guide's and their guidebook's word that it was an inferior structure although so amazingly effective from below; they had looked studiously down upon the city and tried to distinguish its minarets and towers and ancient gates, they had viewed with proper quizzicalness the imprint in the stone parapet of the hoof of that blindfolded horse which the last of the Mamelukes, cornered and betrayed, had spurred from the heights.

So now, no duty upon them, Ryder led them past the Citadel, up the Mokattam hills behind it, to that hilltop on which stood the little ancient mosque of the Sheykh-el-Gauchy, where the sunset spaces flowed round them like a sea of light and the world dropped into miniature at their feet.

Below them, in a golden haze, Cairo's domes and minarets were shining like a city of dreams. To the north, toy fields, vivid green, of rice and cotton lands, and the silver thread of the winding Nile, and all beyond, west and southwest, the vast, illimitable stretch of desert, shimmering in the opalescent air, sweeping on to the farthest edge of blue horizon.

"A nice resting place," said Jack Ryder appreciatively of the tomb of the Sheykh-el-Gauchy.

"I presume the date is given," Mr. Pendleton was murmuring, as he began to ferret with his Baedecker.

Mrs. Pendleton sighed sentimentally. "He must have been very fond of nature."

"He was very distrustful of his wives," said Ryder, grinning. "He had three of them, all young and beautiful."

"I thought you said he was a saint?" murmured Jinny, to which interpolation he responded, "Wouldn't three wives make any man a saint?" and resumed his narrative.

"And so he had his tomb made where he could overlook the whole city and observe the conduct of his widows."

"They could move," objected Miss Jeffries.

"The female of the Mohammedan species is not the free agent that you imagine," Ryder retorted, beginning with a smile and ending with a queer, reminiscent pang. He had a moment's rather complicated twinge of amusement at her reactions if she should know that to an encounter with a female of the Mohammedan species was to be attributed his departure from her party last night.

And then he remembered that he hadn't decided yet what to tell her and the time was undoubtedly at hand.

The time _was_ at hand. The Pendletons were too thorough-going Americans not to abdicate before the young. They did not saunter self-consciously away and make any opportunity for Jack and Jinny, as sympathetic European chaperons might have done; they sat matter-of-factedly upon the rocks while their competent young people betook themselves to higher heights.

Conscientiously Ryder was pointing out the pyramid fields.

"Gizeh, Abusir, Sakkara, Dahsur - and now here, if you look - that's the Medun pyramid - that tiny, sharp prick. If we had glasses...."

"Yes; but why didn't you like the ball?" murmured Jinny the direct.

"I did like the ball. Very much."

"Then why didn't you stay?"

"I - I wasn't feeling top-hole," he murmured lamely, wondering why girls always wanted to go back and stir up dogs that had gone comfortably to sleep.

"Did it come on suddenly?" said Jinny, unsympathetically, her eyes still upon the pyramids.

Something whimsical twitched at Jack Ryder's lips. "Very suddenly. Like thunder, out of China crost the bay."

"I suppose that dancing with the same girl in succession brings on the seizures?"

So she had noticed that!... Not for nothing were those bright, gray eyes of hers! Not for nothing the red hair.

"Well, I rather think it did," he said deliberately. "That girl was a child who hadn't danced in four years - so she said, and I believe her."

And Jinny received what he intended to convey. "Stepped on your buckled shoon and you felt a martyr?... But why bolt? There were other girls who *had* danced within four years - "

"I went into the garden," he murmured. "The fact is, I was feeling awfully - queer," he brought out in an odd tone.

Queer was a good word for it. He let it go at that. He couldn't do better.

Jinny looked suddenly uncertain. Her pique was streaked with compunction. She had been horribly angry with him for running away, and she remembered his opposition to the idea enough to be suspicious of any disappearance - but there was certainly an accent of embarrassed sincerity about him.

Perhaps he *had* been ill. Sudden seizures were not unknown in Egypt. And for all his desert brown he didn't look very rugged.

She murmured, "I hope you hadn't taken anything that disagreed with you."

"H'm - it rather agreed with me at the time," said Jack, and then brought himself up short. "I expect I haven't looked very sharp after myself - "

But Jinny did not wholly renounce her idea. "Does it always take you at dances you don't want to go to?"

"That's unfair. I came, you know."

"You came - and went."

"I'd have been all right if I hadn't come," he murmured, and Jinny felt suddenly ashamed of herself.

"Do you suppose that you would stay all right if you came to dinner?" she offered pacifically. "It's our last night, you know, till we come back from the Nile."

"I wish I could." Ryder stopped short. Now, why didn't he? Certainly he didn't intend -

But his tongue took matters promptly out of his hesitation's hands. "Fact is, I've an engagement." He added, appeasingly, "That's why I was so keen on getting you for tea." And Jinny told him appreciatively that it was a lovely tea and a lovely view.

"We're going to be at the hotel, I expect," she threw out, carelessly, "and if you get through in time - "

Rather hastily he assured her that indeed, if he got through in time -

She was a nice girl, was Jinny. A pretty girl, with just the right amount of red in her hair. Sanity would have sent him to the hotel to dine with her.

Sanity would also have sent him to the Jockey Club with McLean.

Certainly sanity had nothing to do with the way that he kept himself to himself, after his farewells at the hotel with the Pendletons, and took him to an out-of-the-way Greek cafe where he dined very badly upon stringy lamb and sodden baklava.

Later he wandered restlessly about dark, medieval streets where squat groups were clustered about some coffee house door, intent upon a game of checkers or some patriarchal story teller, recounting, very probably, a bandied narration of the Thousand and One Nights. Through other open doors drifted the exasperating nasal twang of Cairene music, and idly pausing, Ryder could see above the red fezes and turbans that topped the cross-legged audiences the dark, sleek, slowly-revolving body of some desert dancing girl.

Irresolutely he drifted on to the Esbekeyih quarters, to the streets where the withdrawn camels and donkeys had left pre-eminent the carriages and motors of that stream of Continental night life which sets towards Cairo in the season, Russian dukes and German millionaires, Viennese actresses and French singers and ladies of no avowed profession, gamblers, idlers, diplomats, drifters, vivid flashes of color in the bizarre, kaleidoscopic spectacle.

It was quite dark now. The last pale gleam of the afterglow had faded, and the blue of the sky, deepening and darkening, was pierced with the thronging stars. It was very warm; no breeze, but a fitful stirring in the tops of the feathery palms.

The streets were growing still. Only from some of the hotels came the sound of music from lighted, open windows.

Jinny would be rather expectant at her hotel. He could, of course, drop in for a few minutes since he was so near.... He walked past the hotel.... Jinny would be packing - or ought to be. A pity to disturb her.... And his dusty tweeds and traveling cap was no calling costume....

He walked past again. And this time he paused, on the brink of a dark canyon of a lane, running back between walls hung with bougainvillea.

Quite suddenly he remembered that he had told that girl, whose name he did not know, that he would come. It was a definite promise. It was an obligation.

He could do nothing less. It might be unwelcome, absurd, a nuisance, but really it was an obligation.

He sauntered down the lane, keeping carefully in the shadow. He loitered within that deep-set door - and felt a queer throb of emotion at the sight of it - and so, sauntering and loitering, he waited in the darkening night, promising himself disgustedly through the dragging moments to clear out and be done with this, but still interminably lingering, his pulses throbbing with that disowned expectancy.

Very cautiously, the gate began to open.

# CHAPTER V

## AT THE GARDEN GATE

Inch by inch the gate edged open. Warily he presented himself. The furtive crack gave him an instant's glimpse of a dark form within the shadows, then, in his face, it closed.

Ryder waited. In a moment it was opened wider, and he saw the dark-shrouded head and the veiled face of the Turkish girl, and out from the blackness the sparkle of young eyes.

"Is it - but who is it?" whispered a doubtful voice, and at his, "Why it is I - the American," quickly drawing off his cap, a little hand darted out of the darkness to pluck him swiftly within and the door was closed to within an inch of its opening.

Then the black phantom, drawing him back among the shrubbery, against the wall, turned with a muffled note of laughter.

"But the costume! Imagine that I - I was looking again for a Scottish chieftain with red kilts and a feather in his cap!"

"And instead - " Ryder glanced down at his tweeds with humorous recognition of his change of figure. Then his eyes returned to her.

"But you are the same," he murmured.

She was indeed the same. The same black street mantle, down

to her very brows. The same black veil, up to her very eyes. And the eyes - ! Their soft mysterious loveliness - the little winged tilt of the brows!

Apparently their effect was disconcertingly the same. He was conscious of a feeling that was far from a normal calm.

"So you were all right?" he half whispered. "Those steps, last night, you know, made me horribly afraid for you - "

"But, yes, I am all right."

As excitement gained upon him, a constraint was falling upon her. They were both remembering that moment, overlooked in the rush of recognition, when they had parted in this place, when he had had the temerity to clasp and kiss her.

Aimee was standing rigid and wary, ready for flight at the first fear. She told herself that she had only come through pride, the pride that insisted upon humbling his presumption. She would let him see how bitterly he had offended.... She had only come for this, she told herself - and to see if he had come.

If he had *not* come! That would have dealt a sorrily humiliating blow.

But he was here. And reassured and haughty, repeating that she was mortally offended, her spirit alternating between pride and shame and a delicious fear, she stood there in the shrubbery, fascinated, like a wild, shy thing of another age.

"That was old Miriam," she explained constrainedly. "My father had come in - with unexpectedness."

"Lord, it was lucky you were back!"

"Yes, it was - lucky," she assented. "If it had been half an hour before - "

She broke off. There came to the young man a sobering perception of the risk she ran, of the supreme folly of this escapade to which they were entrusting themselves.

It was a realization that deserved some consideration. But, obstinately, with young carelessness, he shook it off. After all, this was comparatively safe for her. She was not out of bounds. At an alarm he could slip away and no one could ever know. What risk there might be was chiefly his own.

"When you asked who it was," he murmured, "it occurred to me that you did not know my name - nor I yours. My own," he added, as she stood unresponsive, "is Ryder - Jack Ryder. You can always get a letter to me at the Agricultural Bank. That is the quickest way. My friend, McLean there, always knows where my diggings are. When in Cairo I stop with him; or at the Rossmore House."

"I shall not need to get a letter to you, monsieur," she told him stiffly.

"But, if you did, how would you sign it?"

"Aimee.... That is French - after my mother."

"Aimee. That means Beloved, doesn't it?"

She was silent.

Surely, she thought with a swelling heart, if he were sorry he would tell her now. It was the moment for contrition, for appeasement, for whatever explanation his American ways might have.

She had thought about him all night. She had given his declaration a hundred forms - but always it had been a declaration.

Now she waited, flagellating her sensitive pride.

Ryder was conscious of the constraint tightening about them and in the dragging pause an uncomfortable common sense had time to put its disconcerting questions.

What did it matter what her name meant? What in the world was he doing here?.... And what did she think she was doing here?... Not that he wanted her to go....

And suddenly it didn't matter - whatever they thought. It was enough that they were together in that still, soft, jasmine-scented dark. He was breathing quickly; his pulses were beating; he had a feeling of strange, heady delight.

The crescent moon was up at last, sailing clear of the house tops, sending its bright rays through the filigree of tall shrubs. A finger of light edged the contour of her shrouded head.

He bent a little closer.

"Won't you," he said softly, "take off your veil for me?"

Appalled, she clasped it to her. He had no idea in the world of the shock of that request. It would be only a faint parallel of its impropriety to suggest to Jinny Jeffries that she discard her frock. Even Ryder's acquaintance with Egypt could not tell him how that swift, confident eagerness of his could startle and affront.

"I want to see you so very much," he was murmuring, and met the chill disdain of her retort, "But it is not for you to see my face, monsieur!"

"Who is to see it?" he demanded.

"Who but the man I am to marry," she gave distinctly back.

The word hit him like stone.

He was conscious of a shock. Did she intend to rebuke - or to imply - to question his intention? The steadiness of her low voice suggested a certain steadiness of design.... He had heard of girls who knew their own minds ... girls with unexpectedly far-sighted vision.... Perhaps, poor child, she looked upon him as romantic escape from all that was restrictive in her life. Secluded women go fast - when they start.

The devil take him for that kiss!

A somewhat set look upon his thin face guarded the fluctuations of his soul, but the blood rose strongly under his dark skin.

For a moment he did not venture upon a reply, and in that moment he was suddenly aware that she had caught his meaning from him - and that it was a horrible mistake. It was one of those instants of highly-charged exchanges of meanings whose revelation was as useless to be denied as powerless to be explained.

Then her words came in tumultuous, passionate refutation of his thought. "That is what my father had come to tell me - that he had arranged my marriage. It is a very splendid thing. To a general - a rich general!"

She had not meant to tell him like that! But for the moment she was savagely glad to hurl it at him.

He made no answer. His eyes were inscrutably intent. A variety of things were rearranging themselves in his head.

"You're - you're going to marry him?" he said slowly.

"What else?" But she felt the phrase unfortunate and plunged past it. "It is not for me to say no, monsieur. It is for my father to arrange."

"But his indulgence - ? You were telling me, you know, that he was so fond of you. And that you were one of the moderns - the revolting moderns - "

Jack Ryder's tone was questioningly cynical and its raillery cut through her brief sham of pride.

"So I thought, too, last night." A tinge of infinite disillusionment was in her young voice. "But it is not so."

"Then you accept - ?"

The shrouded head nodded.

"But you can't want to," he broke out with sudden heat. "You don't know him at all, do you - this general?"

"Know him? I have never seen his face nor heard his voice - and I would die first," she added with bitter, helpless fierceness under her breath.

The veil muffled that from him. "But why - why?" he repeated in an angrily puzzled way.

She made a little gesture of weary impotence. Out of the dark draperies her hands were like white fluttering butterflies.

"What can I do?"

"I should think you could do the Old Harry of a lot."

"Weep?" said the girl with a pale irony not lost upon him.

"Weep - or row. Or run," he added, almost reluctantly.

She turned away her head. "I know, I thought once that I could run. For that I stole the key to this gate. But where would I run, monsieur? I have neither friends, nor - nor the resources.... There have been girls - two sisters - who ran away last year - but they were already married and they had cousins in France. For me, my cousins do not exist. I do not know my mother's family. They disowned her for her marriage, my father says. And so - but it is not possible to evade this.... It is not possible. This marriage is required."

"Required - rot! Can't you - don't you - " he paused, looking down upon her in tremendous and serious uncertainty. The impulse was strong upon him to tell her that he would help her. The accents of her voice had seemed to tear at his very heart.

It was utter madness. Where, in the map of Africa, would he hide her? And how would he take care of her? What would he do to her? Make love to her? Marry her? Take home a wife from an Egyptian harem - a surprising acquisition with which to startle and enchant his decorous family in East Middleton!

And a pretty end to his work here, his reputation, his responsibilities -

It was madness. And the fact that the thought had presented itself, even for his flouting mockery, indicated that he was mad. He told himself to be careful. Better men than he had everlastingly done for themselves because upon a night of stars and moonshine some dark-eyed girl had played the very devil with their common sense.

He reminded himself that he had never set eyes on her until last night, that she might be the consummate perfection of a minx, that there might not be a word of truth in all of this.

This general, now! Sudden. Not a word about it last night. And now -

He had an inkling that even Mohammedan fathers do not rush matters at such a pace.

For all he knew the girl might be inventing this general - for some artless reasons of her own. For all he knew she might be married to him and desirous of escape.

But he didn't believe it. She was too young and shy and virginal. The accents of her candor rebuked his skepticism. He merely told himself these things because the last vestige of his expiring common sense was prompting him.

And after all these creditable and excellent exhortations, to the utter extinction of the last vestige of that common sense he heard himself saying abruptly, "But isn't there anything in the world that I can do - ?"

"Nothing, monsieur."

"But for you to submit - like this - "

"It is not to be helped."

"But it *is* to be helped - if you really dislike it," he added jealously.

"I cannot help it, because - because my father - " She hesitated. The honor of her father and her family pride and affection were all involved, yet suddenly the sacrifice of these became more tolerable than to consent to that image of herself which she saw swiftly defining itself in his mind, that slight, weak creature, whose acquiescent passivity submitted to this marriage.

The thought was unbearable. She was burning beneath her veil. She would tell him.... And perhaps she was not averse, in her childish pride, to the pitiful glory of having him see her in the beauty of her filial sacrifice.

"My father has - has done something against the English laws," she faltered, "and Hamdi Bey, this general, knows of it, and will inform unless - unless my father makes this marriage. A cousin of his has seen me," she added, her young vanity forlornly rearing its head, "and told Hamdi that I am not - not too ill-looking a girl - "

Her essay of a laugh died.

Ryder's look deepened its sharp, defensive concentration.

"This is true - I mean your father is not just putting something over - telling you to get your consent?"

Her thoughts flew back to her father's haggard face. "Oh, it is true! I know."

"And he's going to hand you over - What sort is this Hamdi?"

"A general. Old. Evil enough to lay traps to obtain me."

"It's abomination." The anger in the young man surged beyond his control. "You must not do it.... If your father is clever enough to break a law let him be clever enough to mend it - by himself. Such a sacrifice is not required.... You must realize what this means to you. You must realize - Look here, I'll help you. I'll plan some escape. There must be ways. I have friends - "

She stifled the leap of her heart. She held her head high and made what she thought was a very noble little speech. "It is for my father, monsieur. You do not understand. It is to save my father."

He looked at her in silence. He was afraid to answer for a moment; he could feel the unruly blood beating even in the lips he pressed together.

"But don't you understand - " he blurted at last and broke off.

After all, he did not know this girl. If he swayed her judgment now, and dragged her away, what life, what compensation could he offer her? How did he know that she would not regret it? Would she be happier in a world unknown?....

She had been brought up to this sort of thing. It was bred in her.... Marriage was her inevitable game. This very charm she exercised, this subtle, haunting invasion of his senses, what was that but another proof of the harem existence where all influences were forced to serve the ends of sex ...

And she was so maddeningly resigned to taking this general!

A queer hot rage was gaining possession of him. "Oh, well, if you prefer this," he said brutally, with a youthful desire to wreak pain in return for that strange pain which something was inflicting upon him.

A girl who would let him kiss her one night - and on the next inform him that she was giving herself to an unknown - an old Turk.... If she could go like that, to some other's arms and lips ...

He wanted to take her fiercely in his arms and crush her lips against his and then fling her away and say, "Oh, go to him now - if you can!"

And at the same time he wanted to gather her to him as tenderly as if she were a flower he was guarding and tell her that he would protect her against all the world.

He was divided and confused and blindly angry. He felt baffled and frustrated. He was both aching and raging. And yet he was capable of reminding himself, in some corner of his uninvaded mind, that this was undoubtedly the best thing for them both.

What else? For him? For her?

And yet his tongue went on stabbing her.

"If this is what you are determined to do - " he heard himself saying hardly, yet with a hint of deferred finality.

It was as if he had said, "If this, then, is what you are like! If you are the soft, submissive harem creature, the toy, the odalisque - If you will endure undesired love rather than face the world - "

And she knew that was what he was saying to her. The injustice brought a lump of self-pity to her throbbing throat.... That he should not realize and honor the courage of her sacrifice.... That he should reproach, despise.... She had expected other entreaties ... protestations....

Her heart ached with a throb of steady dreariness.

But she did not stir. Not a line of her drooping draperies wavered towards him. And swallowing that lump in her throat, she achieved a toneless, "That is what I am going to do."

At the other end of the garden a sound came from the house.

Ryder seemed to rouse himself. "Good-bye, then," he said, uncertainly.

"Good-bye, monsieur."

He looked oddly at her. "Good-bye," he muttered again, and turned, and stumbled out of the gate.

A pool of moonlight lay without its arches, and he stepped into it as if coming out of the shadows of an enchanted garden. He stood and straightened himself as if throwing off that garden's spell. He put back his shoulders and took a quick step down the lane.

A slight sound drew his eyes back.

She had followed him to the gate; she stood there, in the moonlight, against the inky wells of shadow into which her black robe flowed, and in the moonlight her face, gazing after him, was an exquisite, ethereal apparition, like a spirit of the garden.

She had cast off her veil. He had a vision of her dark eyes shining over rose-flushed cheeks, of deeper-rose-red lips in curves of haunting sweetness, of the tender contour of her young face, fixed unforgettingly in the radiant moonlight - only an instant's vision, for while the blood stopped in his veins the darkness engulfed her, like a magician's curtain.

But he waited while he heard the gate closed. Still he waited while he heard her locking it. And then for all his hot young pride, he turned back and knocked upon it. He called softly. He whispered entreaties.

Not a sound. Not an answer.

In a revulsion of feeling he turned and made his way blindly from the lane.

She had heard his voice. Like a creature utterly spent, she had been leaning against the great gate from which she had withdrawn the key. But she uttered not a breath in answer, and after she had heard his footsteps die away she turned slowly back and groped among the rose roots for the key's hiding place.

Mechanically she smoothed it over and moved on towards the house. All was quiet there. That sound had been no alarm. Unobserved she slipped within the little door, and up the spiral steps.

She had not seen the dark eyes that were watching her, from the other side of the rose thicket. After the girl had gained the house, the old woman came forward and stooped before the marked bush, muttering under her breath at the thorns. After a few moments she gave a little grunt of satisfaction and her exploring hand drew out the key.

Smoothing again the rifled hiding place among the roses, she made her careful way into the house.

# CHAPTER VI

## A SECRET OF THE SANDS

The siesta was past. The sun was tilting towards the west and shadows were beginning to jut out across the blazing sands.

Over the mounds of rubbish the bearers had resumed their slow procession, a picturesque frieze of tattered, indigo-robed, ebony figures, baskets on heads, against a cloudless cobalt sky, and again the hot air was invaded with the monotonous rise and fall of their labor chant.

A man with a short, pointed red beard and an academic face beneath a pith helmet was stooping over the siftings from those baskets, intent upon the stream of sand through the wire screens. Patiently he discarded the unending pebbles, discovering at rare intervals some lost bead, some splinter of old sycamore wood, some fragment of pottery in which a Ptolemy had sipped his wine - or a kitchen wench had soaked her lentils.

Beyond the man were traces of the native camp, a burnt-out fire, a roll of rags, a tattered shelter cloth stuck on two tottering sticks, and distributed indiscriminatingly were a tethered goat, a white donkey with motionless, drooping ears, and a few supercilious camels.

The camp was in the center of a broken line of foothills on the desert's edge. North and south and west the wide sands swept out to meet the sky, and to the east, shutting out the Nile valley, the hills reared their red rock from the yellow drift.

Among the jutting rock in the foreground yawned dark mouths that were the entrances of the discovered tombs, and within one of these tombs was another white man. He was conducting his own siftings in high solitude, a lean, bronzed young man, with dark hair and eyes and, at the present moment, an unexhilarated expression.

It had been two weeks since Jack Ryder had returned to camp. Two interminable weeks. They were the longest, the dullest, the dreariest, the most irritatingly undelighting weeks that he had ever lived through.

But bitterly he resented any aspersion from the long-suffering Thatcher upon his disposition. He wanted it distinctly understood that he was *not* low-spirited. Not in the least. A man wasn't in the dumps just because he wasn't - well, garrulous. Just because he didn't go about whistling like a steam siren or exult like a cheer leader when some one dug up the effigy of a Hathor-cow.... Just because he objected when the natives twanged their fool strings all night and wailed at the moon.

The moon was full now. Round and white it went sailing blandly over the eternal monotony of desert.... Round and white, it lighted up the eternal sameness of life.... He had never noticed it before, but a moon was a poignantly depressing phenomenon.

He couldn't help it. A man couldn't make himself be a comedian. It wasn't as if he wanted to be a grump. He would have been glad to be glad. He wanted Thatcher to make him glad. He defied him to.

He didn't enjoy this flat, insipid taste of things, this dull grind, this feeling of sameness and dullness that made nothing seem worth while.... A feeling that he had been marooned on a desert island, far from all stir and throb of life.

Suppose he did dig up a Hathor-cow? Suppose he dug up Hathor herself, or Cleopatra, or ten little Ptolemies? What was the good of it?

Not Jinny Jeffries herself could have cast more aspersions upon the personal value of excavations.

When he was tired of denying to himself that there was anything unusual the matter with him, he shifted the inner argument and took up the denial that anything which had happened in Cairo those two weeks before had anything to do with it. As if that rash encounter *mattered*! As if he were the silly, senseless sentimental sort of idiot to go mooning about his work because of a girl - and a girl from a harem with a taste for secret masquerades and Turkish marriages!

As if he cared - !

Of course - he admitted this logically and coldly now to himself, as he sat there in the ray of his excavator's lantern, on the sanded floor at the end of the Hall of Offerings - of course, he was sorry for the girl. It was no life for any young girl - especially a spirited one, with her veins bubbling with French blood.

The system was wrong. If they were going to shut up those girls, they had no business to bring them up on modern ideas. If they kept the mashrubiyeh on the windows and the yashmak on their faces they ought to keep the kohl on their eyes and the henna on their fingers and education out of their hidden heads.

It was too bad.... But, of course, they were brought up to it. Look how quickly that girl had given in. She was Turkish, through and through. Submissive. Docile.... And a darned good thing she was, too! Suppose she had taken him at his fool word. Suppose she had really wanted to get away!

Lucky, that's what he'd been. And it would be a lesson to him. Never again. No more masked young things with their stolen keys and their harem entrances. No more whispered tales of woe in a shady garden. No more -

Violently he wrenched himself from his No Mores. Recollection had a way of stirring an unpleasant tumult.

But it was all over. He had forgotten it - he *would* forget it. He would forget *her*. Work, that was the thing. Normal, sensible, every day work.

But there was no joy in this tonic work. Somewhere, between a night and a morning, he had lost that glow of accomplishment which had buoyed him, which had made him fairly ecstatic over the discovery of this very tomb.

For this tomb was his own find. It had been found long before by the plundering Persians, and it had been found by Arabs who had plundered the Persian remains - but between and after those findings the oblivious sands had swept over it, blotting it from the world, choking the entrance hall and the shafts, seeping through half-sealed entrances and packing its dry drift over the rifled sarcophagus of the king and over the withered mummy of the young girl in the ante-room. The tombs had been cleared now, down almost to the stone floors, and Ryder was busy with the drifts that had lodged in the crevices about the entrance to the shaft.

It was really an important find. Although much plundered, the walls were intact, and the delicate carvings in the white limestone walls were exceptional examples. And there were some very interesting things to decipher. A scholar and an explorer could well be enthusiastic.

But Ryder continued to look far from enthusiastic. Even when his groping fingers, searching a cranny, came in contact with a hard substance his face did not change to any lightning radiance. Unexpectantly he picked up the sand-encrusted lump and brushed it off. A gleam of gold shone in his hand. But it was no ancient amulet or necklace or breast guard - nor was it any bit of the harness of the plundering Persians. It was a locket, very heavily and ornately carved.

He stood a moment staring down at the thing with a curious feeling of having stood staring down at exactly the same thing before - that subconscious feeling of the repetition of events which supports the theories of reincarnationists - and then, quite suddenly, memory came to his aid.

In McLean's office. That day of the masquerade. Those visiting Frenchmen and that locket they had shown him. Of course the thing reminded him -

And it was remarkably alike. The same thick oval, the same ponderous effect of the coat of arms - if it should prove the same coat of arms that would be a clue!

With his mind still piecing the recollection and surmise together his fingers pressed the spring. There was a miniature within, but it was not the picture of Monsieur Delcasse. Ryder was looking down upon the face of a girl, a beautiful, spirited face, with merry eyes and wistful lips - dark eyes, with a lovely arch of brow, and rose-red lips with haunting curves.

And eyes and brows and lips and curves, it was the face of the girl who had gazed after him in the moonlight against the shadows of the pasha's garden.

# CHAPTER VII

## TO McLEAN'S ASTONISHMENT

"It is no end of good of you, Jack, to take this trouble," Andrew McLean remarked appreciatively, looking up from his scrutiny of the packet which his unexpected luncheon guest had pushed over to his plate.

"Uncommon thoughtful. It's undoubtedly a twin to that locket, the portrait of the man's wife - whatever his name was."

"Delcasse," said Jack Ryder promptly.

Gratefully he drained the second lemon squash which the silent-footed Mohammed had placed at his elbow. It had been a hard morning's trip, this coming in from camp in high haste, and he was hot and dusty.

"You might have sent the thing," McLean mentioned. "I daresay that special agent chap has left the country, for I recollect he said he was at the end of his search.... And, of course, this isn't much of a clue - eh, what?"

"It's everything of a clue," insisted Ryder. "It shows where this Frenchman was working, for the first thing - "

"Unless it had been stolen by some native who lost it in that tomb."

"Natives don't lose gold lockets. Of course it might have been stolen and hidden - but that's far-fetched. It's much more

MARY HASTINGS BRADLEY

likely that this was the very tomb where Delcasse was working at the time of his death. For one thing, the place showed signs of previous excavation up to the inner corridor, and there I'll swear no modern got ahead of me. And for another thing, it's a perfect specimen of the limestone carving of the Tomb of Thi which Delcasse wrote his book about - looks very much as if it might be by the same artist. There's a flock of hippopotami in a marsh scene with the identical drawing, and there's the same lovely boat in full sail - but there, you bounder, you don't know the Tomb of Thi from a thyroid gland. You're here to administer financial justice, the middle, the high, and the low; your soul is with piasters, not the past. But take my word for it, it's exactly the spot where an enthusiast of the Thi Tomb would be grubbing away.... Lord, they could choose their find in those days!"

"It's uncommonly likely," McLean conceded, abandoning his demolished cherry tart and pulling out his briar. "And if the locket proves the duplicate of the other it indicates that it's a portrait of Madame Delcasse, but it doesn't indicate what has become of Madame Delcasse.... Though in a general way," McLean deduced with Scotch judicialness, "it supports the theory of foul play. The woman would hardly have lost her miniature, or have sold it, except under pressing conditions. In fact - "

Ryder was brusque with his facts.

"That doesn't matter - Madame Delcasse doesn't matter. The thing that matters is - "

As brusquely he broke off. His tongue balked before the revelation but he goaded it on.

"That there is a girl - the living image of that picture."

"I say!" McLean looked up at that, distinctly intrigued. "That's getting on.... You mean you've seen her?"

Ryder nodded, suddenly busy with his cigarette.

"Where is she, now? In Cairo? That's luck, man!... And you say she's like?"

"You'd think it her picture."

"It's an uncommon face." McLean bent over it again. "I fancied the artist had just been making a bit of beauty, but if there's a girl like that - ! Fancy stumbling on that!... But where is she? And what name does she go by?"

"Oh, her name - she doesn't know her own, of course." Ryder paused uncertainly. "She's in Cairo," he began again vaguely. "She'd be just about the right age - eighteen or so. She - she's had awf'ly hard, luck." Distressfully he hesitated.

The shrewd eyes of McLean dwelt upon him in sorrowful silence. "Eh, Jock," he said at last, with mock scandal scarcely veiling rebuke. "I did not know that you knew any of that sort - the poor, wee lost thing.... Tell me, now - "

"Tell you you're off your chump," said Jack rudely. "She's no lost lamb. Fact is, she's never spoken to a man - except myself." He rather enjoyed the start this gave McLean after his insinuations. It helped him on with his story.

"The girl doesn't know her own name at all, I gather. She thinks she's the daughter of Tewfick Pasha. Her mother married the Turk and died very soon afterwards and he brought up this girl as his own. She says she's his only child."

He paused, ostensibly to blow an elaborate smoke ring, but actually to enjoy McLean's astonishment. As astonishment, it was distinctly vivid. It verged upon a genuine horror as Ryder's meaning sank into his friend's mind.

McLean knew - slightly - Tewfick Pasha. He knew - supremely - the inviolable seclusion of a daughter of such a household. He knew the utter impossibility of any man's speech with her.

Yet here was Ryder telling him -

Ryder's telling him was a sketchy performance. He mentioned the girl's appearance at the masquerade and their acquaintance. He touched lightly upon her attempted flight and his pursuit. Even more lightly he passed over those lingering moments at her garden gate and the exchange of confidences.

"She said that her dead mother had been French. And that her name was her mother's - Aimee. So there is - "

"But the likeness, man - her face? She never unveiled to you?"

"Well, the next night - "

"The *next* night?"

It was at this point that Ryder began to lose his relish of McLean's astonishment.

"Yes, the next night," he repeated with careful carelessness.... "I told the girl I would come and see if she got in all right - there had been some footsteps the night before - "

"And you went? And she came?"

"Do you suppose she sent her father?"

"You're lucky she didn't send her father's eunuch," McLean retorted grimly. "Well, get on with your damning story. The girl took off her veil - "

"Nothing of the kind," said Jack a trifle testily - so soon does conventional masculinity champion the conservatism of the other sex! "That was just as I was going - gone, in fact. I looked back and she had drawn her veil aside. The moon was bright on her face - I saw her as clear as daylight, and I tell you that this miniature is a picture of her. She is Delcasse's daughter and she doesn't know it. Her mother was stolen by that disgusting old Turk - "

"Hold on a bit. Fifteen years ago Tewfick could hardly have been thirty and he has the rep of a Don Juan. It may have been a love affair or it may have been plunder.... The girl remembers her?"

"Very little. She was so young when her mother died. She said that the father was so in love that he never married again."

"H'm ... It seems to me that I've heard tales of our Tewfick and of pretty ladies in apartments. Cairo is a city of secrets and tattlers. However - as to this Delcasse inheritance, I'll just notify the French legation - "

"We'll have to look sharp," said Ryder quickly. "There's no time to lose. The girl is to be married."

"Married?... But she'll inherit the money just the same."

"But she doesn't want to be married," Ryder insisted anxiously. "Her father - her alleged father - has just sprung this on her. Says there are political or financial reasons. He's been caught in some dirty work by this Hamdi Bey and he's stopping Hamdi's mouth with the girl.... And we've got to stop that."

"I wonder if we can," said McLean thoughtfully.

"If we can? When the girl is French? When she's been lied to and deceived?"

"She seems to have been taken jolly well care of. Brought up as his own and all that. Keep your shirt on, Jack," McLean advised dryly with a shrewd glance from his gray eyes at the other's unguarded heat.

Then his eyes dropped to the miniature again. A lovely face. A lovely unfortunate creature.... And if the daughter looked like that, small wonder that Jack was touched.... Beauty in distress.

Some men had all the luck, McLean reflected. He had never taken Jack for the gallivanting kind, either, yet here he was going to masquerades with one girl and coming home with another....

Jack was too good looking, that was the trouble with the youngster. Good looking and gay humored. The kind that attracted women.... Women and romance were never fluttering about lank, light-eyed, uninteresting old Scotchmen of twenty-nine!

A mild and wistful pang, which McLean refused to name, made itself known.

"I'll see the legation," he began.

"At once. I'll wait," urged Ryder.

And at once McLean went.

*     *     *     *     *

The result was what he had foreseen. The legation was appreciative of his interest. That special agent had returned to France but his address was left, and undoubtedly the family of Delcasse would be grateful for any information which Monsieur McLean could send.

"Send!" repudiated Ryder hotly. "Write to France and back - wait for somebody to come over! Can't the legation do something now?"

"The legation has no authority. They can't take the girl away from the man who is, at any rate, her step-father."

"They can put the fear of God into him about this marriage. They can deny his right to hand her over to one of his pals. They can threaten him with an inquiry into the circumstances of her mother's marriage."

"And why should they? They may regard it as a very natural marriage. And remember, my dear Jack, that the legation has no desire to alienate the affections of influential Turks, or criticize fifteen-years-ago romances. You have a totally wrong impression of the responsibilities of foreign representatives."

"But to let him dispose of a French girl - "

"He is disposing of her, as his daughter, in honorable marriage to a wealthy and aristocratic general. There can be no question of his motives - "

"Of course, if you think that sort of thing is all right - "

Carefully McLean ignored the other's wrath.

Patiently he explained. "It's not what I think, my dear fellow, it's what the legation thinks. There's not a chance in the world of getting the marriage stopped."

"Then I'll do it myself," declared Ryder. "I'll see this Tewfick Pasha and talk to him. Tell him the money is to come to the girl only when she is single. Tell him the French law gives the father's representatives full charge. Tell him that he kidnapped the mother and the government will prosecute unless the girl is given her liberty. Tell him anything. A man with a guilty conscience can always be bluffed."

In silence McLean gazed upon him, perplexed and clouded, his quizzical twinkle gone. Jack was taking this thing infernally to heart.... And it was a bad business.

"You will let me do the telling," he stated at last, grimly. "What can be said, I'll say. Like a fool, I will meddle."

And so it happened that within another hour two very stiff and constrained young men were ringing the bell at the entrance door of Tewfick Pasha.

# CHAPTER VIII

## TEWFICK RECEIVES

A huge Soudanese admitted them. They found themselves in a tiled vestibule, looking through open arches into the green of a garden - that garden, Ryder hardly needed to remind himself, with whose back door he had made such unconventional acquaintance.

Now he had a glimpse of a sunny fountain and fluttering pigeons, and, on either side of the garden, of the two wings of the building, gay white walls with green shutters more suggestive of a French villa than an Egyptian palace, before the Soudanese marshaled them toward the stairs upon the right.

The left, then, was the way to the haremlik. And somewhere in those secluded rooms, to which no man bat the owner of the palace ever gained admission, was Aimee.

The Soudanese mounted the stairs before them and held open a door into a long drawing-room from which the pasha's modernity had stripped every charm except the color of some worn old rugs; the windows were draped in European style, the walls exhibited paper instead of paneling; in one corner was a Victrola and in another, beside a lounge chair, stood a table littered with cigarette trays
and French novels with explicit titles.

The only Egyptian touch to the place was four enormous oil portraits of pompous turbaned gentlemen, in one of whom Ryder  recognized the familiar rotundity of Mahomet Ali in his

MARY HASTINGS BRADLEY

grand robes.

As a pasha's palace it was a blow, and Ryder's vague, romantic notions of high halls and gilded arches, suffered a collapse.

Tewfick Pasha came in with haste. He had been going out when these callers were announced and he was dressed for parade, in a very light, very tight suit, gardenia in his buttonhole, cane in his gloved hands, fez upon his head. For all their smiling welcome, his full, dark eyes were uneasy.

He had grown distrustful of surprises.

It was McLean's affair to reassure him. Far from fulminating any accusations the canny Scot announced himself as the bearer of glad tidings. A fortune, he announced, was coming to the pasha - or to the pasha's family. A very rich old woman in France had decided to change her will.

There he paused and the pasha continued to smile non-committally, but the word fortune was operating. In the back of his mind he was hastily trying to think of rich old women in France who might change their wills.

"I am afraid that it is my stupidity which has kept you from the knowledge of this for some weeks," McLean went on. "I had so many other matters to look up that I did not at once consult my records. And it has been so many years since you married Madame Delcasse that the name had slipped general recollection.... It was twelve years ago, I believe, that she died?"

Casually he waited and Jack Ryder held his breath. He felt the full suspense of a pause long enough for the pasha's thoughts to dart down several avenues and back. If the man should deny it! But why should he? What harm in the admission, after all these years, with Madame Delcasse dead and buried? And with a fortune involved in the admission.

The Turk bowed and Ryder breathed again.

"Ten years," said Tewfick softly.

"Ah - ten. But there has been no communication with France for twelve years or even longer?"

"Possibly not, monsieur."

"This old aunt," pursued McLean, "was a person of prejudice as well as fortune - hence it has taken a little time for her to adjust herself." He paused and looked understandingly at the Turk, who nodded amiably as one whose comprehension met him more than half way.

"My own aunt was of a similar obstinacy," he murmured. He added, "This fortune you speak of - it comes through my wife?"

"For her inheritors. Madame Delcasse - the former Madame Delcasse I should say - left but one daughter?"

Again the pasha bowed and again Ryder felt the throb of triumph. He looked upon his friend with admiration. How marvelously McLean had worked the miracle. No accusations, no threats, no obstacles, no blank walls of denial! Not a ruffle of discord in the establishment of these salient facts - the marriage of Madame Delcasse to the pasha and the existence of the daughter.

Wonderful man - McLean. He had never half appreciated him.

But the pasha was not wholly the simple assenter.

"Do I understand," he inquired, "that there is a fortune coming from France for my daughter?" And at McLean's confirmation, "And when you say fortune," he continued, "you intend to say - ?" and his glance now took in the silent American, considering that some cue must be his.

But McLean responded. "The figures are not to be

divulged - not until the aunt is in communication with her niece. But they will be large, monsieur, for this aunt is a person of great wealth."

"And yet alive to enjoy it," said Tewfick with smiling eyes.

"An aged and dying woman," thrust in Ryder in haste. "Her only care now is to see her niece before she dies."

"Ah!... But that could be arranged," said Tewfick amiably.

"We have at once communicated with France," McLean told him, "but we came instantly to you, to, inform you - "

"A thousand thanks and a thousand! The bearers of good tidings," smiled their host.

"Because we understand that there is a question of the young lady's marriage," pursued McLean, "and you would, of course, wish to defer this until these new circumstances are complied with."

The pasha stared. "Not at all. A fortune is as pleasant to a wife as to a maid."

"There are so many questions of law," offered McLean with purposeful vagueness. "French wardship and trusteeship and all that. It would be advisable, I think, to wait."

"Absurd," said the pasha easily.

"You would want no doubts cast upon the legality of the marriage," McLean persisted thoughtfully, "and since made-moiselle is under age and the French law has certain restrictions - "

"Pff! We are not under the French law - at least I have not heard that England has relinquished her power," retorted Tewfick not without malice.

"But Mademoiselle Delcasse is French," thrust in Ryder. He knew that McLean had ventured as far as he, an official and responsible person, could go, and that the burden of intimation must rest upon himself. "And under her father's will his family there is considered in trusteeship. So there would be certain technicalities that must be considered before any marriage can be arranged, the signature of the French guardian, the settlement of the dot - this inheritance, for instance - all mere formalities but involving a little delay."

Tewfick Pasha turned in his chair and cocked his eyes at this strange young man who had dropped from the blue with this extensive advice. He looked puzzled. This American fitted into no type of his acquaintance. He was so very young and slim and boyish ... with not at all the air of a legal representative.... But McLean's position vouched for him.

"You speak for the French family, monsieur?"

Unhesitatingly Ryder declared that he did.

"Then you may inform the family," announced Tewfick, bristling, "that my daughter has been very well cared for all these years without advice from France."

"I haven't a doubt of it," said Ryder quickly, "but the French law might begin to entertain doubts of it, if mademoiselle were married off now without consultation with the authorities.... Already," he added a little meaningly, as the other shrugged the suggestion away, "there have been questions raised concerning the mother's marriage and the separation of the little Mademoiselle Delcasse from her relatives in France, and now if she were to be married without any legal settlement of her estate - "

Steadily he sustained the other's gaze, while his unfinished thought seemed to float significantly in the air about them.

"Have a cigarette," said the pasha hospitably, extending a gold case monogrammed with diamonds and emeralds. "Ah, coffee!" he announced, welcomingly, as a little black boy entered with a brass tray of steaming cups.

"I hope, gentlemen, that you like my coffee. It is not the usual Turkish brew. No, this comes from Aden, the finest coffee in the world. A ship captain brings it to me, especially."

Beamingly he sipped the scalding stuff, then darted back to that suspended sentence. "But you were saying - something of a trusteeship?... Do I understand that it is an aunt of Madame Delcasse - the former Madame Delcasse - who is leaving this money?"

"Not of Madame but of Monsieur Delcasse," McLean informed him.

"Ah!... That accounts ... But in that case, then, there need be no concern in France over my daughter's marriage...." He turned his round eyes from one to the other a moment.

"There is no Mademoiselle Delcasse."

"Sir?" said Ryder sharply.

"There is no Mademoiselle Delcasse," repeated the pasha, his eyes frankly enlivened.

"But - we have just been speaking - you cannot mean to say - "

"We have been speaking of my daughter - the daughter of the former Madame Delcasse."

Smilingly he looked upon them. "A pity that we did not understand each other. But you appear to know so much - and I supposed that you knew that, too, that the daughter of Monsieur Delcasse was dead."

Neither of the young men spoke. McLean looked politely

attentive; Ryder's face maintained that look of concentration which guarded the fluctuations of his feelings.

"It was many years ago," the pasha murmured, putting down his coffee cup and selecting another cigarette. "Not long after her mother's marriage to me.... A very charming little girl - I was positively attached to her," Tewfick added reminiscently.

"Well, well, well, what a pity now," said McLean very slowly. "This will be a great disappointment.... And so the present mademoiselle - "

"Is my daughter."

McLean was silent. Ryder could hardly trust himself to speak.

"What did she die of?" he asked at last, in a voice whose edged quality brought the pasha's glance to him with a flash of hostility behind its veil.

But he answered calmly enough. "Of the fever, monsieur.... She was never strong."

"And her grave... I should like to make a report."

"It was in the south ... desert burial, I am afraid. You must know that the little one was hardly a true believer for our cemetery."

"And you would say that she was only five or six years old?" Ryder persisted.

The pasha nodded.

"I should like to get as near as possible to the date if it is not too much trouble.... The father died about fifteen years ago and the mother was married to you soon after?"

"Really, monsieur, you - "

Tewfick was frankly restive.

"I know nothing of the father," he said sullenly. "And as to the child's death - how can one recall after these years? In one, two years after she came to me - one does not grave these things upon the eyeballs."

"But you do remember that it was long ago - when your own daughter was very little?"

"Exactly. That is my recollection, monsieur.... And I recall," said the pasha, suddenly obliging and sentimental, "that even my little one cried for the child. It was afflicting.... Assure the family in France of my sympathy in their disappointment."

"I am sorry that my news is after all of no interest to you," observed McLean, setting the example for rising. "You will pardon my error of information - and accept my appreciation of your courtesy."

"It is I who am indebted for your trouble," their host assured them, all smiles again.

But Ryder was not to be led away without a parting shot.

"The name of the Delcasse child - was Aimee?"

Imperceptibly Tewfick hesitated. Then bowed in assent.

"Odd," said young Ryder thoughtfully. "And your own daughter's name, also, is Aimee.... Two little ones with the same name."

With a slight, vexed laugh, as one despairing of understanding, the pasha turned to McLean. "Your young friend, monsieur, is uninformed that Turkish children have many names.... After the loss of the elder we called the little one by the same name.... I trust I have made everything perfectly clear to you?"

"As crystal," said McLean politely.

*     *     *     *     *

"As lightning," said Jack Ryder hotly, striding down the street. "It was a flash of invention, that yarn. When I spoke about the questions raised by his marriage the old fox sniffed the wind and was afraid of trouble - he decided on the instant that no future fortune was worth interference with his plans, and he cut the ground from under our feet.... Lord, what a lie!"

"Masterly, you must admit."

"Oh, I admired the beggar, even while I choked on it. But fever - desert burial - two Aimees! And the sentimental face he pulled - he ought to have had a spot-light and wailing woodwinds."

McLean chuckled.

"I'll believe anything of him now," Ryder rushed on. "I'll bet he murdered Delcasse and kidnapped the mother - and now he is selling their daughter - "

"I fancy murder's a bit beyond our Tewfick. That's too thick. He's probably telling the truth there - he may never have known Delcasse. And as for the widow - she must have been in no end of trouble with a dead man and a wrecked expedition and a baby on her hands, and Tewfick may have offered himself as a grateful solution to her. You'd be surprised at the things I've heard. And if she looked like her picture Tewfick probably laid himself out to be lovely to her.... I rather like the chap, myself."

"I love him," Ryder snorted. "The infernal liar - "

"Steady now - suppose it's all the truth? Nothing impossible to it. Fact is, I rather believe it," said McLean imperturbably. "It hangs together. If this girl you met thinks she's his daughter, that's conclusive. She'd have some idea - servants' gossip or family whisperings.... And why should he have brought her up as his own?"

"No other children. And he'd grown fond of her, of course. If you could see her!" retorted Ryder.

"Just as well, I can't.... And I think he could hardly have kept her in the dark.... We'd better call it a wild goose chase and say the man's telling the truth."

"If this girl were his daughter she couldn't be more than fourteen years old. And I've seen the girl and she's eighteen if she's a day - you might take her for twenty. *Fourteen!*" said Ryder in repudiating scorn.

Hesitating McLean murmured something about the early maturity of the natives.

"Natives?" Ryder flung angrily back. "This girl's French!"

"As far as we are concerned, Jack, this girl is Turkish - and fourteen.... We can't get around that, and you had better not forget it," his friend quietly advised. "We've done everything that we can and there is no use working yourself up.... If anybody's to blame in this business, I don't think it's Tewfick - he's done the handsome thing by her - but the fool Frenchman who took his baby and his wife into the desert, and it's too late to rag him. Cheer up, old top, and forget it. There's nothing more to be done."

It was sound advice, Jack Ryder knew it. They had done all that they could. McLean had been a brick. There remained nothing now but to notify the Delcasse aunt that Tewfick Pasha claimed the child.

"And I've a notion, Jack," said McLean thoughtfully, "that he might not have done that if you hadn't rushed him so, trying to break off the marriage. That was what frightened him."

"I thought you said she was his own daughter," Ryder responded indignantly, and to that McLean merely murmured, "She will be now, to all time."

It was a haunting thought. It left Ryder with the bitter taste of blame in his mouth, the gall and wormwood of blame and a baffled defeat.

But for that sense of blame he might have taken McLean's advice. He might - but for that - have gone the way of wisdom, and accepted the inevitable.

As it was, he did none of these things.

*　*　*　*　*

He said to himself that all that he could do now - and the least that he could do - was to let the girl know as much of the story as he knew and draw her own conclusions. Then, if she wanted to go on and sacrifice herself for Tewfick, very well. That was none of his affair.

But she had a right to the truth and to the chance of choice.

He did not know what he could do, but secretly and defiantly he promised himself that he would do something, and in the back of his mind an idea was already taking shape. It was manifest in the tenacity with which he refused to send the locket to the Delcasses. He had the case and the miniature photographed very carefully by the man who did the reproductions for museum illustrations, and he sent that, conscious of McLean's silent thought that he was cherishing the portrait for a sentimental memory.

But he had other plans for it.

He did not return to his diggings. He sent a message to the deserted Thatcher, faking errands in Cairo, and he took a room at the hotel where Jinny Jeffries - now up the Nile - had stayed. He spent a great deal of time evenings in the hotel garden, staring over the brick walls to the tops of distant palms beyond, and not infrequently he slipped out the garden's back door and wandered up and down the dark canyon of a lane.

He might as well have walked up and down the veranda of Shepheard's Hotel.

And yet the girl had her key. She could get away if she wanted to and she might want to if she knew the truth.

But how to get that truth to her? That was his problem. A dozen plans he considered and rejected. There were the mails - simple and obvious channel - but he had a strong idea that maidens in Mohammedan seclusion do not receive their letters directly. And now, especially, Tewfick would be on his guard.

Then there was the chance of a message through some native's hands. The house servants - ? There were hours, one day, when Ryder sauntered about the streets, covertly eyeing the baggy-trousered *sais* who stood holding a horse in the sun or the tattered baker's boy, approaching the entrance with his long loaves upon his head, but Ryder's Arabic was not of a power or subtlety to corrupt any creature, and he stayed his tongue.

Bitterly he regretted his wasted years. If he had not misspent them in godly living he would now be upon such terms of intimacy with some official's pretty wife who had the entree to a pasha's daughter that she could be induced to make use of it for him.

Desperately he thought of remedying this defect. There were several charming young matrons not averse to devoted young men, but the time was short for establishing those confidential relations which were what he required now.

Jinny Jeffries would do it for him if she could, but Jinny would not return for another week. And if she changed her mind and took the boat back - as he, alack! had advised - instead of the express, then she would be longer.

And meanwhile the days were passing, four of them now since he and McLean had heard the Soudanese locking the door behind them.

There seemed nothing for it but to trust to that idea which had been slowly shaping in his mind.

# CHAPTER IX

## A WEDDING PRESENT

In a room high in the palace a young girl was trying on a frock. Before a tall pier glass she stood indifferently, one hip sagging to the despair of the kneeling seamstress, her face turned listlessly from the image in the glass.

Through the open window, banded with three bars, she looked into the rustling tops of palms, from which the yellow date fruit hung, and beyond the palms the hot, bright, blue sky and the far towers of a minaret.

"A bit more to the left, h'if you please, miss," the woman entreated through a mouthful of pins, and apathetically the young figure moved.

"A bit of h'all right, now, that drape," the woman chirped, sitting back on her heels to survey her work.

She was an odd gnome-like figure, with a sharp nose on one side of her head and an outstanding knob of hair on the other. Into that knob the thin locks were so tightly strained that her pointed features had an effect of popping out of bondage.

She was London born, brought out by an English official's wife as dressmaker to the children, remaining in Cairo as wife of a British corporal. Since no children had resulted to require her care and the corporal maintained his distaste for thrift, Mrs. Hendricks had resumed her old trade, and had become a familiar figure to many fashionable Turkish harems, slipping in and out morning and evening, sewing busily away behind the bars upon frocks that would have graced a court ball, and lunching in familiar sociability with the family, sometimes having a bey or a captain or a pasha for a vis-a-vis when the men in the family dropped in for luncheon.

As the girl did not turn her head she looked for approbation to the third person in the room, a tall, severely handsome Frenchwoman in black, whose face had the beauty of chiseled marble and the same quality of cold perfection. This was Madame de Coulevain, teacher of French and literature to the *jeunes filles* of Cairo, former governess of Aimee, returned now to her old room in the palace for the wedding preparations.

There was history behind madame's sculptured face. In an incredibly impulsive youth she had fled from France with a handsome captain of Algerian dragoons; after a certain matter at cards he had ceased to be a captain and became petty official in a Cairo importing house; later yet, he became an invalid.

Life, for the Frenchwoman, was a matter of paying for her husband's illness, then for his funeral expenses, and then of continuing to pay for the little one which the climate had required them to send to a convent in France.

There was, at first, the hope of reunion, extinguished by each added year. What could madame, unknown, unfriended, unaccredited, accomplish in France? The mere getting there was impossible - the little one required so much. Her daughter was no dependent upon charity. And in Cairo madame had a clientele, she commanded a price. And so for the child's sake she taught and saved, concentrating now upon a dot, and feeding her heart with the dutifully phrased letters arriving each week of the years, and the occasional photographs of an ever-growing, unknown young creature.

It was to madame's care that Aimee had been given when the motherless girl had grown beyond old Miriam's ministrations, and for nearly nine years in the palace madame had maintained her courteous and tactful supervision. Indeed, it was only this last year that madame had undertaken new relations with the world outside, perceiving that Aimee would not longer require her.

"Excellent," she said now in her careful, unfamiliar English to Mrs. Hendricks, and in French to Aimee she added, with a hint of asperity, "Do give her a word. She is trying to please you."

"It is very nice, Mrs. Hendricks," said the girl dutifully, bringing her glance back from that far sky.

The little seamstress was instantly all vivacity. "H'and now for the sash - shall we 'ave it so - or so?" she demanded, attaching the wisp of tulle experimentally.

"As you wish it.... It is very nice," Aimee repeated vaguely. She picked up a bit of the shimmering stuff and spread it curiously across her fingers. A dinner gown.... When she wore this she would be a wife.... The wife of Hamdi Bey.... A shiver went through her and she dropped the tulle swiftly.

In ten days more....

Gone was her first rush of sustaining compassion. Gone was her fear for her father and her tenderness to him. Only this numb coldness, this dumb, helpless certainty of a destiny about to be accomplished.... Only this hopeless, useless brooding upon that strange brief past.

There was a stir at the door and on her shuffling, slippered feet old Miriam entered, handing some packages to Madame de Coulevain. Then she turned to revolve about the bright figure of her young mistress, her eyes glistening fondly, her dark fingers touching a soft fold of silver ribbon, while under her breath she chanted in a croon like a lullaby, "Beautiful as the dawn ... she will walk upon the heart of her husband with foot of rose petals ... she will dazzle him with the beams of her eyes and with the locks of her hair, she will bind him to her ... beautiful as the dawn...."

It was the marriage chant of Miriam's native village, an old love song that had come down the wind of centuries.

Mrs. Hendricks, thrusting in the final pins, paid not the slightest attention and Madame de Coulevain displayed interest only in the packages. If she saw the stiffening of the girl's face and the rigid aversion of her eyes from the old nurse's adulation she gave no sign.

Towards Aimee's moods madame preserved a calm and sensible detachment. Never had she invited confidence, and for all the young girl's charm she had never taken her to her heart in the place of that absent daughter. As if jealously she had held herself aloof from such devotion.

Perhaps in Aimee's indulged and petted childhood, with a fond pasha extolling her small triumphs, her dances, her score at tennis at the legation, madame found a bitter contrast to the lot of that lonely child in France. Certainly there was nothing in Aimee's life then to invite compassion, and later, during those hard, mutinous months of the girl's first veiling and seclusion, she had not tried to soften the inevitable for her with a useless compassion.

So now, perceiving this marriage as one more step in the irresistible march of destiny for her charge, she overlooked the youthful fretting and offered the example of her own unmoved acceptance.

"What diamonds!" she said now admiringly, holding up a pin, and, examining the card. "From Seniha Hanum - the cousin of Hamdi Bey."

A moment more she held up the pin but the girl would not give it a look.

"And this, from the same jeweler's," continued madame, while the dressmaker was unfastening the frock, aided by Miriam, anxious that no scratch should mar that milk-white skin.

"How droll - the box is wrapped in cloth, a cloth of plaid."

Aimee spun about. The dress fell, a glistening circle at her feet, and with regardless haste she tripped over it to madame.

"How - strange!" she said breathlessly.

A plaid ... A Scotch plaid. Memories of an erect, tartan-draped young figure, of a thin, bronzed face and dark hair where a tilted cap sat rakishly ... memories of smiling, boyish eyes, darkening with sudden emotion ... memories of eager lips....

She took the box from madame. Within the cloth lay a jeweler's case and within the case a locket of heavily ornamented gold.

Her heart beating, she opened it. For a moment she did not understand. Her own face - her own face smiling back. Yet unfamiliar, that oddly piled hair, that black velvet ribbon about the throat....

Murmuring, madame shared her wonder.

It was Miriam's cry of recognition that told them.

"Thy mother - the grace of Allah upon her! - It is thy mother! Eh, those bright eyes, that long, dark hair that I brushed the many hot nights upon the roof!"

"But you are her image, Aimee," murmured the French-woman, but half understanding the nurse's rapid gutturals, and then, "Your father's gift?"

With the box in her hands the girl turned from them, fearful of the tell-tale color in her cheeks. " But whose else - his thought, of course," she stammered.

That plaid was warning her of mystery.

The dressmaker was creating a diversion. Leaving, she wished to consult about the purchases for to-morrow's work, and madame moved towards the hall with her, talking in her careful English, while Miriam bent towards the dropped finery.

Aimee slipped through another door, into the twilight of her bedroom, whose windows upon the street were darkened by those fine-wrought screens of wood. Swiftly she thrust the box from sight, into the hollow in the mashrubiyeh made in old days to hold a water bottle where it could be cooled by breezes from the street.

Leaning against the woodwork, her fingers curving through the tiny openings, she stared toward the west. The sky was flushing. Broken by the circles, the squares, the minute interstices of the mashrubiyeh, she saw the city taking on the hues of sunset.

Suddenly the cry of a muezzin from a nearby minaret came rising and falling through the streets.

"*La illahe illallah Mohammedun Ressoulallah - *"

The call swelled and died away and rose again ... There is no God but *the* God and Mahomet is the Prophet of God ... From farther towers it sounded, echoing and re-echoing, vibrant, insistent, falling upon crowded streets, penetrating muffling walls.

"*La illahe illallah - *"

In the avenue beneath her two Arabs, leading their camels to market, were removing their shoes and going through the gestures of ceremonial washing with the dust of the street.

"*La illahe -* "

The city was ringing with it.

The seamstress and the Frenchwoman, still talking, had passed down the hall. In the next room Miriam's lips were moving in pious testimony.

"*Ech hedu en la illahe -* ! I testify that there is no God but *the* God."

In the street the Arabs were bowing towards the east, their heads touching the earth.

And in the window above them a girl was reading a note.

*     *     *     *     *

The last call of the muezzin, falling from the tardy towers of Kait Bey drifted faintly through the colored air. With resounding whacks the Arabs were urging on their beast; Miriam, her prayers concluded, was shaking out silks and tulle with a sidelong glance for that still figure in the next room, pressing so close against the guarding screens.

She could not see the pallor in the young face. She could not see the tumult in the dark eyes. She could not see the note, crushed convulsively against the beating breast, in the fingers which so few moments ago had drawn it from the hiding place in the box.

Ryder had not dared a personal letter. But clearly, and distinctly, he stated the story of the Delcasses. He gave the facts which the pasha admitted and the ingenious explanation of the two Aimees. And for reference he gave the address of the Delcasse aunt and agent in France and of Ryder and McLean at the Agricultural Bank.

*     *     *     *     *

The pasha did not dine with his daughter that night. He had been avoiding her of late, a natural reaction from the strain of too-excessive gratitude. A man cannot be continually humble before the young! And it was no pleasure to be reminded by her candid eyes of his late misfortunes and of her absurd reluctance towards matrimony.

As if this marriage were not the best thing for her! As if it were a hardship! To make sad eyes and draw a mouth because one is to be the wife of a rich general.... Irrational ... The little sweetmeat was irritating.

To this point Tewfick's buoyancy had brought him, and all the more hastily because of his eagerness to escape the pangs of that uncomfortable self-reproach. To Aimee, in her new clear-sightedness of misery, it was bitterly apparent that he was reconciled with her lot and careless of it.

So blinded had been her young affection that it was a hard awakening, and she was too young, too cruelly involved, to feel for his easy humors that amused tolerance of larger acquaintance with human nature. She had grown swiftly bitter and resentful, and deeply cold.

And now this letter. It dazed her, like a flame of lightning before her eyes, and then, like lightning, it lit up the world with terrifying luridity. Fiery colored, unfamiliar, her life trembled about her.

Truth or lies? Custom and habit stirred incredulously to reject the supposition. The romance, the adventure of youth, dared its swift acceptance. How could she know? Intuitively she shrank from any question to the pasha, realizing the folly and futility of exposing her suspicion. If he needed to lie, lie he would - and in her understanding of that, she read her own acceptance of the possibility of his needing to lie.

Madame de Coulevain? Madame had never known her mother. Only old Miriam had known her mother and Miriam was the pasha's slave. But the old woman was unsuspecting now, and full of disarming comfort in this marriage of her wild darling.

Through dinner she planned the careless-seeming questions. And then in her negligee, as the old nurse brushed out her hair for the night, "Dadi," said the girl, in a faint voice, "am I truly like my mother?" and when Miriam had finished her fond protestation that they were as like as two roses, as two white roses, bloom and bud, she launched that little cunning phrase on which she had spent such eager hoping.

"And was I like her when I was little - when first she came to my father?"

"Eh - yes. Always thou wast the tiny image which Allah - Glory to his Name! - had made of her," came the nurse's assurance.

"I am glad," said Aimee, in a trembling voice.

She dared not press that more. Confronted with her unconscious admission the old woman would destroy it, feigning some evasion. But there it was, for as much as it was worth....

Presently then, she found another question to slip into the old woman's narrative of the pasha's grief.

"Eh, to hear a man weep," Miriam was murmuring. "Her beauty had set its spell upon him, and - "

"And he lost her so soon. Three or four years only, was it not," ventured Aimee, "that they had of life together?"

It seemed that Miriam's brush missed a stroke.

"Years I forget," the nurse muttered, "but tears I remember," and she began to talk of other things.

But it seemed to Aimee that she had answered. As for that other matter, of the dead Delcasse child, she dared not refer to it, lest Miriam tell the pasha. But how many times, she remembered, had she been told that she was her mother's only one!

Yet, oh, to know, to hear all the story, to learn Ryder's discovery of it! It was all as strange and startling as a tale of Djinns. And the life that it held out to her, the enchanted hope of freedom, of aid - Oh, not again would she refuse his aid!

She had no plans, no purposes. But that night over her hastily-donned frock she slipped the black street mantle and when at last, after endless waiting, the murmuring old palace was safely still and dark, she stole down the spiral stair and gained the garden. And then, a phantom among its shadows, she fled to the rose bushes by the gate.

Breathlessly she knelt and dug into the hiding place of that gate's key. To the furthest corner her fingers explored the hole, pushing furiously against the earth. And then she drew back her hand and crushed it against her face to check the nervous sobs.

The hole was empty. The key was gone.

# CHAPTER X

## THE RECEPTION

In Tewfick Pasha's harem everything was astir.

It was the morning of the marriage, almost the very hour when the wedding cortege would bear the bride from her father's home to the house of her husband.

The invited guests were already arrived and streaming through the reception rooms, a bright, feminine tide in evening toilettes, surrounding the exhibited gifts or pausing about tables of cool syrups, and their soft, low voices, the delicious musical tones of highbred Turkish women, rose like a murmuring of somnolent bees to the tenser regions about, tightening the excitement of haste.

The bride was not yet ready. Still and white, she was the only image of calm in that fluttering, confusing room. Her nearer friends were hovering about her, and her maids of honor, two charming little Turks in rose robes, were draping her veil while old Miriam, resplendent in green and silver, endeavored jealously to outmaneuver them.

On her knees, the gnome-like Mrs. Hendricks was adding an orange blossom to the laces on the train. Then she sat back on her heels, her head a-tilt like a curious bird's, her eyes beaming sentimentally upon the bride.

"The prettiest h'I h'ever did see," she pronounced with satisfaction, "H'as pretty as a wax figger now - h'only a thought *too* waxy."

And like a wax figure indeed, immobile, rigid, the bride was standing before them, arrayed at last in the shimmering white of the sweeping satin, overrich of lace and orange flowers, and shrouded in the clouding waves of her veil. White as her robes, pale as death and as still, the girl looked out at them, and only that sick pallor of her face and the glitter of her dark eyes betrayed the tumult within.

"Your diadem, my dear - you are keeping us attending," came Madame de Coulevain's voice from the door.

The diadem, that heavy circlet of brilliants which crowned the Eastern bride in place of the orange wreath of Western convention, must not be touched by the bride's fingers but placed by one of her friends, married and married but once, and exceptionally happy in that marriage.

Ghul-al-Din, Aimee's selection from her friends, stepped hastily forward now, a soft, dimpled, slow-smiling girl, her eyes drowsy with domesticity. No question of Ghul-al-Din's happiness! She extolled her husband, a young captain of cavalry, and she adored her infant son, a prodigy among children. Life for her was a rosy, unquestioning absorption.

A shaft of irony sped through Aimee, as she bent her head for its crowning at this young wife's hands, and received the ceremonial wishes for her crowning of happiness, a crowning occurring but once in her lifetime. Irony was the only salvation for the hour; without that outlet for her tortured spirit she felt she would grow suddenly mad, hysterical and babbling or passionate and wild.

So many moods had stormed through her since that night when she had found all hope of rescue gone with her lost key! So many impulses seethed frantically now beneath her quiet, as she faced for the last time that white-misted image in the glass. She had a furious longing to tear off that diadem and veil and heavy robe, to scatter the ornaments and drive out all those maddening spectators, all those interested, eager, unknowing, uncaring spectators of her humiliation.

Arranging her veil, draping her satins, as if gauze and silk were all that mattered to this hour! Wishing her happiness - as if happiness could ever be hers now for the wishing! Smiling, fluttering, complimenting, lending to the ghastly sacrifice the familiar acceptances of every day....

If only she could wake from this nightmare and find that it was all a dream. If only she could brush this confusion from her senses and from her heart its dumb terrors.... If only she had the courage for some desperate revolt, some outburst of strength -

"I am ready," she said faintly, turning from the glass, and moved towards the door, while a young eunuch bent for her train, that train of three yards length, which stretched so regally behind her in her slow descent of the stairs.

In the French drawing-room below her father was waiting for the ceremonial farewell, in which the father received the daughter's thanks for all his care of her.

Mechanically Aimee advanced. She stood before him, she lifted her eyes - and there passed from them a look of such strange, breathless, questioning intensity that it was like something palpable.... She had not foreseen this, sudden crisping of her nerves, this defiant passion of her spirit....

Her father? Was he her father? Was it a father who had sold her so, careless, callous - or was it only a father's semblance, and did there lie in the background of those petted, childish years some darker shadow, of a tragedy that had wrecked her mother's life and broken her heart - ?

Like flashing light that look passed between them. It penetrated Tewfick's nonchalant guard and brought the unaccustomed color to his olive cheeks. His handsome eyes turned uneasily aside. A girl's pique perhaps, at the situation, her last defiance of his power, - but for all his reassurance there was something deeper in that look, something tenable, accusing, which went into his soul.

It was a moment in which the last cord of their relationship was severed forever.

She did not speak a word. She bent, not to kiss his hand as custom dictated, but to sweep a long, slow courtesy, that salutation of a maid of spirit to a conqueror, a bending of the pliant back, but with the head held high and the spirit unsurrendered.

And yet there was wretchedness in those proud eyes and a blind fear and supplication.

Useless to beg now. She knew it, and yet the eyes implored.

And then she smiled. And before that smile Tewfick faltered in his paternal benediction and hastened the phrases.

Little murmurs flew back and forth as she turned away, and then a hasty chatter sprang up as the guests hurried into their tcharchafs for the journey to the bridegroom's house.

That day Aimee did not put on her veil. On either side of her, as she went out her father's gate, huge negroes held up silken walls of damask, and between those walls she walked into the carriage that awaited her, followed by Madame de Coulevain and the two little maids of honor.

It was when the carriage began to move that the panic inside of her grew to whirlwind. The horse' hoofs, trotting, trotting, the motion of the wheels, seemed to be the onbearing rush of fate itself. If she could only stop it! If she could only cry out, tear open the windows, scream to the passers by. She knew these were only the impotent visions of hysteria, but she indulged them pitifully.

She saw herself, in those moments, helpless, and hopeless, passing on into the slavery of this marriage - Aimee, no longer the daughter of Tewfick Pasha, but Aimee Delcasse, child of a dead Frenchman, inheritor of freedom, sold like any dancing girl....

And her own lips had assented. In the supreme, silly uselessness of sacrifice she had given herself for the safety of that man who had spent such careless indulgence upon her ... that man whom perhaps her mother had loved and perhaps had hated....

Faster and faster the horses were trotting, leading the long file of carriages and impatient motors that bore the relatives and guests and trousseau, rolling on under the lebbeks and sycamores of the wide Shubra Avenue, once the delight of fashionables before the Gezireh Drive had drained it of its throngs and its prestige.

Now some bright-eyed urchins ran out from their games in the dust to curious attention, and through a half open gate Aimee caught once a glimpse of a young, unveiled girl watching eagerly from the tangled greens and ruined statuary of an old garden. Farther on came glimpses of farm lands, the wheat rising in bright spears, and of well-wooded heights and in the distance the white houses of Demerdache against the Gibel Achmar beyond.

But where were they bearing her? Aimee had a despairing sense of distance and desolation as the carriage turned again - Abdullah, the coachman, having traversed unnecessary miles to gratify his pride before the house of his parents - and made a zigzag way towards the river, where old palaces rose from the backwaters, their faces hidden by high walls or covered with heavy vines and moss.

Deeper and deeper grew the girl's dismay. It was a different world from that bright, modern Cairo that she knew; this was as remote from her daily life as the old streets of Al Raschid. Her thoughts flew forward to that unknown lord, that Hamdi Bey, whose image she had refused to assemble to her consciousness. Now she comforted her terror with a sudden assumption of age and dignity and kindness, of a courtesy that would protect her and a deference that would assuage the horror of a life together, when unknown, fearful familiarities would alone vibrate in the empty monotonies.

Before a high wall the carriage had stopped. A huge, repellent Ethiopian was standing before an opened doorway, through which a rich carpet was spread.

"Ah, but he looks like an ogre, that new eunuch of yours, Aimee," murmured one of the little Turks. The other, more touched with thought, gave her a disturbed glance, and laughed in nervousness.

Madame, alone serene, ignored the dismaying impression.

"The palace is of a fine, ancient beauty, I am told," she mentioned cheerfully.

For one wild instant Aimee thought to plead with her, to implore her to tell Abdullah to drive on, to give her the freedom of flight, if only flight down those deserted streets. And then a mad vision of herself in her bridal robes in flight, brought the hysterical laughter to her throat. The time for flight had gone by ... And as for madame's pity on her - this was not the first time that Aimee had thought of invoking her aid, but she had always known, too well, that thought's supreme futility.

Sympathetic as Madame de Coulevain might be in her inmost heart - and Aimee divined in her an understanding pity for the necessities of existence - never would that sympathy betray her to rashness. She never would believe that in serving Aimee she would not be ruining her; and even if assured of Aimee's safety, she could never be brought to betray her own reputation for truthworthiness among the harems of Cairo.... As well appeal to the rocks of the Mokattam hills.

The carriage stopped. The negroes extended the damask walls, and one sprang to open the carriage door and bear the bride's train. In one moment's parting of the silken walls the girl saw a sun-flooded cluster of staring faces, thronging for her arrival, and then the damask intervened and through its lane, followed by her duenna and her maids of honor, she entered the arched doorway.

She was in a garden, a great gloomy place, over-spread with ancient, moss-encrusted trees. A broken, marble fountain flung up waters into which no sunlight flashed, and the heavy stepping stones, leading to it, were buried in untrodden grass. A garden in which no one lingered.

The Ethiopian was marshaling them to the left, to an entrance in the dark palace walls before them. Behind them the oncoming guests were streaming out in veiled procession.

He opened a door. Ancient, beautiful arches framed a long vestibule and against a background of profuse cut flowers a man's figure stepped forward in the glittering uniform of the Sultan's guard. Aimee had a confused impression of a thin, meager, dandified figure with a waspish waist ... of a blond mustache with upstanding ends ... of sallow cheek-bones and small, light eyes smiling at her in a strained, eager curiosity....

Through all her sinking dismay she had a flash of clear, enlightening irony at that look's suspense. If she were not as represented! If his cousin's fervor had misled his hope - !

But in that instant's encounter his eyes cleared to triumph and gayety, and he smiled - a smile curiously feline, ironic, for all its intended ingratiation - a conqueror's smile, winged to reassure and melt.

He stepped forward. There were formal words of welcome to which she returned a speechless bow, and then he offered his arm and conducted her slowly up the stairs, his sword rattling in its scabbard, to the apartment which was to be her home, and the prison for the spirit and the body.

She knew in a moment that she hated this man and that he inspired her with fear and horror.

Across a long expanse of drawing-room he conducted her to the ancient marriage throne upon its platform, surmounted by a pompous crown from which old, embroidered silks hung heavily.

Then with an unheard phrase, and another bow, he left her to the day-long ordeal of the reception while he withdrew to his own entertainment at her father's house. She would not see him again until night, when he would pay her a call of ceremony.

She saw his figure hesitating a moment, as he faced the oncoming guests, such a flood of femininity, unmantled now and unveiled, sparkling in rainbow hues of silks and tulle and gauze that he had never before faced and never would again. Like a bright wave the throng closed about him and then surged on towards the bride upon the throne.

How often, in the last years, Aimee had pitied that poor puppet of a bride, stuck there like some impaled, winged creature, helpless for flight, to the exhibition of the long stream of passersby! How often she had promised herself that never would this be her fate, never would she be given to an unknown! And now -

She was smiling as she faced them, that light, fixed smile she had seen so often on others' lips, the smile of pride trying desperately to hide its wounds from the penetrating glances of the curious. Satiric, cynical, or sympathetic, that light smile defied them all, but beneath its guard she felt she was slowly bleeding to death of some mortal hurt.

The sympathy unconsciously betrayed, was hardest. The whispers of her young maids of honor, "Really, Aimee, he looks so young! One would never surmise," were more galling in their intended consolation, more revealing in their betrayal of her friends' own shrinking from that arrogant, dandified old man than the barbed dart of the uncaring, inquisitive, "How do you find him, my dear? He has the reputation for conquest!"

They were all there, her friends, young, slim, modish Turkish girls whose time had not yet come, glancing quizzically about the ancient drawing room, with its solid side of mashrubiyeh, its old wall panelings of carvings and rare inlay, and then pointing their glances back at her, as if to ask, "And is this our revoltee? Is this her end, in this dim, old palace among the ghosts of the past?"

Some, the frankest, murmured, "But why did you not refuse?" and others attempted consolation with a light, "As well the first as the last - since we must all come to it."

Of the married women there were those who raised blank, bitter eyes to her, and others, more mild, romantic, affectionate, tried to infuse encouragement into their smiles as if they said, "Come - courage - it's not so bad. And what would you? We are women, after all; we do not need so much for happiness.

"Those dreams of yours for love, for a spirit to delight in your spirit in place of a master delighting in your beauty alone, what are they, those dreams, but the childish stuff of fancies? For other races, perhaps - but for you, take hold of life. There are realities yet in it to bring you joy."

It was all in their eyes, their voices, their intonations, their pressure of her hands.

And she stood there among them all, smiling always that smile demanded of the bride, looking unseeingly into their eyes, listening unhearingly to the sea of voices breaking on her ears, responding in vague monosyllables and a wider smile, while all the time her eyes saw only that face, that smirking, cynical old face, and the tide of terror rose higher and higher in her soul.

Never had she given way to her fear, never since the black night when she found the key was gone.

Then, after frenzied searching in impossible places she had stolen back to her room and buried her face in her pillow to stifle the breaking sobs of rebellion and despair - and of a longing so deep and so terrible that it seemed to rend her with a physical anguish, a pain so fiery that her heart would forever bear the scar.

Never again would she see him now.... Never would she know - never would she know all. She had refused his aid. And he might believe her still aloof, incredulous.... It was finished - forever and ever.

She had told herself that before. But always there had been the key. And now there was no key and no escape and her heart broke itself against the iron of necessity.

She had cried the night through. Morning had brought her exhaustion, not peace but a despairing submission. Why struggle when the prison gate is shut? And if there was never to be freedom for her ... never again the sight of that too-remembered face and the sound of that voice - why, then, as well one fate as another. And it was too late now to recede.

So she had called upon her pride and summoned her spirit to play its part to protect her from whispers, and surmise and half-contemptuous pity. She would surrender to this man because she must, and she would win his respect by her dignity and worth, but her soul she would keep its own, in its unsullied dreams ... and in its memories.... Life would be nothing but a hardship, nobly borne.

But now she had seen the man. Now this wild dislike, this sickening terror.

To be alone with him, to have only the few days grace of courtship which the Mohammadan custom imposes upon the bridegroom, to be forever at his mercy in this solitary palace, with its echoing corridors, its blackened walla, its damp breath of age....

She thought wildly of death.

And all the time she was smiling, bending her cheek to the kiss of a friend, feeling the fingers of some well-wisher press upon her, listening to praises of her beauty....

For she was beautiful. No image of wax now. The scarlet of her frightened blood was staining her cheeks, her eyes were bright as the jewels in her diadem, and beneath the thrown-back veil her dark hair revealed its lovely wealth.

"Is she not a rose - will he not adore her, our Hamdi?" she heard that stout cousin of Hamdi's say to a companion, and the two stared on appraisingly at the young girl, in her freshness and virginal youth, as if at some toy to invite the jaded appetite of a satiated master.

And still the throng filed by, a strange throng beneath the flickering light and shadow of the mashrubiyeh, slender young Turks or blonde Circassians in their Paris frocks, their eyes tormented or malicious, and here and there, like a green island of calm, some rotund matron grave and serene, her head encircled with an old fashioned turban of gauze, her stout flesh encased in heavy silks, bought at Damask so as not to enrich the Unbelievers at Lyons.

*     *     *     *     *

And then the spectacle changed, the black street mantles appeared, yashmaks and tcharchafs, for now the doors were opened to all the feminine world, and there came strange, unknown women, slipping out from their grills for this pleasuring in a palace, old-timers often, draped and turbaned in the fashion of some far province of their youth; women, incredibly fat, in rich stuffs of Asia, their bright, deep-sunken eyes spying delightedly upon the scene, or furtive, poor women, keeping courage in twos and threes.

Now, too, at four, came the women from the Embassies, a Russian girl with whom Aimee had played tennis in ages past, rosy now with yesterday's sun and sleepy with last night's dance, who touched the bride's hand as if it were the hand of one half-dead, already consigned to the tomb; other girls she did not know, who stared at her with the avid eyes of their young curiosities; older women, experienced, unstirred, drinking their tea and smoking cigarettes and gossiping of their own affairs, and occasionally among them a tourist agog with wonder and exultation, storing away details for a lifetime of talk, asking amiably the most incredible questions....

"And is it true you have never met your husband? Listen, Jane - she says she has never met him - "

A girl in a creamy white silk came forward a little uncertainly. She was a pretty girl, with a curve of ruddy hair visible under her smart straw, and very bright eyes, where shyness was at variance with a friendly smile.

Indeed Jinny Jeffries was extraordinarily intimidated by the occasion. She had a distinct sense of intrusion mingling with her delight at having intruded, and she murmured her good wishes in an almost inaudible tone.

"It is very good of you to let us come ... I wish you every happiness," she said.

Beside her a tall slender figure , in black tcharchaf and

MARY HASTINGS BRADLEY

yashmak, made its appearance.

Aimee's eyes slipped past the pretty American; the mechanical smile was frozen on her lips. Over the black veil she saw the hazel eyes, bright with excitement, vivid as speech; the eyes of the masquerader in the Scotch costume, the eyes of the man at the garden gate - Jack Ryder's eyes ... the eyes of her dreams.

# CHAPTER XI

## THE FORTY DOORS

When Ryder had despatched from the jeweler's who had polished the locket for him, that package with its secret note, and its warning plaid, he had no real assurance that the message would fall into Aimee's hands. But he could think of nothing better, and he argued very favorably for his stratagem.

That miniature should have some effect, and given the miniature, and the bit of plaid cloth, Aimee's quick wit ought to divine a message.

She had always the key, he remembered, and the power of egress from her prison. And surely it ought not to be difficult for her to devise some way of getting a letter into the post.

So his hope fluctuated between the garden gate and the daily mail at the Bank, and he rather surprised McLean by the frequency and brevity of his visits, and by the duration of his stay in Cairo.

For that he had an excuse, both to McLean and to the deserted Thatcher, at the excavation camp, two excuses in fact - some belated identification work to be done at the Museum and a cracked wisdom tooth.

Chiefly he spoke of the necessity for dentistry and accounted for his moods with his molar.

Of moods he had many. Moods when he contemplated his

behavior lightly and brightly or darkly, in unrelieved disgust, moods when he refused to contemplate it at all. But he stayed. That was the conspicuous and enduring thing. He stayed.

Jinny Jeffries returned from the Nile by express to find him ensconced at her hotel, and her bright confidence suffered no diminution of its self respect. And it was through Jinny that chance set another straw of circumstance dancing his way.

Jinny had a frock she wished repaired. Mrs. Heath-Brown, whom she had met upon the Nile, recommended to her a Mrs. Hendricks, wife of a British soldier and a most clever little needle woman. Jinny looked up Mrs. Hendricks and found it impossible to secure her for some days as she was busy refitting for a fashionable wedding in the Mohammedan world.

A night later, and two nights before the wedding, Jinny made a narrative of the circumstances for Jack Ryder's benefit.

"Such frocks h'as h'I 'ave to do - and the young lady no more caring!" had been a saying of the Hendricks that Jinny passed interestedly on to Jack. She had no memory of the young lady's name, but distinctly she recalled that she was young and beautiful and to marry a general.

It was enough to launch Jinny's eager interest in Mohammedan marriages and foster the wish that she might attend one. She regretted Mrs. Heath-Brown's absence and her lack of acquaintance, and suggested that Jack ought to know some one -

"Better than that, *I'll* take you," said Jack with a promptness that brought a light to Miss Jeffries' eyes.

There was also a light in Jack Ryder's eyes, a swift burning of excitement and adventure.

Why not? The thing was possible. Muffled in a tcharchaf and veiled with a heavy yashmak, armed with enough Arabic for the briefest of encounters, he might dare the danger. Who in the world would discover him? Who would ever know?

The thing was unthinkable. It was a desperate desecration, comparable only, in his vague analogies, to the Mecca pilgrimage and profanation of a Holy Tomb. But its very improbability would prevent detection.

Only Jinny had to keep her mouth extremely shut - before and afterwards.

He impressed this upon her so thoroughly, as they did their shopping for the costume together the next morning, that she had compunctious moments of solicitude when she said he really ought not to.... She would feel responsible....

Thereupon he laughed, and dared her to be game, and she grew all mirthful confidence again.

But that night, sitting alone in a native cafe over his Turkish coffee, Ryder was grimly serious.

He knew that it was a mad thing to do. He felt, not so much the danger he ran from discovery, but the danger to his already shattered peace of mind from another glimpse of that strange girl ... that young unknown, on whom he had spent such time and thought, of late, that she seemed a very part of his existence.

What was the good of going to her wedding reception? Feebly he told himself that it was his only chance to inform her upon the history of the Delcasses. There might have been reasons for her non-appearance at the gate, for her not writing.... He could have no glimmering of what went on behind those barred windows. This was his only chance - he meant to say, to tell her - but his eager senses murmured, to see her again.

That was it - to see her again. He owned the lure, at last, with a bitter ruefulness. But - he brightened up at that - it was partly his duty to himself. Now he had all sorts of fool imaginings about this girl. He was remembering her as something lovelier than a Houri, more enchanting than fairy magic, more sweet than spring. He owed it to himself to rout these imbecile prepossessions and prove clearly and dispassionately that the girl was just a very nice little girl, a pretty bride, marrying into a very distinct life from his own - and a girl with whom he would not have an idea in common. A girl, in fact, far inferior to any American. A girl not to be compared to Jinny Jeffries.

Besides, there was fun in the thing. It tempted him tremendously. It was adventurous, romantic forbidden.

He heard the word echoed in Turkish behind him.

So engrossed in his thoughts had he been that he had been inattentive to the rhythm of old Khazib, the tale teller's voice, as he held forth, from the divan, beside his long-stemmed pipe, to his nightly audience, of men and boys, camel drivers, small merchants, desert men from the long caravans who were the frequenters of this cafe.

To-night there were few about the old man, and Ryder had small difficulty in drawing nearer the circle. A green-turbaned Arab, with the profile of a Washington and the naive eyes of youth, whispered to him courteously that it was the tale of the Third Kaland, and the Prince Azib was in the palace of the forty damsels who were farewelling him, as they were to depart, according to custom, for forty days.

Khazib, with a faint salutation of his turban towards the newcomer, went slowly, sonorously on with his tale.

"We fear," said the damsel unto Azib, "lest thou contraire our charge and disobey our injunctions. Here now we commit to thee the keys of the palace which containeth forty chambers and thou mayest open of these thirty and nine, but beware (and we conjure thee by Allah and by the lives of us!) lest thou open the fortieth door, for therein is that which shall separate us forever."

For a moment the cafe faded from Ryder's eyes. He was in the gloom of a garden, a shadowy darkness just touched by a crescent moon, and beside him in the shrubbery a dark-shrouded form, shaking its shawled head at him in denial, and whispering, lightly but tremblingly. "It is a forbidden door ... forbidden as that fortieth.... There are thirty and nine doors in your life, monsieur, that you may open, but this is the forbidden...."

He had meant to look up that tale. And now chance was reminding him of it again. A superstitious man - Ryder's great grandfather, perhaps, would have felt it an omen of warning, and a devout man - Ryder's grandfather, perhaps - would have taken it for a sign from Heaven to divert his steps. Ryder reflected upon coincidence.

"When I saw her weeping," Khazib was intoning, and now Ryder attended, his scanty knowledge of the vernacular straining and overleaping the blanks, "Prince Azib said to himself, 'By Allah, I will never open that fortieth door, never, and in no wise!'"

"A wise bird," thought Ryder to himself, drawing on his cigarette.

"And I bade her farewell," continued the voice slipping into the first person. "Thereupon all departed, flying like birds, leaving me alone in the palace. When evening drew near, I opened the door of the first chamber and found myself in a place like one of the pleasances of Paradise. It was a garden with trees of freshest green and ripe fruits of yellow sheen. And I walked among the trees and I smelt the breath of the flowers and heard the birds sing their praise to Allah, the One, the Almighty."

"*Allhamdollillah*," murmured Ryder's neighbors reverently.

"And I looked upon the apple, whose hue is parcel red and parcel yellow ... and I looked upon the quince whose fragrance putteth to shame musk and ambergris ... and upon the pear whose taste surpasseth sherbet and sugar, and the apricot, whose beauty striketh the eye as she were a polished ruby...."

"On the morrow I opened the second door and found myself in a spacious plain set with tall date palms and watered by a running stream whose banks were shrubbed with rose and jasmine, while privet and eglantine, oxe-eye, violet and lily, narcissus, origane and the winter gilliflower carpeted the borders; and the breath of the breeze swept over those sweet-smelling growths...."

How inadequate, Ryder realized, had been the description given by the Book of Genesis to the Garden of Eden.

"And the third door," droned on the rhythmic voice, "into an open hall, hung with cages of sandal-wood and eagle-wood; full of birds which made sweet music, such as the mocking bird, and the cusha, the merle, the turtle dove - and the Nubian ring-dove."

A trifle restively Ryder stirred. He liked birds but he wanted to be getting on to that fortieth door and this was slow progress. Not a sign of impatience marred the bright, absorbed content of the other listeners, intent now upon the wonders behind that the fourth chamber revealed, stores of "pearls and jacinths and beryls, and emeralds and corals and carbuncles and all manner of precious gems and jewels such as the tongue of man could not describe."

The story teller proceeded, "Then, quoth Prince Azib, now verily am I the monarch of the age, since by Allah's grace this enormous wealth is mine; and I have forty damsels under my hand nor is there any to claim them save myself."

The handsome Arab beside Ryder inhaled his pipe luxuriously. "By the grace of Allah!" he said reverently.

"Then I gave not over opening place after place until nine and thirty days were passed and in that time I had entered every chamber except that one whose door I was charged not to open. But my thoughts ever ran upon that forbidden fortieth and Satan urged me to open it for my own undoing...."

"I see his finish," said Ryder interestedly to himself - and he thought of the analogy.

"So I stood before the chamber, and after a few moments' hesitation, opened the door which was plated with red gold and entered. I was met by a perfume whose like I had never before smelt; and so sharp and subtle was the odor that it made my senses drunken as with strong wine, and I fell to the ground in a fainting fit which lasted a full hour. When I came to myself I strengthened my heart, and entering found myself in a chamber bespread with saffron and blazing with light.... Presently, I spied a noble steed, black as the murks of night when murkiest, standing ready saddled and bridled (and his saddle was of red gold) before two mangers one of clear crystal wherein was husked sesame, and the other, also of crystal containing water of the rose scented with musk. When I saw this I marveled and said to myself, 'Doubtless in this animal must be some wondrous mystery, and Satan - '"

"Satan the Stoned!" murmured Ryder's neighbor religiously.

"Satan cozened me, so I led him without and mounted him ... and struck him withal. When he felt the blow he neighed a neigh with a sound like deafening thunder and opening a pair of wings flew up with me in the firmament of heaven far beyond the eyesight of man. After a full hour of flight he descended and shaking me off his back lashed me on the face with his tail, and gouged out my left eye, causing it to roll along my cheek. Then he flew away."

On rolled the voice, narrating the prince's descent to the table of the other one-eyed youths, but Ryder was unheeding. And at the close he inclined his head with the other listeners, murmuring "May Allah increase thy prosperity," as he felt in his pockets for the silver which the others were drawing from turban and sleeves and sash to lay in the patriarch's lap, and then raised his head to question diffidently, "Would you interpret, O Khazib, the meaning of that door? For I hear that it hath now become a saying of a forbidden thing."

The sage hesitated, sucking at his pipe. Then he said slowly, "To every man, O Youth, is there a forbidden door, beyond which waits the steed of high adventure ... with wings beyond man's riding. And so the rider is lost and his vision is gone."

"But for him who could ride?" Ryder suggested.

"Inshallah! Who can say till he has tried his destiny - and better are the nine and thirty chambers of safe pleasance than the lonely sightlessness of the outcast one.... It is a tale which if it were written upon the eye-corners with needle-gravers, were a warning to those who would be warned."

For a moment their eyes held each other, smiling but grave. Ryder's thoughts were of the morrow, of that forbidden entry he was planning to make, of the risks, the wild uncertainties....

Wisdom and counsel looked significantly out at him out of those patriarchal eyes. Prudence and sanity clamored within him for a hearing.

And then he smiled, the whimsical, boyish smile of young adventuring.

"But whoever, O, my father, had opened that forbidden door the veriest crack, and breathed its scent and glimpsed its dazzlement - then for him there is no turning back," he confided.

He rose and Khazib's eyes followed him.

"Luck go with you, my son," he said clearly, "in Allah's name," and smiling in faint ruefulness, "May Allah heed thee!" Ryder murmured piously.

# CHAPTER XII

## THE UNINVITED GUEST

Now as he stood before Aimee, and saw her eyes widen with recognition, he knew that he would have need of all his luck and all his wit. He stepped hastily forward.

"*Alhamdolillah* - Glory to God that he has permitted me to behold you this day," he murmured, in the studiously sing-song Arabic that might be expected from a humble Turkish woman in plain mantle and yashmak. "May Allah continue to spread before thee the carpet of enjoyment - " and then lower, almost muffled by the thick veil, "Can you give me a moment - ?"

Eagerly, significantly, his eyes met hers.

Half fearfully, Aimee flashed an excited look around her. The space before the marriage throne had thinned, for there were no more arrivals waiting to offer their congratulations and the guests were clustering now about the tables for refreshment or drifting into the next salon where behind firmly stretched silken walls a stringed orchestra was playing.

Miss Jeffries alone was lingering near, but she moved off now - at a secret look from Ryder - with an appearance of unconcern.

"I am going to try my vernacular on the bride," Ryder had told her. "Don't linger or look alarmed. I won't give the show away."

So there was no one to overhear a low-toned colloquy between the bride and the veiled woman, no one to note or wonder that the veiled woman was speaking, strangely enough, in rapid English.

"When I didn't hear from you I had to come, to know if you received the package and letter I sent - "

With a swift gesture of her little ringed hand Aimee drew from the laces on her bosom that heavy gold locket.

"Indeed I have it - and the note, too, I found. But I could not write you. There was no way - no one to trust to mail it. And they had stolen my key," she whispered, and the confessing words with their quiver of forlornness told Ryder something of the story of those helpless days and nights.

He murmured, "I didn't dare write you more personally for fear they would find the note."

"I understood. That plaid about the box - that was so clever a warning. I kept the box and hunted in it."

"I wanted to tell you more about that locket. I dug it up myself from the tomb I was excavating - do you remember how you wished that I would dig from the sands whatever secret I most desired? And I found that.... And it happened that at McLean's I had met the French agent who was searching for any trace of the Delcasses, of the wife and child of the explorer who had disappeared fifteen years before. That miniature was your image, and I guessed at once. McLean and I went to the pasha - Oh, I didn't tell him I'd met you!" he flung in, his eyes twinkling, "and we pretended we knew all about his marriage to Madame Delcasse and he owned up without a quiver. But when we tried to claim you for the French family, he doubled like a hare. He said the Delcasse child was dead, died when his own child was a baby, and that you were his own. But I was sure that you were more than fourteen, and that he was simply putting it over on us so as to have this marriage go on without interference - and so I tried to get the story to you. Even now I thought you ought to know," he added, as if in palliation of his invasion here.

For he realized now how tremendous an invasion it was.

All the guests about him had not given him that feeling, all that sea of femininity, those grave matrons whose serenely unveiled faces would burn with shame to be beheld by this stranger, those bright, slim girls in their extravagant frocks, their tulle, their lace, their pearls, their diamonds, all the hidden charms that no man had yet seen stirred in him no more than an excited and adventurous curiosity.

But the vision of Aimee - that delicate beauty in its tragic irony of throne and diadem! It touched him to tenderness and to an actual sense of sacrilege at the freedom of his gaze. No moonlight vision this, ethereal and dream-like, but a vivid, disquieting radiance of dark, shining eyes and rose-flushed cheeks. He had never seen her hair before, midnight hair, escaping little curls from the veil and the diadem. And he had never really seen her mouth - wistful and gay, like the mouth of the miniature ... nor her chin, so tender and willful ... nor her skin, satin-soft, in its veiling from the daylight....

She was more than young and sweet and fair. She was beauty, beauty with its elusive, ineluctable spell, entangled with the appeal of her helplessness.

A bright blush flooded her now and her eyes fell in confusion, before the prolonging of his look.

"But it is dangerous - your being here," she murmured.

"The fortieth door," he reminded her.

Under her breath, "Ah, you remember?"

"I remember. And but last night I heard Khazib, the story

teller, tell the tale, and I thought of you and your warning - of the door that hid you, that it was forbidden for me to open."

"And so you opened it, monsieur." Faintly she smiled, with downcast lashes.

"And I came as you first came to me - in mantle and veil."

For a moment their thoughts fled back to that masquerade, which seemed so long ago.

"But it is too late," she said tremulously.

"*Is* it too late - for me to help you?"

At that her eyes rose to his again in a swift flash of hunted fear.

"Oh, take me away from him!" she breathed suddenly, unpremeditately. "Somehow - somewhere - "

Another figure came towards them. Madame De Coulevain in all her severe elegance of black.

"Come and join your friends at the supper, my dear; there is no need for you to be pilloried here any longer," she observed with an indifferent scrutiny of the persistent veiled woman, and Ryder moved slowly away while Aimee came dutifully down from the throne, a huge black bending to hold her train.

"I thought you were *never* coming! What *were* you talking about?" demanded a voice in Ryder's ear, and he found Jinny Jeffries at his side, her bright gray eyes pouncing upon him with curiosity.

"Oh, I wished her joy - native phrases - that sort of thing," he answered mechanically as they drew back into an embrasure of the mashrubiyeh that formed one side of the great room.

"But you were talking forever. I saw you holding forth at a

tremendous rate. Why wouldn't you let me stay and listen - ?"

"You'd have put me off my shot, I had to feel unobserved to play up."

"You must be fearfully good at Arabic," said Jinny guilelessly. "And what did she say?"

"Why - she didn't say anything in particular - "

"But what was that she was showing you? I saw her bend forward with a locket or something - ?"

A plague upon Jinny's bright eyes! "Oh, yes, the locket," said Ryder with an effort. "She - ah - she showed it to me."

"But *why*? Wasn't that awfully funny - "

"Oh, I believe it's a custom, courtesy stunt you know, to show a poor guest some of the presents," he explained, manufacturing under pressure.

"I wish she'd show *me* her rings. Did you ever see so many? It was the only thing about her you'd call really Eastern - all those glittering diamonds on her fingers. And did you notice her hands?" Jinny went on enthusiastically. "Jack, I never knew there was anything so lovely as that girl in the world. She's simply *exquisite*.... I suppose it's her whole life," Miss Jeffries reflected, "keeping herself beautiful." Her eyes rested curiously on the feminine groups before them. "They haven't anything else to do or think about, have they?"

"I understand some of them are remarkably educated young women."

"What's the use of it?" said the practical daughter of an American college. "They can't ever meet any men, but just a husband - "

"They can read for themselves, can't they? And talk to each other. And - well, what do you girls do with your education anyway? You don't lug anything very heavy about the golf course and the ball room."

"Who wants us to? But we do bring something to committees and clubs and - and welfare work," Miss Jeffries maintained stoutly. "And we are always into arguments at dinners. While these girls, they can't dine out, they haven't anybody but themselves to argue with, and it doesn't matter a straw politically what they think - they can't even change the customs that their great, great, great grandfathers imposed.

"If I were one of these girls," she declared positively, "I wouldn't bother about Kant and chemistry and history - I'd stuff myself full of sweetmeats and loll around on a divan and not care what happened outside. Or else I'd be miserable."

"Perhaps they are miserable."

"They ought to fight. Think, *think*," said Jinny dramatically, "of marrying some man you've never seen - the way that lovely girl is doing. Suppose she doesn't like him? Suppose he's dull and cranky and mean and greedy? Suppose he bores her? Suppose she actually hates him? Why, Jack, it's horrible! And yet she submits - she *submits* to it - "

"Suppose she has to submit, that she hasn't a soul on earth to help her? How would you fight, I wonder - "

"Well, you don't need to shout about it! That woman's looking now - that one with the green turban and the stuffed-date eyes."

Nervously Jinny glanced around.

"It's a fearful lark," she murmured, "but I don't believe I'd ever have had the nerve if I'd realized.... What do you suppose they would *do*, Jack, if they found you out?... Those big blacks look

MARY HASTINGS BRADLEY

so - so uncivilized."

Her eyes rested upon the huge eunuch at the far entrance of the salon, a huge hideous fellow, with red fez, baggy blouse and trousers, and a knife handle sticking piratically from a sash.

"He has on English oxfords," said Ryder lightly. "That's a saving something. But they aren't going to find out..... I have an idea we ought to make our getaway now, and that we had better not go together. You go first and then I'll stroll along, and whisk off these duds in some quiet corner.... I have to meet a man to-night, but I'll probably see you to-morrow. And *don't*," he entreated, "don't as you love your life, liberty and the pursuit of happiness, breathe a word of my being here like this to any one - any time - anywhere. I was an unmitigated ass to link you up with it. So be wary."

"Oh, I shall!" Jinny Jeffries promised vividly and with a last look about the old palace, the empty marriage throne and the dissolving knots of guests, she gave a little nod to her veiled companion, sauntered without visible trepidation past the staring eunuch at the door, went down the long stairs where other departing guests were drawing on mantles and veils, and so made her way across a shadowy garden and out the gate that another black opened.

And then she drew a sudden breath of relief and glanced up at a sky of sunset fires and felt the free airs play with her hair and face and so shook off, lightly and gratefully, that darkening impression of shuttered rooms and guarding blacks.

Little rivers of wine and fire were bubbling in Aimee's veins. She was gay at supper, as a bride should be gay. It was enough, for those first few moments, that she had seen him again, that he had dared to come and try to help her - that he cared enough to come!

Her heart sang little paeans of joy and triumph. She sketched impossible scenes of escape - she saw herself, in a shrouding mantle, slipping with him past the guests at the door, she saw them speeding away in a motor, she saw France, the unknown Delcasses - a bright, gay world of freedom and romance.

Or, perhaps, if not to-night, then to-morrow.... They would plan ... she would obtain permission to take a drive and there would be a signal, a waiting car....

But, better now. She could not endure even the call of ceremony from that man who called himself her husband. The very memory of his eyes on her....

Decidedly, it must be to-night. And Ryder would think of a way. She must get back to him ... he would be lingering. She must get away from this hateful table, these guests and companions....

A wild impatience tore at her. She grew uneasy, anxious, fretted at the frightening way that time was slipping past....

Her radiance vanished, her smile was nervous, forced, as she sat at her table of honor, amid the circle of her friends, with a linked wreath of candelabra sending its sparkle of lights over the young faces and jewel-clasped throats, over the glittering silver on the white satin cloth among the drift of pink and white rose petals.

She began to bite her lips nervously... she did not hear what her bridesmaids were chattering about ... her eyes went often, with that stealth that invites regard, to the tiny platinum and diamond watch upon her wrist.

Would they never finish? Would they never be free? She wondered if she dared feign an illness to rise and leave them; but no, that would mean solicitude, companions....

And now the slaves were bringing still another round of trays....

Oh, hurry, hurry, her tightening nerves besought.

At last! The older women were going. Not even for a wedding would they deeply infringe upon that rule which keeps the Moslem women indoors after the sun has set. Ceremoniously each made to the bride her adieux and good wishes, and ceremoniously a frantically impatient Aimee returned the formal thanks due for "assistance at the humble fete."

She did not see that black mantle anywhere.

Her heart sank. Stupid, she told herself with quivering lips, to dream that he could dare to linger, that he had any way to get her out. By help he meant no more than getting letters to France for her.... And yet his eyes when they had met hers.... Surely he had meant - but when she had disappeared from the reception room to attend the supper, when there seemed no way of speaking again to her, and all the outsiders, all but the invited guests were departed, he had been, obliged to go, too.

Perhaps some one had begun to notice him.... She wondered if he had been careful about his shoes, his hands.... How had he managed about the dress anyway?

And then she remembered that girl, that pretty American with the ruddy hair to whom she had seen him talking, and she conjectured that there was feminine aid and confidence....

A wave of bitterness swept over her. He had told that girl about her - he knew that girl well enough to tell her! And perhaps he was only sorry for the poor little French girl in the Turkish harem, perhaps they were *both* sorry....

Had he told that girl, she thought with bitter mutiny, that he had kissed her?

That girl must have been very sure of him not to be jealous of his interest in herself!

And now they could be somewhere together, perhaps talking her over, while she was here ... here forever....

She was so white now, so silent, so distrait, that all the chatter of the younger girls who were lingering around her could not dispel the feeling of depression. They cast covert glances of discomfort at each other, begged for more music from the orchestra, tallied with an effort of the size and spaciousness of the palace and the magnificence of the feast.

She had told herself that she had ceased to hope. She did not know how false it was until the eunuch brought his message. Then hope really died.

The general was below and begged to be announced to madame.

"We fly!" whispered a lingerer with nervous laughter, and hastily the young people hurried into their tcharchafs and veils, murmuring among themselves, with sidelong glances at that white figure whose cold hand and cheek they had just touched, hastily they sped, like light-footed nymphs in some witches' robes, down the long room, while Madame de Coulevain drew back a strand of the girl's dark hair and murmured, "But smile, my dear," to the still figure and escaped with the guests.

And then Aimee was alone in the great room, deserted of its throngs, a darkening room, full of burned-down candles and fallen flower petals, with here and there the traces of the revelers, a scented handkerchief ... a fan ... a buckle from some French slipper ... or a feather from some ancient turban clasp....

Like the ghost of some deserted queen, with her regal satins and glittering circlet, she waited. There was a moment of grace in which she tried, to turn a gallant face toward the next moment.

Then he came, advancing.... It may have been her distorted

fancy, but down the long perspective, that figure looked more mincing, more waspish, more unreal than ever. And she was conscious of that swift rising of dislike, of antagonism touched with reasonless fear.

# CHAPTER XIII

## THE BEY RETURNS

He kissed her hands. She caught the murmur of compliments and the mingled scent of musk and wine. He had been dining at his reception for the men, but he called now for a table and more refreshment.

A small table was brought to the end of the room near the marriage throne where all the day she had paraded; a richly embroidered cloth of satin was flung over it, and from crowding candelabra fresh lights shed down a little circle of brilliance.

Faintly Aimee protested that eat she could not, and then she made a feint of eating, lingering over her sherbets, because eating was, after all, so safe and uncomplicated a thing.

The black brought champagne in its jacket of ice and filled their glasses.

The general rose. "*A notre bonheur* - to our happiness," he declared, holding out his glass, and she clinked her own to it and brought her lips to touch the brim, but not to that toast could she swallow a single one of the bubbles that went winking up and down the hollow stem.

The glass trembled suddenly in her hand as she set it down. An overpowering sense of fatigue was upon her. With the death of her poor hope, with the collapse of all those flighty, childish dreams , the leaden weight of realities seemed to descend crushingly upon her. She felt stricken, inert, apathetic.

It was all so unreal, so bizarre. This could not possibly be taking place in her life, this fantastic scene, this table set with lights and food at the end of a dark, deserted old room opposite this grimacing, foppish stranger....

She could barely master strength for her replies. How had it all gone? Excellently? She was satisfied with her new home? With the service? The appointments?

He plied her with questions and she tried to summon her spirit: she achieved a few perfunctory phrases, the words of a frightened child struggling for its manners. She tried to smile, unconscious of the betrayal of her eyes.

He told her, sketchily, of his day. A bore, those affairs, those speeches, he told her, gazing at her, his wine glass in his hand, a flush of wine and excitement in his face. She found it unpleasant to look at him. Her glance evaded his.

She stammered a word of praise for the palace. It must be very ancient, she told him. Very - interesting.

He waved a hand on which an enormous ruby glittered. He could tell her stories of it, he promised. It had been built by one of the Mamelukes, his ancestor. Its old banqueting hall was still untouched - the collectors would give much to rifle that, but they would never get their sharks' noses in. Nothing had been changed, but something added. Once the Mad Khedive had borrowed it for some years and begun his eternal additions.

"Forty girls, they say, he kept here," smiled Hamdi Bey. "They gulped their pleasure, in those days. It is better to sip, is it not?"

He smiled. "But these are no stories for a bride! I only trust that you will not find your palace dull. It is very quiet now, very much of the old school. You may miss your pianos, your electricity, all your pretty Parisian modernity."

She glanced at the glittering table.

"But I do not find this so - so much of the old school. Here one does not eat rice with the fingers!"

"And I?" said the bey, leaning suddenly towards her on his outspread arm. "Do you find me too much of the old school? Eh? eh?"

" But you, monsieur , " she stammered, still looking down, "you - I do not know you - not yet."

"Not - yet. Excellent! There will be time."

"I confess that now I am weary - "

"Ah, - and that diadem is heavy. Your head must ache with it," he said solicitously.

Perhaps it was the diadem that gave her that leaden, constricted sense of a band tightening about her forehead. She put up her hands to it.

"Permit me," he said quickly, springing to his feet. "Permit me to aid you."

He stepped behind her and bent over her. She held her head very still, stiff with distaste, and felt the weight lifted. He surveyed the circlet a moment then placed it upon the marriage throne behind her. She had an ironic memory of the false omen of her crowning, of soft, satisfied little Ghul-al-Din's bestowal of her own happiness.... Happiness, indeed....

"And that veil - surely that is incommoding?" suggested the suave voice, and she felt the touch of his hands on her hair where the misty veil was secured.

She stammered that it was quite light - she would not trouble him -

Then she held herself rigid, for suddenly he had swept the veil aside and bent to press his lips to that most hidden of all veiled sanctities, for a Moslem, the back of her neck.

She did not stir. She sat fixed and tense. Then slowly the blood came back to her heart, for he was moving away from her again to his place at the table.

Laughing a little, pulling at his blond mustache in a gesture of conquest, his kindling eyes glinting down at her, "You must forgive the precipitateness - of a lover," he murmured. "You do not know your own beauty. You are like a crystal in which the world has thrown no reflections. All is pure and transparent - "

If she did not find words to answer him, to divert his admiration, she felt that she was lost.

"You are not complimentary - a bit of glass, monsieur, instead of a diamond! But I am too weary to be exacting.... If now, you will permit me to bid you good evening and withdraw - "

"Little trembler," said the general facetiously, and reached out a hand to touch her cheek, the light, reassuring caress that one might give a petted child, but it almost brought a cry of nervous terror from her lips.

She thought that if he touched her again she would scream. He inspired her with a horrible fear. There was something so false, so smiling in him... he was like an ogre sitting down to a delicate dish of her young innocence, her childish terrors, her frank fears....

She could not have told why she found him so horrible, but everything in her shrank convulsively from him.

And the need of courtesy to him, of propitiation - !

The cup was bitterer than her darkest dreams.... She wondered how many other women had drained such deadly brews... had sat in such ghastly despair, before some other bridegroom, affable, confident, masterful....

She told herself that she was overwrought, hysterical. The man was courteous. He was trying to be agreeable, to make a little expected love. He had drank a little too much - another time she might find him different. He was probably no worse than any other man of her world.

It was not in her world, each young Turkish girl said in those days, that one could find love.

But it was *not* her world! It was an alien world, enforced, imprisoning.... That was the bitterest gall of all the deadly cup.

"There is no need for haste," he was assuring her. "In a moment I will call your woman. Fatima, her name is, an old slave of our house."

"I could wish," said Aimee, "that I had been permitted to bring my old nurse, Miriam, without whom I feel strange - "

"No old nurses - I know their wiles," laughed the bey, setting down his drained cup with a wavering hand. "They are never for the husbands, those old nurses - we will have no old trot's tricks here!"

He laughed again. "This Fatima is a watch dog, I warn you, my little one ... but if she does not please you, we can find another. And as for the rooms - I have assigned this suite to you, the suite of honor. This is the salon, and there," he pointed to a curtained door behind them, opening into a small room that Aimee had already seen, "there is your boudoir and beyond that, your sleeping apartment. I have had them done over for you, but you shall choose your own furnishings - everything shall be to your taste, I promise you. You are too sweet to deny. You have but to ask - "

Certainly, she thought, he was drunk. He moved his head so jerkily and his whole body swayed so queerly. Desperately she fought against her horror. Perhaps it was better for him to be drunk.

Drunken men grow sleepy. Perhaps he would fall down and sleep. Perhaps she ought to urge him to drink. Long ago the black had left the bottle at his elbow and gone out of his room.

But she did not move. She sat back in her chair, withdrawn and shrinking, watching him out of those dark, terrified eyes.

"You are beautiful as dreams," he told her, leaning towards her with such abruptness that his sword struck clankingly against the table. "Beyond even the words of my babbling cousin - eh, Allah reward her! - but she did me a good turn with her talk of you!"

Fixedly he stared at her, out of those intent, inflamed eyes.

"I did not know that there was anything like you in the harems of Cairo. You are like a vision of the old poets - but I suppose that you do not know the ancient poetry. You little moderns are brought up upon French and English and music and know little of the Arabic and the Persian.... I daresay that you have never heard of the poet Utayyah."

Still leaning towards her he began to intone the stanzas in a very fair tenor voice, and if his movements were at all unsteady, his speech was most precise and accurate.

"From her radiance the sun taketh increase when
She unveileth and shameth the moonlight bright."

He chuckled.... "Ah, I shall put the triple veil upon you, my little moon.... How Is this one?

"'On Sun and Moon of Palace cast thy sight,
Enjoy her flower-like face, her fragrant light,

Thine eyes shall never see in hair so black
Beauty encase a brow so purely white.'"

He got up and drew his chair closer to her. "That is the song
for you, little white rose of beauty."

Back went her own chair, and she rose to her feet.

"I thank you for the compliment, monsieur. But now have I
your permission to retire? For it has been a long day and I am
indeed fatigued - "

To her vexation her voice was trembling, but she steadied it
proudly.

"I bid you good evening."

"Nonsense, my little white rose. This is not so fatiguing - a few
words more. But you are like the flower that flies before the
wind.... But your room, yes, to be sure. Shall I show you the
way?"

"I can discover it, monsieur."

"Monsieur - fie on you, my little dove.... Hamdi, I tell you,
your lover Hamdi."

He laughed unsteadily, and put a hand on her arm. "You are
running away, I know that. And I have so much to tell you ...
Oh, it was tedious in that villa of your father's! 'Yes,' I thought
to myself, 'that is a fine story, a funny story, but I have heard
them all before. And you are in no haste, you revelers - you
have no little bride waiting for you at home.'... That one
glance at you - I tell you it was the glance of which the poet
sings - the glance that cost him a thousand sighs. I was on fire
with impatience.... For I am beauty's slave, little dove.... You
may have heard - but no matter. A wife must be a pearl
unspotted.... I am not as the English who take their wives from
the highways, where all men's glances have rested upon them.

Have I not been at their balls? Their women dance in other men's arms. They marry wives whose hands other men have pressed. Sometimes - who knows? - their lips have been kissed.... And then a husband takes her.... Oh, many thanks!"

He laughed sardonically and waved his hands a little wildly. "Oh, I know English - all the Europeans. I have seen their women. I have seen them selling their wares - stripping themselves half bare in the evenings, the shameless - For me, never! My wife is a hidden treasure. You know what the poet says:

"'An' there be one who shares with me her love
I'd strangle Love tho' Life by Love were slain,
Saying, O Soul, Death were the nobler choice,
For ill is Love when shared twixt partners twain.'"

"You are fond of your poets," said Aimee with stiff lips.

"You - you kindle poetic fires, my little one. You - I - " He stammered a moment, then forgot his fierce speech against foreign ways. "You have the raven hair - "

His hand went out to it. He smoothed it back out of her eyes, then tried to draw her to him.

Desperately she resisted. "Monsieur, one does not expect a gentleman - "

"Expect! Ho - what should one expect when a man has such a little sweetmeat, such a little syrup drop, such a rose petal - Come, come, you would not struggle - "

But it was not the struggling hand of the frightened girl that sent the general back.

It was a brown, sinewy hand on his shoulder, a hand protruding from a well tailored gray sleeve and lilac striped cuff, that caught Hamdi Bey by the epauleted shoulder and sent him spinning about.

Another hand was holding a revolver very directly at him.

"Silence!" said Jack Ryder in his best Turkish and repeated it, with amplification, in English. "Not a sound - or I'll blow your head off."

Aimee gave a strangled gasp.

He had not gone, then! He had hidden there, in some nook of that boudoir behind those shadowy curtains, waiting to protect her, to rescue....

Over one arm he had the black mantle and veil, "Better put these on," he suggested, without taking his eyes from the rigid bey, "and then run for it."

"But you - you - ?"

"I'll take care of myself. After you are out of the way. Dare you try that? Or what do you suggest?"

"Oh, not alone. Together - "

"So - so - " said Hamdi Bey inarticulately, his head nodded, he staggered, his knees gave way and he crumpled very completely upon the floor, and lay like a felled log.

After a quick look down at him Ryder turned to Aimee. "Quick, then. We'll make a run for it - "

He did not finish. Hamdi Bey, upon the floor, fallen half under the folds of the white cloth, made a swift and very expert roll and darted to his feet beside Aimee, whirling her about, with pinioned elbows, for his shield.

And so screened, he gave a shrill whistle.

# CHAPTER XIV

## WITHIN THE WALLS

Ryder sprang forward, trying to reach the bey, but he dodged skillfully; his holding Aimee blocked Ryder in his attack.

He knew that high, peculiar whistle had been a signal, a call for aid, and he flung a lightning glance down that long room, tightening his hold on the revolver - but he did not see the small door that opened in the shadowy paneling behind him, nor the shadow that grew into the gorilla-like shape of the black as it launched itself through the air upon his back.

He only heard Aimee's scream, and then before the crashing weight upon his shoulders he staggered and went down.

The bey flung Aimee aside and rushed upon the prostrate figure, kicking the revolver from the outspread hand. The black knelt swiftly down, unfastening his silken sash.

Giddily the room whirled about Aimee.... In the candle light, leaping in the rush of conflict, she saw the bey and the black, and their distorted shadows in a goblin blur.... And beneath them she saw Ryder, helpless, his hands and feet pinioned.... With the madness of despair she rushed forward, but the general intercepted her.

"He is quite helpless.... You need not be alarmed for my safety, madame!"

The cold, biting fury of his voice steadied her. She saw his face was distorted, livid with anger. His breathing was stertorous.

She stood helplessly by the table; the general turned and looked down upon the face of the man who had dared to violate the sanctity of his harem and attempt to steal his bride; beyond the man's head Yussuf, the black, was squatting with a grinning, dog-like watchfulness.

But Ryder did not require watching. That sash had been tied strongly about his hands and feet. He was as helpless as a baby.

But the peculiar flavor of his helplessness was not so much fear before the fanatic fury of this man he had outraged, although he had a clear notion that his position was not enviably secure, but a bitter, black chagrin.

To have had the game in his hands and have bungled it! To have been surprised by that simple strategy, taken off his guard by a feigned collapse! The wily old Turk for all his champagne had the clearer, quicker brain....

To have let him get to Aimee and call in his black! To have been thrown, disarmed.... It was crass stupidity. It was outrageous mismanagement, abominable, maddening....

And Aimee must pay for it. He tried to think very quickly what could best clear her.

He fixed his eyes on those glittering eyes, staring down upon him.

"I realize I owe you an explanation," he said grimly. "If you will let me tell you - "

The bey turned to Aimee with a smile that was the lifting of a lip and the distention of his nostrils.

"This fool thinks he has the time to talk - his English."

Desperately Ryder grasped for his vernacular. "I want to tell you - why I came. This - this young lady doesn't know me."

Past the general he shot a look of warning at the girl.

"I was trying to get hold of her for her family in France - She is really a French girl. Tewfick Pasha is not her father but her - " he could not find the word and dropped into English. "Her step-father - do you understand? And he had no business to marry her off, so I tried to steal her for the French family. It was a mad attempt which has failed - but for which the young lady should not be blamed. She had never seen me before. She had no idea I was here."

After a pause, "A remarkable story," said the general distinctly. He turned about to the table and drank off the last of a glass of champagne, then wiped his mouth with the back of a hand that trembled.

He turned back to stand over his prostrate invader. "Now, you - you dog of Satan," he snarled in a sudden snapping of restraint, "how did you get here? Who admitted you?"

And at that, for all his trussed and helpless plight, Jack Ryder grinned. He moved his head slightly. "That blackbird of yours here."

"Yussuf - never!"

"The very one. But he didn't know it - I was in that black mantle - and veil."

"Oh, the mantle, I had forgot. So you stole in, disguised, to violate my hospitality, to outrage my harem, to gaze upon the forbidden faces of women and to steal the bride - "

"I tell you I was trying to rescue the girl for her French family. She *is* French and Tewfick Pasha is only - "

"And what is that to me? Do I - " the bey broke off and then turned to the silent girl who stood leaning towards them, a trembling ghost in white.

"And you, my little one," he murmured sardonically with a savage irony of restraint, "you, the little dove secluded from the world, who trembled at a kiss, the crystal vase who had never reflected the blush of love, whose virginal praises I was chanting when I was so oddly assaulted, do you support this idiot's story?"

Mechanically her head moved in assent, her eyes, dilated with fear, were like the dark, fascinated eyes of some helpless bird.

"You never saw this young man?" the bey pursued. "And yet you were ready to run off with him - a pretty character you give yourself, my snowdrop! - and you liked his eyes and hastened to obey?"

Aimee was silent. From his ignominy upon the floor Ryder hastened to interpose.

"It is true she had never seen me, but I had already written to her and acquainted her with the story. I tried to reach her first through her father but that was useless so I resorted to these desperate means."

"Oh you wrote! And you told her you would be here, and murder her husband - "

"I told her nothing of the kind. She didn't know that I was coming until I spoke to her here, and then she had no idea that I was going to wait and carry her off - "

"In the name of Allah! Do you take me for a dolt, an ass? You, with your writing and your masquerade and your secrets! Do any families try to recover their relatives with such means? Daughter or step-daughter, it is nothing to me - "

"But it is true," Aimee insisted, in a trembling voice. "My father was Paul Delcasse - "

"*Yahrak Kiddisak man rabbabk* - curse the man who brought thee up! Delcasse or devil, it is Tewfick Pasha who is your step-father, your guardian, who gave you to me for wife - what has your genealogy to do with this affront upon my honor?"

"But he did not intend to affront your honor - only to aid the family in France - "

"I ask you again, do I resemble an ass that you should put such a burden of lies upon me? As if I did not know why young men risked their lives, in the dead of night, in other men's rooms! If I did not know what turns their brains to mush and their hearts to leading strings! And you - you - you little white rose of seclusion - !"

His venom leaped out at her in his voice. It was a terrible voice, the cold, grating menace of a madman.

"You, who had never seen this man but who fluttered to him like a white moth to a fire, you who cowered from your husband's hand but who turned to follow this strange dog into the streets - there will be care taken of you later. But now - you complained of fatigue. Surely this scene is overtaxing for your delicacy. If you will come to your rooms - "

She drew back from the hand he laid upon her. "Do not injure him! By Allah's truth! He is rash, mad, but a stranger. He did not know - "

"He needs enlightenment. He needs to learn that a nobleman's harem is not a cafe of dancing girls, where all may enter and stare and fondle. *Bismallah* - he shall learn!... And now come - "

"I shall not go," she said breathlessly.

"What - struggle? But your father has been strangely remiss with his discipline.... Permit me."

His hand tightened in a grasp of iron.

"My train is caught," she said in a tone of sudden pettishness; she stooped to lift it with her hand that was free.

"My train - !" he mimicked her in a quivering falsetto. "Have a care of my frock - do not crush my chiffons.... And these are the women for whom men break their heads and hearts!"

"I tell you, sir," came urgently from Ryder, "that the girl is innocent of all - "

"Keep your tongue from her name - and your eyes from her face!... Come, madame."

With his iron grasp on her elbow he thrust her towards the boudoir at the end of the drawing-room, behind whose curtains Ryder had so long been hiding.

The chamber was in darkness, lighted only by a pale gleam from the other room. Aimee stumbled across the rug and found herself upon a huge divan against a window screen.

"Fatima is in the next room to come at a call. But perhaps you would prefer to wait for me alone? I shall not be long."

Desperately she caught at his arm, imploring, "I beg you, monsieur. He has done no real harm. Let him go. He is a stranger - he did not know. And he will never trouble you again. I will do anything - everything you desire - if only you will not injure him - "

"You trouble yourself strangely for a stranger."

"He is a stranger in danger for my sake. For it was in his duty to my - my family - " her trembling lips stumbled over the ridiculous lies, "that he has blundered into this. He has no idea how shocking a thing he has - "

"And you had no idea, either, I suppose. You had never heard of honor or treachery or - "

"I was wrong, oh, I was wrong! I did want to go to France - I own it. And I was not ready for marriage. And I had heard that you - I was afraid. But now - if you will let him go for my sake, if you will not visit my sins upon him, oh, I should be so grateful - so grateful that anything I can ever do - "

"But you will be grateful, anyway, my little blossom. I promise you that you will learn to be very grateful - "

"It is easier to die than to learn to love a hated one," she reminded him softly, leaning towards him. "I can die very willingly, monsieur.... And you would not want a wife before whom there was always an object of terror - "

Through the dusk her great eyes sought his.

"Be generous - and harm him not," she breathed. "I beg of you, I implore - "

"And if I am - lenient - you will always be grateful?"

Mutely she nodded, her eyes trying pitifully to read that shadowy mask of mockery he turned towards her.

"And how grateful could you be, little dove?"

Pitifully she smiled.

"Could you," he murmured, "could you learn to kiss?"

He leaned nearer and involuntarily she shrank back. Faintly, "At this moment - I beg of you, monsieur - "

"Oh, if it is to be an affair of moments! We shall never find the right one. But you were so full of promises - "

"I will do anything," said Aimee, convulsively, "if you will promise me - "

"Come, then a kiss. A peck from my little dove."

She looked at him out of wretched eyes.

"And you promise to free him, not to hurt him - "

"I promise not to hurt a hair of his head. Come, that is generous, isn't it? As to freeing him - h'm - that is for later. Perhaps, if you are very good. A kiss then... and later...."

He bent over her. She shut her eyes and heard the taunt of his laugh. She kissed him, and he laughed again.

"What is it the Afghan poets say? 'Kissed lips lose no sweetness, but renew their freshness with the moon.' Certainly if you have ever been kissed, little bud, you have lost no dew.... Delicious.... I shall hurry back."

He cast a hard look down at her as she sat there, her arms drooping at her sides. He looked about the room as if consideringly, then nodded at an unseen door at the right.

"Fatima is there if you want lights or assistance.... And Alsamit, Yussuf's brother, is at the other door beyond. Do not stir, little bird. I shall be back very soon."

"And he - you promised - "

"I shall not hurt a hair of his head."

But he was smiling evilly in the darkness as he drew shut the door and returned to the bound figure by the guarding black.

For a moment he stood silent, considering, while Yussuf looked up with glistening-eyed intentness like an eager dog ready for the word of attack.

Then in hasty Turkish the general gave his directions and the black nodded and strode to a portiere, jerking it down, which he wrapped about Ryder's helpless form.

Then he hoisted his burden over his huge shoulder and bore it on after the general.

Across the great room they went and down the long stairs up which that day a most complacent Hamdi Bey had escorted his just-glimpsed bride.

Now at the bottom of the stairs a shadowy figure of a sleeping eunuch was stretched.

Hamdi Bey spoke sharply, giving a quick order. The black scrambled to his feet, yawned, nodded, and strode away into the main vestibule and out into the garden to investigate a shadow which the general had just reported, and when he was out of sight the general and Yussuf, with his unwieldy burden, came quietly down the stairs and turned back into a long, dark hall.

For a moment they paused outside a wide, many-columned banqueting room, and there Hamdi Bey stood listening, straining attentive ears for the faint sounds from the service quarters on the other side of the room. He caught the guttural of a half inaudible voice, and the wash of water and clink of a dish, showing that the belated work of the reception was going draggingly on, but it was all far away and invisible.

Satisfied he went on a few steps to a pointed door set in the heavy stone. From a nail he took down a lantern of heavy, fretted brass and lighted it, not without some difficulty, for his hands were still trembling. Then he took from the black a cumbersome key which he fitted into the lock and turned heavily.

Drawing back the door he motioned Yussuf ahead, and followed, drawing the door shut. Down a steep, stone spiral stair they went, and at the bottom, at the general's order, the black set Ryder down from his shoulder and flung aside the portiere.

From its muffling folds Ryder looked out bewilderedly into the darkness about him, illumined only by the yellow flare of the ancient lantern. The general cautioned him to silence while Yussuf knelt and untied the strip that bound his feet, then, his arms still bound, he was ordered to march on before them.

This, he said to himself, as he silently obeyed that order, this really was the time to pinch himself and wake up! Of all the dark, eerie nightmares! This slow procession through these underground halls, the giant black on his heels, the general's lantern throwing its flickering rays over the huge, seamed blocks of granite foundations.

It made him think of the Catacombs. It made him think of the Serapeum. It made him think of those damp, tortuous underground ways of the Villa Bordoni....

They seemed to be in the wine cellars. He saw bins and barrels and barred vaults that would have done credit to an English squire, and he reflected fleetly that wine bibbing was forbidden to Mohammedans and that Hamdi Bey was a fanatic Moslem.... Then he saw open spaces of ancient stuffs, broken tables and dismantled caiques and a broken oar. His earlier observation of the palace had told him that it had a water gate and he thought now that they might be near some opening.

He wondered if they were going to throw him, pinioned, into the river. He wouldn't put it past this livid, silent, shaking man - and yet the thing appeared so impossible, so theatric, so utterly unrelated to any of the ways that he, Jack Ryder, might be expected to end his days, that it couldn't possibly send more than a shiver of speculation down his spine.

And yet men *had* been thrown into rivers - this very river. And men had disappeared from just such palaces as this. There was the story about young Monkton. He knew it perfectly; he had reminded himself of it the last evening while he reflected upon this escapade, but he had never actually appreciated the peculiar poignancy of the thing until now.

Monkton had met - so rumor reported - a Turkish lady of position, flirted with her, it was said, while on horseback outside her motor when caught in the crush at Kasr-el-Nil bridge. There had been a meeting or two in the back of shops, and then he had boasted, lightheartedly, of a design to take tea in her harem.

He had never boasted about the tea. No one had ever seen Monkton again and he was generally reported, after a stifled inquiry, to have been thrown from his horse in the desert, or spilled out of his sailing canoe.

The government, English or Egyptian, assumed no interest in the matter of gentlemen found in other gentlemen's harems.

There were other stories, too. There was one of a little Viennese actress who after a dramatic escape reported a whole winter of captivity in one of these old palaces, and there was a vaguer rumor of a rash young American girl, detained for days....

Ryder had always known these stories. They were part of the gossip and thrill of Cairo. But he had never till now realized how exquisitely possible was their occurrence.

Anything, everything might happen in these hidden, secret chambers. These Turks were as much masters here as their old predecessors who had reared these stones. This black upon his heels might have been the grinning, faithful executioner of some Khedive or Caliph - he might have been the very Masrur, the Sworder of Vengeance of Al Raschid.

He told himself that it was no time to think of the past. His business - acutely - was the present. If only he could get his hands untied! If only he could get those untied hands upon that demoniac Turk!

But, strain as he could upon the knots, they held.

It seemed to him that they had been walking for an interminable distance, in odd, roundabout ways. Once they had stopped and he had involuntarily glanced back over his shoulder, but at a word from the general he had kept his head forward again, while he heard the black behind him gathering something that clinked. Later, a stolen glance had revealed the eunuch with some tools in one hand and bag slung over his shoulder.

The bag disquieted him. Bags filled a foreboding place in the Eastern literature of vengeance. He wondered if he were to go into the river in that bag, with the tools for weight.

He decided, feeling now a very odd and definite disturbance in the region of his stomach, that he would tell that general that he was a cousin of the late Lord Cromer and a nephew of Lord Kitchener. Something insistent would have to be done about this.

They were passing now through a strange, open space, between old arches that for an instant arrested his excavator's interest. He saw in the shadows about them, a crumpled, crumbling dome and broken shafts, with half a wall of masonry pierced with Arabesques. Traces of old ruins, fragments of some old, forgotten mosque over which the palace had spread its foundations in bygone days.... Buried treasure, looted, some of it, for the palace overhead, but still rare and lovely.... That was a gleam of lapis lazuli that winked at him from the crumbling mortar under his feet.

Then they were between other walls, not crumbling ones, but the solid, pillared blocks of the palace masonry with here and there broad arches of old brick.

They stopped. Between two arches the general held his lantern high, flashing it over the surface while Yussuf swung down his sack and knocked with the handle of his tool.

Suddenly he stopped and looked at his master, nodding cheerfully. The general lowered his light and stepped back and Yussuf reared the pickaxe in his powerful arms and sent it dexterously at the wall, between two broken bits of brick.

It caught, and sent the mortar spraying; another blow and another loosened a hole in which the black inserted a short iron and began nervously grinding and prying.

Ryder, watching with oppressed and helpless fury, saw the bricks at last break and tumble faster and faster in a cloud of dust, and saw a pocket in the wall become revealed, a long, upright niche, the size, perhaps, of a man's coffin, on end.

He tried, very suddenly, to talk. His tongue felt thick and swollen and there seemed no words in all the world to fit his need of overcoming this fanatic madman, - and after all, he had no chance for them, for Yussuf, with a huge palm upon his mouth, urged him suddenly backwards towards that horrible niche.

"Gently, Yussuf, gently," said the general, suavely and with a slow distinctness that was for Ryder's ears. "I gave my word that I would not hurt a hair of his head - "

Grinning, the black lifted him over the remaining wall, and set him down into the niche, leaving him standing in there like a helpless statue, tasting to the full fury of his heart the bitterness of his helplessness and the ludicrous impotence of all struggle.

"Good God, sir, you must be mad," he said in a strained sharp voice that his ears would not have known as his own. "Do you realize - there will be an inquiry - there is such a thing as law - "

It seemed to him that he talked, in English and stammering Arabic, for a long time. The black was kneeling, out of sight, stooping over a basin of water and his abominable sack, and Ryder was facing that silent, sardonic face, with its fantastic mustache, its evil, gloating eyes....

He stopped for very shame. The man was mad. Mad and drunk - and there was no appeal from Philip drunk to Philip sober.... Mad or drunk, he had devised his vengeance shrewdly.

Upon Ryder's helpless body a cold sweat of incredulous horror broke softly out.

At his feet he heard the black beginning to fit his bricks and smooth his mortar.

"You do well to save your breath," said Hamdi Bey at last, as Ryder still stood silent. "You will need it in this chamber I am providing.... But it may be," he said thoughtfully, "that your breath will last your need. Thirst may be the more impatient for her victim; they tell me thirst is an obtrusive visitor. As you were, this evening.... Still, why do you not cry out a little? It will amuse my black."

Yes, this was real, Ryder reminded himself. And these things could happen - had happened. He remembered suddenly the hideous scene, outside the dungeons, in "Francesca da Rimini," when that bestial brother goes in to the helpless prisoners. He remembered the sick horror of those groans....

He remembered also various excursions of his in the Tower of London and the Seigniory of Florence, and the sight of old rings and stakes and racks and the feeling of their total unrelatedness to every actuality.

And yet they had happened. And this thing, for all its fantastic medieval horror, was happening. Brick by brick the imprisoning wall was rising. Brick by brick it intervened between him and sane, sensible, happy, normal life.

Eye for eye he gave the general back his look. He had always wondered about the poor devils in underground torture chambers. Had wondered how they had the stuff to hold out, against such odds, for some belief, some information.... Now he knew the stiffening stuff of a personal hate, upholding to the very grave....

That sardonic, devil's face.... That face which was going back upstairs to Aimee.... But he must not think of that or he should give way and begin to babble, to plead.... He must simply stand and meet that glance....

And there came the incredible, insane moment when Ryder looked out on that face through one last breathing space, and then saw the fitted brick, settled into place, blot the world to darkness before his eyes.

# CHAPTER XV

## UNDERGROUND

Alone in the gloom of that strange room, Aimee sat rigid. Listening. Not a sound, beyond the closed door, from the long drawing room. Not a sound, beyond the other door, from the room where the slave, Fatima, waited to assist in her disrobing.

Silence everywhere - save for a low lapping of water against the masonry beneath her windows.

The palace was on the river, then, or on some old backwater. She remembered glimpses of dark canals on her drive that morning - had it only been that morning? The sound of that soft, hidden water added to her feeling of isolation and remoteness from everything that had been her life before - she thought fleetingly, almost indifferently of her friends, Azima, who to-day had crowned her for happiness, and fond, foolish old Miriam and Madame de Coulevain and Tewfick Pasha, weakly cruel, but amiable; she thought of them all, as unreal figures from whom she had long taken leave.

The old life was over. It had died for her when she passed through the dark doorway and met that arrogant, sardonic, fatuous man, the master of this palace....

Or more truly that old life had died for her when she had flung a black mantle about her chiffon frock and a street veil across her sparkling face and had stolen, daring and breathless, into the lights and revelry of that hotel masquerade. There, when she had shrunk back from the Harlequin and had looked up to meet the kindling glance of that mask in tartans - yes, there, the old life had died for her forever if only she had known it.

And now - she would only like to die, too, she thought miserably, after she had been assured of Ryder's safety. She was tense with fear for him, distrusting in every fiber the assurance of that fanatic, outraged Turk.

She was not utterly resourceless. When Ryder's revolver had dropped to the floor she had maneuvered, unseen by Hamdi Bey, to get her train over it, and when she had stooped for her train her one free hand had closed over the revolver handle beneath the satin and lace.

Now the revolver lay on the divan, and very eagerly she drew it out, feeling it in the darkness, curling her finger about the trigger. Never in her life had she fired a shot, for her most formidable weapon had been the bows and arrows of the Children's Archery Contest of the English Club, but she felt in herself now that highstrung tensity which at all cost would carry her on.

Carefully she bestowed the small, steel thing in the bosom of her dress, then she stared questioningly at the dress itself, hastily unpinning the veil, and tying the long train up to her girdle. Then, with a wary glance for the closed door behind which waited that Fatima she dreaded, she stole to the door the general had shut and pressed it softly ajar, peering out into the deserted throne room.

Like a great cave of darkness the room stretched before her, peopled with goblin shadows from the dying candles upon the disordered, abandoned table; she saw the chair pushed back where she had risen to struggle with the bey, the long folds of white cloth, sweeping the floor, behind which Hamdi had rolled so agilely; a stain was still spreading about an upset glass, and from the overturned cooler the ice water was dripping, dripping with a steady, sinister implication.

She thought of flight.... There was another black, the general had warned her, beyond the door, and there would be bars and bolts on any egress from the harem, but with the revolver in her possession some desperate escape might be achieved.

But Ryder.... No, the gun was for another purpose.... She would not squander it yet upon herself....

From the boudoir she moved slowly, carrying one of the gilt candelabra from the table to light the room. She would need light for her plan....

For ages, long, unending ages, she sat there, waiting.... A hundred times it seemed to her that she could stand no more, that she must make her way out at all costs, must discover what fate they were dealing to Ryder, but still she forced herself to sit there, her pulses racing, her heart sick with suspense, but desperately waiting....

She felt a sudden wave of weakness go through her at an advancing step from the next room. But her chin was up, her eyes fixed and desperate as the figure of the general appeared in her opening door.

"Ah, light! This is more cheerful, little one."

She had risen, half moved towards him. "Is he safe?"

"The stranger? Safe as treasure - buried treasure, little one."

The bey laughed, and that laughter and the glittering satisfaction of his eyes, filled her with foreboding although his next words came with smiling reassurance.

"Not a hair of his head is hurt, I give you my word."

"But where is he - what have you done?"

"Shut him up, to be sure. Kept him as hostage for your sweet humility - a novel way to win a bride, oh, essence of shyness!"

Malevolently he smiled down at her and in the back of her frightened mind she realized that this man did well to be angry, that the affront to him had been immeasurable, and that many a Turk would have simply driven his dagger through the intruder's heart - and her own, too.

But though she tried to tell herself that there was forbearance in him, she felt, instinctively, that there was deeper kindness in direct, thrusting fury than in this man's sinister mockery.

She had sunk back upon the divan on the bey's approach; now as he stood before her with that mask of a smile upon his face, drawing a silk handkerchief across a forehead she saw glistening in the candlelight, she leaned towards him again, her hands involuntarily clasping.

"Monsieur, I seem to have done you a great wrong," she said tremblingly, "but it is not so great as you suppose. Will you listen to me? I - "

"Useless, useless." He waved the handkerchief negligently at her. "I have had words enough. You are not the daughter of Tewfick Pasha - you are his step-daughter - your French family desires to capture you - I know the rigmarole by heart, you observe. And of course when a French family desires to obtain possession of a charming step-daughter, on the eve of her marriage, that family always employs a handsome young man to break into the bride's chamber - and point a gun at the husband - "

His mustache lifted in a grimacing sneer.

"But it *is* true, and I *am* French," she interposed swiftly.

"Excellent - I do not object in the least." He shot his handkerchief up his cuff, and turned to her with eyes that lightly mocked the agonized appeal of the young face. "French blood is delightful - quicksilver and champagne. You will enliven me, I promise you."

"But the marriage - it is not legal, monsieur," she said desperately, summoning all her courage. "Tewfick Pasha has no right to give me to you - "

Indulgently he smiled down at her, then his narrowed eyes traveled slowly about the room.

"But this is a strange time - and place! - to talk of legalities. Do not distress yourself - your step-father is your guardian and your marriage will be as binding as the oaths of the prophet. Have no qualms.... And now, if your French blood will smile a little - "

He started to seat himself beside her, but in that instant she was on her feet. With all the courage in her beating heart she whipped out that revolver and pointed it at him.

"If you call - I shoot," she said breathlessly.

The round mouth of the gun shook ever so slightly in the excited hand gripping it, but in the blazing look she turned on him was the unshaken, imperious passion of a woman swept absolutely beyond all fear.

Meeting that look Hamdi Bey stood extremely still and made no sound.

"There are plenty of shots - for you, at the first noise, and for the servants, if they come," she went on in that fierce undertone, and then, passionately, "What did you do to him? Take me to him - at once!"

Irresolutely the man stood and looked up at her under his half-lowered lids. He was near enough for a spring - and yet if that excited finger should press.... The girl was capable of anything. She was possessed.... And men had died of such accidents before that....

"May I speak?" he murmured, in a tone scarcely audible, yet preserving somehow its flavor of sardonic amusement.

"Under your breath. One sound, remember - and I am a very good shot."

"But what a wife," he sighed. "All the talents - "

"I tell you that I will see him for myself. Take me to him, this moment - "

"Shall I give orders and have him brought here? He is quite safe, I assure you."

"Orders? If you summon a servant I will shoot. No, lead the way, and I will follow you. And if you make one sound - one false move - "

Decidedly the girl was possessed. She stood there like a white image of war, her hand on that infernal automatic.... He hesitated, gnawed his mustache, then swung sullenly upon his heel.

Like some fantastic sculpture from an Amazonian triumph, they crossed the long drawing-room, the erect, gilt-braided general preceding, very slowly, the white-clad feminine creature, who held one hand extended, with something boring almost into his shoulder blades.

He did not lead her down the long stairs, past the guarding eunuch. He took, instead, an inner way through the late supper room which led down into the pillared hall of banquets. That way was safe of servants now; crossing the pillared hall there were no more sounds of late work from the service quarters beyond. Oblivious of the wild developments of that wedding reception, the tired servants, stuffed with the last pasty, warmed with the last surreptitious drop of wine, were asleep at last.

Outside the door in the stone wall the bey took down the lantern which so short a time before he had replaced upon its nail and lighted its still smoking wick. He had not restored the key to Yussuf, and he drew it now from his pocket and fitted it into the lock, drawing back the door.

"These stairs are steep," he murmured. "I hardly like you to descend them unaided, but if you insist - "

"Go on," she said imperiously.

Down he went, and after him she came, following the way he led her down the long stone underground ways.

"We have, of course, very pleasant stairs down to our water gate," he murmured apologetically, "but since you prefer this way - really not the way that I would have chosen to have you first explore your palace, madame! These, you perceive, are the cellars and old storerooms - "

"I do not want you to talk," she said urgently.

"But you would not shoot me for it? Only for raising an alarm? And surely you cannot be unreasonable about a few words - you must be very careful, here, this doorway is low - "

It was not past the old ruined mosque, included in the palace's underground world, that he was leading her, but down a narrow branching way, between walls so low that the general's head was bowed in caution.

"This part of the palace is very old," he murmured, over his shoulder. "An ancestor of mine, Sharyar the Wazir, raised these walls during the wars - for the dispensing of that sacred duty of hospitality which Allah enjoins upon the faithful. It is reported that he was host here to fifty of the enemy during their remaining lifetime - although they had the delicacy not to cumber him with overlong living. It is not, as I said, a pleasant place, but the walls are strong and so I selected a spot here - "

Here, somewhere, then, in these grim ruins, Ryder was penned, helpless and questioning the to-morrow. The girl trembled with excitement when she thought of his joy, his deliverance - and at her hands. For their escape she had no plans, only the decision to thrust the gun into his hands and follow him unquestioningly ... Perhaps they could leave the general in his place and he could wear the general's uniform for disguise....

Everything was possible now that she was nearing him and his safety was at hand. She thrilled with a reanimating excitement that flew its scarlet banners in her cheeks ... Only a few steps now....

"Go on," she said breathlessly.

The bey had stopped and now flashed his lantern over a low, timbered door, studded with ancient nail heads in a design whose artistry did not arrest her. From a peg beside it he took down a key of brass, fitted it to the lock and turned it with a deliberation maddening to her tense nerves.

Her heart was beating as if it would burst its bounds. Only a moment or two -

He had trouble with that door. It took his shoulder; at last he set it swinging inward slowly on its creaking hinges. Then he stepped back and with a wave of his hand invited her to enter.

"Not a chamber of luxury, you understand, but substantial, as you will see - "

"Go first," she ordered.

He laughed. "Ever distrustful, little thorn-of-the-rose! Follow, then," and he stepped within, into the darkness, which his failing lantern but little illumined, calling out in a louder tone in his halting English, "A visitor, my friend. A tourist of the subterranean."

She had followed him to the threshold, seeing nothing in the blackness but the seamed blocks of stone within the lantern's rays, afraid always to turn her eyes from him or her hand from its outstretched pointing.

He said very quickly to her in Turkish, "If you will wait by the door. The floor is bad and there is another lantern, here on the wall - "

At her left he fumbled along the stone wall. She heard him mutter ... and then reach.... And then - she did not know what was happening. For the very ground on which she stood, the solid block of stone began to slip swiftly beneath her feet - she staggered - and felt herself falling, falling, into some precipitately opened abyss....

She gave a wild scream, flinging out her arms in terror, and then cold waters closed above her, and the scream ended in a gurgling cry.

It was no great distance that she fell. What the dropped stone had revealed, answering the signal of the old lever in the wall that the general had pressed, was a stone well, narrow, deep, implanted there by some ingenious lord of the palace in bygone days, for the subtle elimination of friend or foe or rival.

But it was not part of Hamdi's plan to leave the young girl there and close the obliterating stone. Scarcely had the waters met above her head than he was flinging down a rope ladder whose upper ends were fastened to rings in the floor and descending this with swift agility until the waters reached his waist.

Then he leaned out and clutched the floating satin bubbling and ballooning yet unsubmerged above the stagnant depths and drew it towards him. As the struggling girl came gasping within his reach, he carried her panting up the ladder again, and laid her down in the darkness, while he drew up the ladder and closed the stone by pressing that hidden lever.

But the stone which had dropped so swiftly, was slow and heavy in slipping back in place, and when he turned again to Aimee, she had ceased her choking cough and was sitting up, thrusting back the dripping hair from her black eyes, staring bewilderedly about the gloom as murky as any genie's cave.

The lantern light was almost out. In its expiring gleams she saw no more inky water, but only the damp, moss-grown stones, on which a pool was widening from her wet garments, and the half-defined figure of the general stooping over to squeeze the streams from his own wet clothes.

The nightmarish horror of it overwhelmed her. For a moment she could have screamed with horror, and then she felt a cold and terrible despair lay its paralyzing hand upon her heart.

Somewhere, she felt, beneath those secret stones lay Ryder, drowned ... And she was living, in her helplessness ... No revolver now. That was gone ... in the water, perhaps....

There was no resource, now, no refuge.... Strength went out of her, and passive in a dream of evil darkness she felt herself being hurried, stumblingly, back through the secret corridors and the dark halls.

# CHAPTER XVI

## OUT OF THE DARKNESS

There was no measure of time for Ryder in that walled coffin of death. The seconds seemed hours, the minutes ages.

He drew quick, short breaths as if economizing the air that was so soon to fail him; he tugged at his bonds till the veins rose on his forehead, but the silk held and the confines of the prison permitted him no room for struggle; then he leaned forward, to press with all his might upon the bricks before him; he grunted, he sweated with the agony of his exertions, but not a brick was stirred, not a crack was made in the mortar that gripped them tighter every instant.

He died a thousand deaths in the horror that invaded him then. Already he felt strangling, and the painful pumping of his heart seemed the beginning of the end.

Cold sweat stood out all over him; it ran down his face in trickling streams and his body was drenched with that clammy dew of fear.

He tried to count the minutes, the hours, to estimate how long he would hold out....

And then he heard his own voice saying very distinctly and clearly and dispassionately, "This thing is absurd."

It was absurd. It was idiotic. It was utterly irrational. It was an impossible end for an able-bodied young American, an excavator of no mean attainments, a young scholar and explorer of twentieth century science, a sane, modern, harmless young man, to die immured in the ancient walls of a Turkish palace - because he had invaded a marriage reception and intervened between man and wife.

Violent death in any form must always appear absurd to the young and energetic. And the fantastic horror of his death removed it definitely from any realm of possibility. The thing simply could not happen.... He thought of the amazement and the incredulity of his friends....

Dangers in plenty they had warned him against, to his youthful amusement - sand storms and chills and raw fruit and unboiled waters, but they had not warned him against veiled women and the resentments of outraged lords and masters.

He thought of his mother's consternation and dismay. He thought of his father's stern amazement.... What an awful jolt it would give them, he reflected, with an irrational tickling of young humor.

But no, it would not. They would never know. Not a word of this fate would percolate into the world without. Not a comment upon his true end would enliven the daily columns of the East Middleton *Monitor*. Never would it regret the tragic and romantic interment of a young native son of talent, buried alive by a revengeful general of the Sultan....

He amused himself by writing the paragraph that would never be written. Then he told himself that he was lightheaded and hysterical and that he had better wonder what would actually be written. What explanation would be found?

A desert storm perhaps, or some accident. McLean would poke about - but for all McLean knew he might be on his way back to camp that very moment. And sometimes he went by sailing canoe, and a rented horse, and sometimes by the accredited steamer and a camel, and sometimes by tram or train to the nearest station. Even McLean's mind and McLean's Copts wouldn't make much of all the alternatives that his unsettled habits had afforded.

Was there any possibility of his being traced, of any rescue reaching him? He thought hard and long upon his last free moments. Jinny Jeffries knew that he was in the palace, and Jinny had been reiteratedly warned about the danger of betraying that knowledge. It would take some little time for alarm before Jinny said anything. And it would take a little time for Jinny to begin to worry.

He had not been so instant in attendance upon Jinny of late, for all their residence in the same hotel, that she would suspect that his absence of twenty-four hours was due to actual incarceration.

His cursed passion for freedom in which to ramble up and down that deserted lane without Tewfick Pasha's garden! His inane love of solitary mooning....

No, Jinny would not soon wonder about him. She had not expected to see him that evening, anyway - he had muttered something to her about a man and an engagement.

She *would* rather look to see him the next day and talk about their adventure.... But still she would feel no more than pique at his absence; positive worry would not develop until later.

Besides, all the revelations that Jinny could make would do no good. Jinny could only report that he had maintained a disguise at a wedding reception, and talked a few moments, apparently undetected, to a bride. Hamdi Bey, and Hamdi's eunuchs, would be blandly ignorant of such a scandal. What his disappearance would indicate would be some further frolic on his part, some tempting of a later Providence before he had abandoned his disguise.... If he were discovered, for instance, in some of those native quarters, behind a woman's veil....

Decidedly the only effect of Jinny's revelations would be an unsavory cloud upon his character.

There was no hope to be looked for.

And yet he could not believe it. There were moments when the black terror mastered him, but involuntarily his young strength shook it off. He could not believe in its reality. He could not believe that he was actually here, bricked and bound, in this infernal coffin....

But, indisputably, the evidence was in favor of belief.... Only to believe was to feel again that horror....

He tried to tell himself that it didn't matter. One had to die some time. Everybody did. One might as well go out young and strong and still interested in life.

But that was remarkably cold comfort. He didn't want to go out at all. He didn't want to die, not for fifty or sixty years yet, and of all the ways of dying, he wanted least to smother and choke and stifle like a rat walled in its hole in the wall.

He recalled, with peculiar pain, a woodchuck that he had penned up as a boy, and he hoped with extraordinary passion that the poor beast had made another hole. Never again, he resolved, would he pen up a living creature, never again, if only again he could see the light of day and breathe the free air....

He thought of Aimee. And when he thought of her his heart seemed to turn to water. Useless to repeat to himself now those old reminders that he had seen her so little, known her so slightly. Useless to measure that strange feeling that drew him by any artifice of time and acquaintance.

She was Aimee. She was enchantment and delight. She was appeal and tenderness. She was blind longing and mystery. She was beauty and desire....

Even to think of her now, in the infernal horror of this cramping grave, was to feel his heart quicken and his blood grow hot in a helpless passion of dread and fear. She was alone, there, helpless, with that madman.

He tried to tell himself that she was not wholly helpless, that she had wit and spirit and courage, and that somehow she would manage to quell the storm; she might persuade Hamdi to their story, make him remember that this was the twentieth century wherein one does not go about immuring inconvenient trespassers as in the earlier years of the Mad Khedive - years which had probably formed the general's impulses - but in telling himself this there was no comfort for the thought of the price that Aimee would have to pay.

It was pleasanter to pretend that Hamdi was really only joking, in a shockingly exaggerated, practical way, and that presently, when the suitable time had elapsed, he would present himself, smiling, to end the ghastly, antiquated jest.

For some time he continued to tell himself that.

And then suddenly he told himself that the time for intervention had surely come. It was very hard to breathe.

The next minute he was assuring himself that this was merely some devil's trick of his apprehensive imagination. There must be a great deal of air left.... But he was distressingly ignorant of the contents of air, and his calculations were lamentably unsupported by any sound basis of fact.

Mistake, not to have gone in for chemistry and physics. A chap who'd done time in those subjects wouldn't now be rocking with suspense; he'd comfortably and satisfactorily know just how many hours, minutes and seconds were allotted before his finish and he could think his thoughts accordingly.

Undoubtedly, so he insisted to himself, there was air enough here to last him till morning. This gasping stuff was all imagination. He wanted to keep cool and quiet. But for all his reassurance there *was* something a little queer with his lungs, and his heart was lurching sickeningly in his side, like a runaway ship's engine.

And then he heard his own voice repeating very tonelessly, "O God, O God," and the horror of it all came blackly over him and a feeling of profound and awful sickness....

It *was* a sound. The faintest scraping and knocking without that wall. It went through him like an electric current.... And then a roar burst from him that fairly split his ears, the reaction of his quivered nerves and racking fears of his uncertainties, his tightening terrors.

But now - nothing. He could not hear a thing. A delusion? A torture of his final hours?... No, it came again. More definitely now, a little grinding and scraping.

Faster and faster, a muffled, driving thud.

A jubilant reassurance sang gayly through him. He had expected this - this was what he had predicted. Hamdi was no foul friend. He was a devilish uncomfortable customer with antiquated notions of revenge, but now he had shot his wad and was going to undo his tricks.

Ryder braced himself to present a carefree jauntiness - an air somewhat difficult to assume when one is trussed like a spitted bird, in a hot coffin space, with hair falling dankly over a steaming brow, with a collar like a string, and an indescribable pallor beneath the bronze of one's face.

Something stirred. One end of a brick was driven in against his chest. Then he felt the blind working of some tool that caught it and worried it free.

It seemed to him that through that dark aperture a current of cold, delicious air came rushing in about him. The blows sounded against the adjoining bricks and he thought of the glorious joy of seeing out again, feeling that he would welcome even the sight of Hamdi's blond mustache and the eunuch's hideous grin.

Now the aperture admitted a pale gleam upon his chest. Staring steadily down he caught a glimpse of the fingers curving about a brick, and his heart that had steadied, began to race again wildly. For they were not the fingers of the black nor yet the wiry joints of the general.

They were soft, white fingers, with a gleam of rings.

Aimee! Somehow, somewhere, she had managed to come to him, to achieve this rescue....

"Aimee!" He breathed the name.

"S-sh!" came a warning little whisper, and impatiently he waited until that opening should be greater and permit of sight and speech.

His helplessness was maddening. If only he could raise his hands, could get those bonds off! He twisted, he writhed, he tried to lift his elbows and get his wrists in reach of the opening, but the coffin was too diabolically cramped for movement until the hole was very much larger. Then with a convulsive pressure he swung his wrists within reach and after a moment's wait he felt a thin blade drawn across the silk.

The relief was glorious. He swung his hands free, rubbing the chafed wrists, then thrust an opened hand out into the opening, and with instant comprehension a short, pointed bit of iron was put within it.

Now he could do something! With furious strength he attacked the bricks edging the hole and as he pried free each brick he could again get a glimpse of those white delicate fingers lifting it carefully away.

MARY HASTINGS BRADLEY

And now the hole was large enough. He twisted about and thrust out a leg, and then, with a feeling of ecstasy which made the official literary raptures of saints and conquerors but pale, dim moods, he wormed his way out of that jagged hole and turned, erect and free, to the shrouded figure of his rescuer.

She had drawn back a little against the wall, a gauzy veil across her face. Beside her, upon the stone floor, a solitary candle sent its flickering rays into the shadows, edging with light her slender outlines.

Ryder took one quick step to her, his heart in his throat, and put out eager arms. But in the very moment that he was gathering her to him, even when he felt her pliant body, at first resistant, then softly yielding, swept against his own, he felt, too, a little palm suddenly upon his mouth.

"Hsh!" said the soft, whispering voice, cutting into his low murmur of "Aimee!" and then, in slow emphatic caution, "Be - careful!"

He had need of that caution. For under the saffron veil was not the face of Aimee. He was clasping a young creature that he had never seen before, a girl with flaming henna hair and kohl darkened brows, a vivid blazoning face that smiled enigmatically with a certain mockery of delight at the amazement he reflected so unguardedly.

# CHAPTER XVII

## AZIZA

From the slackening grip of his astounded arms she stepped backward, still smiling faintly and holding up in admonishment the palm she had pressed against his mouth.

"But what - what the dev - " muttered Ryder.

She nodded mysteriously, and beckoned.

"Come," she whispered, catching up her candle, and after holding it high for a moment, staring at him, she extinguished it suddenly, and turned to lead the cautious way across the stone spaces while Ryder closely followed.

Not Aimee, then. But some messenger, he could only suppose. Some confidante, at need. A handmaid? The whisper of her silks, the remembered gleam of jewels in the henna hair flouted that thought, and not troubling his ingenuity with alternatives he was content to follow her swift steps.

They were now in those open rubbishy spaces where he remembered the crumbling masonry and broken arches of old, disregarded mosques; now they were again enclosed in narrow stone walls, winding past cellars and store rooms.

The girl's advance grew more cautious. Often she stopped and listened, peering ahead into the darkness, and now, as she took another turning, her care redoubled and Ryder needed no exhortation to imitate it. Obeying a gesture of her arm, he followed at a greater distance, prepared, at the warning of a sound, to flatten himself against the wall or dart into some cranny of retreat.

They were now in the cellars. The corridor was widening out before them with a pallid showing of light, crossed with many bars, at some far end.... They stole towards it. It was a window, or barred gate, he saw, and he heard again that lapping of restless water against stone.

He could see, too, in the dimness the curve of a stair near the gate.

Abruptly his guide checked him. Wary and noiseless he waited while she stole forward to those stairs, peering up into the gloom, attentive for any sound from above.... Apparently satisfied, she went on towards the barred gate, and bent down over a spot of darkness which Ryder had taken for a shadow.

He saw now that it had some semblance to a human outline.

Closely the girl bent and he caught the pallor of her hands, searching swiftly, and then a muffled clink.... Next moment, a wraith with soundless steps, she was back at his side again, urging him on with her. They passed the stairs; he felt the soft yield of carpet beneath his feet; they passed that recumbent figure and now he heard the rhythm of a sleeper's heavy breath, escaping muffledly from the folds of a thick mantle which the sleeper's habits had wrapped about his head. For all the mantle he was aware of the fumes of wine.

"I saw that Ja'afar had his drink," said the girl suddenly in softly whispered Turkish, her head close to his. "He is my friend. I do not neglect him," and under her breath she laughed, as she exhibited the great bunch of keys she had taken from the imbiber.

Stooping now before the gate she fitted the key into the lock. Then over her shoulder she looked up at the young man, and asked him a quick question.

He did not understand. That was the trouble with his vernacular. It would go on very well for a time, when he had a clue to the sense, or when it was a question of every day expression, but a sudden divergence, an unexpected word, was apt to prove a hopeless obstacle.

Now she repeated her question again, more slowly, and again he shook his head.

Now she stood up, frowning a little and began again in English, "You - no, I not know - This way? You do it?" A sudden smile broke over her face as she made a swift pushing gesture with her hands, that, with her pointing to the water outside, sent Ryder a sudden enlightenment.

"Swim? You mean - do I swim?"

She nodded. "Not go - " She made a swift downward movement of her hands and then pointed again to that water just outside the gate.

"Not go down - not sink?" interpreted Ryder. "No, indeed, I can swim," he assured her, and revisited with smiling satisfaction she knelt again before the barred gate.

Open it swung with so sharp a crack that both glanced at the figure behind them, and then at the shadowy gloom of the stairs. But no alarm sounded. Outside the gate Ryder saw the darkness of fairly wide rippling waters, visited with floating stars, and beyond a low-lying, dun bank.

Escape was there. Freedom. Safety. He felt an exultant longing to plunge in and strike out, but he turned, questioningly, to the mysterious rescuer.

"Aimee?" he asked, under his breath. "Where is she?" He repeated it in the vernacular, distrusting her English, and in the vernacular she answered, "You want her? You want to take her away with you?"

She laughed softly at the quick flash in his eyes and hardly waited for his speech.

"Good - what a lover! You are not afraid?"

Mendaciously he assured her that he was not.

"Good!" she said again, with a showing of white teeth between her carmined lips. "You take her - you take her away from him. That is what I want. You understand?"

Very suddenly he understood.

# CHAPTER XVIII

## AZIZA IS OFFENDED

This was no emissary from Aimee. This was no philanthropic bystander. It was some girl of the palace, jealous and daring, conspiring shrewdly for the removal of her rival.

"Take her away," she was saying urgently. "Out of this palace. We want no brides here." Lowering and sullen, she turned bitter on the word.

"To-night, I was watching," she went on swiftly. "I heard - the noise - and then the whispering.... The darkness has ears and eyes - and a tongue. And so I waited out there...."

He could not distinguish all the quick flow of her speech, but he caught enough to understand how she had lurked in the halls, jealously spying, defying the eunuchs' authority, and how she had caught with passionate delight that stifled alarm of scandal. Later, hanging over some banister, she had seen the Ethiopian pass with his burden and had stolen down afterwards, stalking like a cat, and had discovered the lantern gone, the door unlocked.... And then she had watched until the pair emerged without the burden.

She had not been able to get hold of the key to the door. But she had resolved to explore and so she had furnished the waterman with his wine, drugged, Ryder gathered, and so stolen past him on the other route to those underground foundations to which her suspicions had been directed by the mortar and dust upon Yussuf.

Evidently she knew the possibilities of the place and the mind of its master. And when she found the old niche freshly bricked and the mortar at hand she had not needed more to assure her that here was the burial place of her rival's lover.

Now, for the boon of his life, he was to relieve her of that rival. Or try to.

"For once - he might not kill her," she whispered, " but if again - " Her eyes glowed like a cat's in the dark. "Take her away. Make her name a spitting and a disgrace.... Her memory a shame and a sting.... Is she beautiful?" she broke off to demand. "They say – but slaves lie - "

"Can you believe a lover?" he said whimsically for all his impatience. "She is a pearl - a rose - a crescent moon - "

"They say she is very pale and thin - "

"She is an Houri from Paradise," he said distinctly. "And now, in the name of Allah, let me get to her. Tell me the way - "

"Will she go gladly with you?" the low, insistent voice went on, and at his quick nod, "Holy Prophet, what a bride!"

She clapped her two ringed hands to smother the impish joy of her laugh. "A warning to those who can be warned - he will not be so eager for another stripe from that same stick! - It was his cousin, Seniha Hanum - Satan devour her! - who made this marriage. Always she hated me.... But now I will tell you how to get to her. Look out, with me."

Kneeling at the gate, over the dark flow of the water, she drew him down beside her, and thrusting out her veiled head, she pointed upward and to the right to a jutting balcony of mashrubiyeh, where a pale light showed through the fretwork.

"There - you see? That is my room. And if you climb up, I can let you in.... There... Up," she repeated in English, resolved to make certain.

"I see. I can get there," he assured her, measuring with his eye the dim distance.

"At once," she said. "I will be there. I cannot take you with me through the upper hall - it is dangerous even for me to be caught. But no eunuch wants my displeasure."

He could believe it, watching the subtle, malicious daring of her face. Even in the gloom he caught the steady-lidded arrogance of her kohl-darkened eyes and the bold insolence of a high cheek bone. She had a hint of gypsy....

"And you can get me in? You're a wonder!" he whispered. "I can't thank you enough - "

"Rid me of her," said the girl swiftly. "But not - not him. You must swear - what is it that Christians swear by?" she broke off to demand. "By the grave of your father? Yes? You will swear not to hurt him, to hurt Hamdi, by the grave of your father? Yes?"

Ryder nodded quickly. His father, to be sure, was in no grave at all. He was, allowing hastily for the difference in time, in his treasurer's cage at the bank in East Middleton, but he did not wait to explain this to the girl.

"I swear it," he repeated. "I won't hurt your Hamdi, since that's your condition. But we're wasting time - "

"Up, then. And if you fall down - do like this."

Smiling mischievously, she made the gesture of swimming. "Allah go with thee - and with me also," he heard her murmur, as he stepped out to the ledge of the entrance, twisted himself agilely about and climbing up the opened gate swung himself up to the stone carving overhead.

Below him, he heard the gate swing shut. He did not hear her lock it. Fervently he hoped she had not, since it was a possible exit for any one in a hurry, but at any rate, he need not worry about a way out of the place until he had got into it again.

And the getting in was not any too simple. It was work for a mountain goat, he reflected, after a short interval devoted to tentative reaches and balancing and digging in of hands and feet. The distances were far greater than the first-glimpsed, foreshortened perspective had allowed him to guess, and there was only the starlight to illumine the gray face of the palace.

He had no idea of the time. Somewhere about the middle of the night or early morning, he judged vaguely by the stars, although it seemed impossible that so few hours had passed.

The river was all silence and darkness. No nuggars with their sleeping crews were moored below. He seemed the only living, breathing thing clambering across the face of time and space.

Gingerly he kicked off the nondescript black shoes he had worn with his disguise that afternoon and essayed a perilous toehold while he reached for the interstices of a mashrubiyeh window just overhead.

Once gripping the rounds he pulled himself up, reflecting that it was well it was night and that no lady was sitting within her shelter to be affrighted at this intrusion of fingers and toes.

From the jutting top of this projection he surveyed his further field of operation. The window with a light was two stories higher yet and to the right. There were two other windows with lights on the second story, very much farther along, and he wondered painfully if these were the rooms of Aimee.

That boudoir in which he had hidden through the end of the long reception had been upon the water. And there had been a door into an adjoining room, for he had seen a sallow-faced attendant passing in and out.

A wild longing seized him to crawl on and over into those windows. But it was a difficult, almost an impossible distance, and even when there he would be like a fly on the outside of a pane with no way of getting in.

The unknown girl had promised him a way through her window and he had confidence in her ingenuity and daring.

So he went on, worming cautiously along old gutters and ledges and jutting balconies until at last he was clasping the lower grill of that mashrubiyeh from which her light gleamed.

Instantly the light went out.

"Wait!" he heard her voice say sharply over his head. She was standing by the window fumbling with the woodwork, and in a moment he heard the click of a knob and then, just opposite his head, the screening grill slipped aside and an aperture appeared.

"Quick!" admonished the voice, and quickly indeed he drew himself up and in, reflecting whimsically as he did so that this girl had first helped him out of a hole and then into one.

The next moment she had moved the grill into place and lifted the cover she had placed over her triplet of candles on a stand.

Triumphant, her eyes dancing, her teeth a gleam of light between those scarlet lips of hers, she looked at him for the admiration she saw twinkling back at her in his eyes.

"But not me - no!" she protested, her supple hands gesturing towards the magic casement. "I found it here. It is very old - you understand? Some other, long ago, found time dull and so - "

Delightedly she shared the flavor of that secret of the vagabond lady of long ago who had devised this cunning entrance for her lover.

On some dark night like this, with the gatekeeper drowsy with old wine, some other stripling had climbed that worn facade before him and slipped through the secret space and stood triumphantly before some daring, laughing girl who had cast aside for him her veil and her fear of death.

What ingenuity, Ryder wondered fleetly, had smuggled in the carpenter for the contrivance, what jewels had gone to the bribing, what lies had been told!... And what had been the end of it all?

Evidently not the discovery of the opening....

He hoped, with singular intensity, for the safety of the daring young lovers, that unknown youth whose feet had foreworn the path for his feet and that dead and gone young girl, who had dared anything rather than endure the mortal ennui of those hours behind the veil....

These thoughts all went through him like one thought as he stood there, his eyes roving about the dim, shadowy room of old divans and Eastern hangings, and then turning back to the glimmering figure of its mistress.

She was staring frankly at him, her eyes boldly curious and examining. They were not dark eyes, he saw now; that had been the impression given by the kohl about them and the black line of the brows penciled into one line; they were yellow eyes, golden and glowing, scornful and lazy-lidded.

As she looked at him, these eyes smiled slowly. She was seeing in this lover of her rival a singularly delightful looking young man, for all his dust and disarray, a slender, bronzed, hardy-looking young man, with dark, disordered hair straying across a white brow, and audacious, eager eyes in which the fear of death, so lately glimpsed, had left no daunting refection.

Slowly she lifted her hand and with deliberate softness put back that straying hair of his.

"Poor boy," she said slowly in English, and then, smiling ruefully, she held out her hands for his inspection. The grime of the bricks had discolored their scented delicacy and he saw bruised finger tips and a torn nail.

"I'm infernally sorry," he said quickly.

Her smile deepened at his look of concern, as he held, a little helplessly, the witnesses of her work of rescue which seemed somehow to stray into his keeping.

"It is nothing - but you - poor boy," she said again, in that English of which she seemed naively proud.

"If you could give me some water," he suggested, and drank deep with delight the last drop she brought him from an earthen jar. It seemed to wash from his throat the taste of that dust and fear.

"I can't begin to thank you," he murmured. "I only wish that I could do something for you - "

She looked up at him. They were standing close together, their voices cautiously low.

"Perhaps, yes, you can - "

"It's not doing anything for you to save Aimee," he told her. "That's what you are doing for her and for me.... But if ever you want me for anything after this - my name is Ryder, Jack Ryder, and you can reach me at the Agricultural Bank."

He had a vague vision of some day repaying his enormous debt by assisting this girl, grown tired of her Hamdi, out of this aperture and into a waiting boat. He would do it like a shot, he told himself gladly; he would do anything on God's green earth if only she helped him get Aimee away from that infernal villain.

"Jack," she repeated, under her breath, and then in her slow English, "I like - Jack."

"Don't forget it. I'll always come and do anything for you. And if you'll tell me your name - "

"Aziza."

"Aziza. I'll never forget that. And now, if you'll tell me how I can get to her and then the best way out - "

"Why you so hurry - "

"Why?" he looked a little blank. "I can't lose a minute - he may be with her - "

She came a little nearer to him, her head tilting back with a slow, indolent challenge.

Gone was the silken mantle that had been about her below stairs and he saw now that she was a vivid, exotic shimmer of gauzy green against the saffron veil that fell from her henna hair. There was barbaric beauty in her, in the bold, painted face, the bare, gold-banded arms, the slender, sinuous lines, and there was barbaric splendor in the heavy jewels that winked and flashed....

It struck Ryder that she was gotten up regardless.... In pride, perhaps, on her rival's wedding night?... Or had there been some defiant, desperate design upon Hamdi - ?

She did not miss that sudden prolonging of his look upon her.

"You like me - yes?" she murmured, and then slipping back into the vernacular, "I - I am not the stupid veiled girl of the seclusion - not forever. I come from the west, the deserts. I have seen the world: Men - men, I know ... I danced before them, not the dances of the Cairene cafes," she uttered with swift scorn, "but the dance of the two swords, the dance of the serpents.... Men threw the gold from their turbans about my feet when I had danced to them ... And others, English, French - "

She broke off, but her eyes told many things. "Then - Hamdi," she said slowly. "Him I ruled - and his palace.... But I have known other things."

Closer yet she came to him. Her eyes, golden fires of eyes, were smiling up into his, her scarlet lips gathered in soft, sensual curves ... her whole silken scented body seemed to slip into his embrace. A bare arm touched his neck, resting heavily.

"Sweet - heart," she said slowly, in her difficult English.

It was the deuce of a position.

No man can rudely snatch from his neck the arm of the lady who has just saved him from a harrowing death. And a lady who was risking more than her life in sheltering him - decidedly the situation was delicate.

It was not the lady's fault that her impetuosity, the impetuosity which had been his salvation, now plunged her into amorous caprice. There were obvious handicaps, moral, social and ethical, in her upbringing. She was a child of nature, a nature undisciplined, unruly, tempestuous.

And even queening over Hamdi and his palace must have offered little diversion to a wild dancing girl familiar with the excitement of more varied conquest.

Ryder was horribly embarrassed. He was visited with a fearful constraint, a chivalrous wish not to hurt her feelings, and a sharp prevision of the danger of offending her.

He took the first turn of least resistance.

He did not need to bend his head; their eyes were on a level.

He simply kissed her. And she kissed him back.

He hated himself for the leap of his blood... and for the Puritanical discomfort of his nature....

Her arm about his neck was pressing closer. It was the moment for action and Ryder acted. Very firmly he put his hand upon her hand, withdrew it from its clasp about him, and raised it to his lips.

His kiss was respectful gratitude and an abdication of the delights of dalliance.

"Good-bye, my dear," he murmured. "Now, if you will show me the way out - "

Her eyes agleam between half-closed lids, she studied him. It occurred to Ryder that probably never before had her hands been detached - and kissed - and put away. He must be a phenomenon, an enigma.

Then her lips parted in a faintly scornful smile.

"You afraid - you? You want - run?"

"I'm horribly afraid," he said earnestly. "I want to get out of here as quick as I can."

That was putting, he considered, the very wisest construction upon it.

Negligently her gesture reminded him of the opening in the window. "Here you are safe." she murmured in the vernacular. "And the doors are locked - "

"Yes, but - but Aimee isn't safe, you know - and I must get her out of here."

"Aimee?" In those yellow eyes he caught the flash of capricious resentment at the reminder. Then, indifferently, she brushed the distraction away.

"There is time enough for Aimee. She is not lonely now."

"Not lonely?" he shivered at the cold carelessness of her tone. "I must get to her quickly then."

"But that is not safe.... A little - later."

Uncomfortably he tried to infuse his glance with innate innocence and utter lack of understanding.

"I shan't hurt him - if I have the chance," he told her. "I've given you my word - "

"And I trust you - much." Her gaze sought his in a trifle of impatience at such simplicity. "But it is not safe for you now.... Later ... By and by."

"You don't want him to have a chance to make love to her, do you?" said Ryder sharply. "I thought that was the very thing you *didn't* - "

Her smile was a subtle, confessing caress. "I shall have my revenge," she murmured, and pressed closer to him again, every sensuous, sumptuous line of her a challenge and an enticement.

"I give you life," she whispered, very low in her throat. "You give me, perhaps, an hour - ?"

"I *haven't* an hour," said Ryder very desperately and unhappily. "Not when Aimee is with that devil - "

It took every thought of Aimee to get the words out.

He felt a brute about it, a low, ungrateful dog. She *had* given him life and every fiber in him clamored to save her pride and

MARY HASTINGS BRADLEY

champion her caprice.

It seemed so dastardly to wrench away from her now, like some self-centered Joseph, leaving that beastly stab in her vanity.... And she was a stunning creature, lawless, elemental, hot and cold like the seventh wind of the inferno....

But it was Aimee who was in his blood like a fever.... Aimee, that frail white rose of a girl, in her bonds of terror....

He saw the flame in Aziza's eyes. He saw the stiffening of her defiance, of half-incredulous affront. Then, her form drawn up, her bared arms outflung, her vivid, painted, furious face challenging him. "I am not beautiful - like Aimee?" she said in a voice of venom, and in the English, for double measure, "You not like me - no?"

"You *are* beautiful and I *do* like you," Ryder combated, feeling a bungling fool. And then went on to thrust into that half-second of suspended fury, a faint breath of appeasing. "But - don't you see - it's my duty - "

"You go - ?" she said clearly.

Even in that moment he had a sharp prescience of the unwisdom of his rejection. A cold calculator of chance and probabilities would have reckoned that a half hour of assuagement here would have been a wiser investment of his mortal moments than any virtuous plunge into single-hearted duty.

But Ryder did not calculate. He could not, with Aimee under that beast's hand. His heart and soul were possessed with her danger and his heart and soul carried his body instinctively back from the dancing girl's advance, and he whispered, "I must go. There is no time - "

She flung back her fiery-hued head with a gesture of intolerable rage. Her eyes were lightnings.

"Dog of a Christian!" she said chokingly and flew to the doors.

Back she thrust the heavy hangings, turning a quick key in the lock and wrenching the door wide. And before Ryder could understand, before he could bring himself to realize that she was not simply violently expelling him from her room, she gave a shriek that rang wildly down the long-unseen corridors.

At the top of her lungs, with one hand out to thrust him back or cling to him if he attempted to pass, she shrieked again and again.

Instantly there came a running of feet.

# CHAPTER XIX

## AN INTERRUPTION

When Hamdi Bey had taken Aimee back to her apartments he pulled sharply upon a bellcord. In a few moments the slave woman, Fatima, made her appearance, no kindly-eyed old crone like Miriam, but a sallow, furtive-faced creature, with an old disfiguring scar across a cheek.

The general pointed to the wet and fainting girl huddling weakly upon the divan.

"Your new mistress has met with an accident, out boating - a curse upon me for gratifying forbidden caprice!" he said crisply. "Be silent of this and array her quickly in garments of rest. I will return."

Very hurriedly he took himself and his own wet condition away. He was furious, through and through. What a night - what a wedding night! Scandal and frustration... a bride with a desperate lover... a bride who, herself, drew revolvers and threatened.

It was beyond any old tale of the palace. For less, girls had had his father's dagger driven through their hearts - his grand-father, at a mere whisper from a eunuch, had given his favorite to the lion. The whisper was found incorrect at a later - too late - date, and the eunuch had furnished the lion another meal.

His modern leniency in this case would have outraged

his ancestors.

But it was not in the bey's nature to deal the finishing stroke to anything so soft and lovely as Aimee. He had no intention of depriving himself of her. If she were red with guilt he would feign belief in her, to save his face until his infatuation was gratified.

But actually he did not believe in any great guilt of hers. Tewfick Pasha, for all his indulgent modernity, would keep too strict a harem for that. What he rather believed, had happened was that the young American - now so happily immured in his masonry - had become aware of the girl through the story of her French father, and in that connection had struck up the clandestine and romantic correspondence which had led to their mutual infatuation and his desperate venture there that afternoon.

The young man had been dealt with - and the thought of the very summary and competent way he had been dealt with drew the fangs from the bite of that night's invasion.

His fury felt soothingly glutted.

He had been a match for them both. He recalled his own subtlety and agility with a genuine smile as he exchanged his dripping uniform for more informal trousers and a house coat. He had taught that young man a lesson - a final and ultimate lesson. And he was beginning to teach one to that girl. Before he was done with her ...

He felt for her a mingled passion for her beauty and a lust for conquest of her resistant spirit that fed every base and cruel instinct of his nature.

A find - a rare find - even with her circumvented lover! He would have his sport with her.... But though he promised this to himself with feline relish, apprehension and chagrin were still working.

The fond fatuity with which he had welcomed that starry-eyed little creature had been rudely overthrown. And his pride smarted at the idea of the whispers that might echo and re-echo through his palace. He was too wise an old hand to flatter himself that it would preserve its bland and silent unawareness of this night.

So far, he believed, he had been unobserved. In Yussuf's silence he had absolute confidence.... But of course there were a hundred other chances - some spying, back-stairs eye, some curious, straining ear....

And for this matter of the boating mishap - he cursed himself now, as he combed up his fair mustaches and settled a scarlet fez upon his thinned thatch of graying hair, cursed himself roundly for his malicious resort to that old oubliette. Anything else would have done to frighten and overwhelm her and yet he had gratified his dramatic itch - and now had paid for it with that idiotic story of the boating expedition.

He had reason to trust Fatima - there was history behind the old sword scar upon her cheek, and he had a hold over her through her ambition for a son. But Fatima was a woman. And she - or some other who would see that drenched satin would be curious of that boating story....

And of course they could find out from the boatman.

It occurred to him to go and see the boatman and order him away so that afterward the man could say he had been sent off duty, and the story of a nocturnal river trip would not appear too incredible. It was a small concession to stop gossip's mouth.

So drawing on a swinging military cloak, the general stole down through the stair of the water entrance into the lower hall, where the pale light gleamed through the cross-barred iron of the gate and the gatekeeper slept like a log in his muffling cloak.

The soundness of that slumber - loudly attested by the fumes of wine - afforded the general a profound pleasure. He took the man's keys softly, and went to the gate; it afforded him less pleasure to observe that the gate was unlocked, but he put this down to the keeper's muddleheadedness.

Carefully he turned the lock and pocketed the keys - for a lesson to the man's overdeep sleep in the morning and to attest his own presence there that night; then he went back and brought out an oar, which he placed conspicuously beside the smallest boat, drawn up just within the gates.

He was afraid to alter the boat's position lest the noise should prove too wakening, but he considered he had laid an artistic foundation for his story and with a gratifying sense of triumph he mounted the stairs.

He was not conscious of fatigue. He had always been a wiry, indefatigable person, and the alarms and emotions of this night had cleared his head of its wines and drowsiness. He felt the sense of tense, highstrung power which came to him in war, in fighting, in any element of danger.

Youth! He snapped his fingers at it. Youth was buried in his masonry - and helpless in its shuttered room. Power was master - power, craft, subtlety.

But his elation ebbed as he crossed again that long drawing room with its faded flowers about the marriage throne, and its abandoned table with its cloth askew, its crystal disarrayed, its candles gutted and spent.

The memory of that insolent moment when a man's hand had gripped him, had whirled him from Aimee - when a man's voice and gun had threatened him - that memory was too overpowering for even his triumph over the invader to lay wholly its smart of outrage.

He felt again the tightening of his nerves, like quivering wires, as he crossed the violated reception room and entered the boudoir. It was empty, but on the divan the flickering candle light revealed the damp, spreading stain where Aimee's drenched satins had been.

He thrust aside a hanging and pushed open the door into the room beyond.

It was a small bedroom evidently very recently furnished in new and white shining lacquer of French design, elaborately inlaid with painted porcelains and draped with a profusion of rosy taffeta. Among this elegance, surprisingly unrelated to the ancient paneled walls, stood the hastily opened trunk and bags of the bride, their raised lids and disarranged trays heaped with the confusion of unaccustomed, swiftly searching hands.

Aimee herself, in a gay little French boudoir robe of jade and citron, sat huddled in a chair, like a mute, terrified child, in the hand of her dresser, who was shaking out the long, damp hair and fanning it with a peacock fan.

At the bey's entrance Fatima suspended the fanning, but with easy familiarity exhibited the long ringlets.

Curtly the bey nodded, and gestured in dismissal; the woman laid down her fan, and with a last slant-eyed look at that strangely still new mistress she went noiselessly out a small service door.

With an air of negligent assurance Hamdi Bey gazed about the room and yawned. "Truly a fatiguing evening," he remarked in his dry, sardonic voice. "But you look so untouched! What a thing is radiant youth."

He sauntered over to her, who drew a little closer together at his approach, and lifted one of the long dark curls that the serving woman had exhibited.

"The ringlets of loveliness," he murmured. "You know the old saying of the Sadi? 'The ringlets of the lovely are a chain on the feet of reason and a snare for the bird of wisdom.'... How long ago he said it - and how true to-day ... Yet such a charming chain! Suppose, then, I forgive you, little one, since sages have forgiven beauty before?"

She was silent, her eyes fixed on him with the silent terror with which a trapped bird sees its captor, in their bright darkness the same mute apprehension, the same filming of helpless despair.

Ryder was dead, she thought. This cruel, incensed old madman had killed him, for all his oaths. Somewhere beneath those ancient stones he was lying drowned and dead, a strange, pitiable addition to the dark secrets of those grim walls.

He had died for her sake, and all that she asked now of life, she thought in the utter agony of her youth, was death. And very quickly.

"I am so soft hearted," he sighed, still with that ringlet in his lifted hand, his hand which wanted palpably to settle upon her and yet was withheld by some strange inhibition of those fixed, helpless eyes. "Who knows - perhaps I may forgive you yet? You might persuade me - "

"He is dead," she said shiveringly.

"Dead? He?... Ah, the invader, the intruder, the young man who wanted you for a family in France!" The bey laughed gratingly. "No, I assure you he is not dead - I have not harmed a hair of his head. He is alive - only not with quite the widest range of liberty - "

He broke off to laugh again. "Ah, you disbelieve?" he said politely. "Shall I send, then, for some proof - an ear, perhaps, or a little finger, still very warm and bleeding, to convince you?... In five minutes it will be here."

Then terror stirred again in her frozen heart. If Ryder were alive and still in this man's power -

"You are horrible," she said to him in a voice that was suddenly clear and unshaken. "What is it you want of me - fear and hate - and utter loathing?"

Her unexpected spirit was briefly disconcerting. The Turk looked down upon her in arrested irony and then he smiled beneath his mustaches and bent nearer with kindling gaze.

"Not at all - nothing at all like that, little dove with talons. I want sweetness and repentance - and submission. And - "

"You have a strange way to win them," she said desperately.

"You have taken a strange way with me, my love! Little did I foresee, when I escorted you up the stairs this morning - " He broke off. "There are men," he reminded her, "who would not consider a cold bath as a complete recompense for your bridal plans."

She was silent.

"But I," he murmured, "I am soft hearted." He dropped on one knee before her and tried to smile into her averted face. "I can never resist a charming penitent.... I assure you I am pliability itself in delicate fingers - although iron and steel to a threatening hand.... If you should woo me very sweetly, little one - "

She could not overcome and she could not hide from his mocking eyes the sick shrinking that drew her back from his least touch. But she did fight down the wild hysteria of her repugnance so that her voice was not the trembling gasp it wanted to be.

"How can I know what you are?" she told him. "You mock me - you threaten to torture that man - it would be folly not to think that you are deceiving me. If you would only prove to me so that I could believe - "

"If you would but prove to *me* so that *I* could believe - ! Prove that you are mine - and not that infidel's. Prove that you bring me a wife's devotion - not a wanton's indifference." He caught her cold hands, trying to draw her forward to him. "Prove that you only pity him," he whispered, "but that your love will be mine - "

She felt as if a serpent clasped her. And yet, if that were the only way to win Ryder's safety - if it were possible for her sickened senses to allay this madman's suspicions and undermine his revenge -

Quiveringly she thought that to save Ryder she would go through fire.

But the hideous, mocking uncertainties! Her utter helplessness - her lost deference....

It was not a sudden sound that broke in upon them but rather the perception of many sounds, muffled, half heard, but gaining upon their consciousness. Running feet - a stifled voice - something faint and shrill -

Aimee sprang to her feet; the general rose with her and turned his head inquiringly in the direction. Then he jerked open the door through which Fatima had disappeared; it led to a dark service corridor and small anteroom, from whose bed the attendant was absent. An outer door was ajar.

No need to question the sounds now. Faint, but piercingly shrill shrieks were sounding from above, while the footsteps were racing, some down, some up -

The bey flung shut the door behind him and hurried towards the confusion.

# CHAPTER XX

## BEYOND THE DOOR

Ryder had stood stock still with amazement when the girl began to scream. She had gone mad, he thought for an instant, in masculine bewilderment, and then her madness revealed its treacherous cunning, for she began crying wildly for help against an invader, an infidel, a dog of a Christian who had stolen into her rooms.

She had chucked him to the lions, Ryder perceived; one furious flash of lightning jealousy and Oriental anger had overthrown, in that wild and lawless head, every other design for him for which she had risked so much.

He had scorned her.... He had flouted her caprice.... He had dared to refuse the languors of those dangerous eyes....

The hurrying footsteps appeared to him the tread of a legion in action, and he had no desire to rush out upon the oncomers; he had, indeed, distinct doubts of his ruthless ability to pass that supple, clawing, incensed creature at the door.

He whirled and made a bolt for the window, striking at the fastened grill. He heard the snapping of wooden bolts and the splintering of wood and out through the hole he climbed to a precipitous, head-long flight that fairly felt the clutching hands upon his ankle.

He had meant to make a jump for it. A three-story plunge into the Nile appeared a gentle exercise compared to the alternative within the palace, but in the very act of releasing his hold he changed his mind.

Quicker than he had ever moved before, in any vicissitude of his lithe and agile youth, he clambered up, not down, and crouching back from sight upon the jutting top of the window, he sent his coat sailing violently through space.

He dared not look over for its descent upon the water, for other heads were peering from below and he could hear an excited outburst of speech, that broke sharply off.

Evidently they were hurrying down to the water gate. Swiftly he utilized this misdirection for his own ends.

The roofs. That was the refuge to make for. Flat, long-reaching roofs, from which one could climb off onto a wall or a palm or a side street.

He had only a story to ascend and he made it in record time, fearful that the searchers whom he heard now launching a boat below would turn their eyes skywards.

But he gained the top without an outcry being raised and found himself upon the roof where the ladies of the harem took their air unseen of any save the blind eyes of the muezzin in the Sultan mosque upon the hill. There were divans and a little taboret or two and a framework where an awning could be raised against the sun.

There was also a trap door.

And here, tempestuously he changed his mind again. He abandoned the goal of outer walls and chances of escape. He wrenched violently at that trap door. It was bolted but the bolt was an ancient one and gave at his furious exertions, letting him down into a narrow spiral staircase between walls.

Down he plunged in haste, before some confused searcher

should dash up. It was no place to meet an opposing force. Nor was the corridor in which he found himself much better.

It was black and baffling as a labyrinth, with unexpected turnings, and he kept gingerly close to the wall with one hand clutching a bit of iron which he had taken into his possession and his pocket when Aziza had led him out of the underground walls - the very bit of pointed iron, it was, with which the volatile creature had effected his rescue.

He considered it an invaluable souvenir and twice, in his nervous apprehension, he almost brought it down upon shadows.

Direction he judged vaguely by the screaming which was still going on at a tremendous rate - evidently the girl had gone off into genuine hysterics or else she had determined not to leave her agitation at the intrusion in any manner of question. No doubt the outcries were a relief to her mingled emotions - remorse at her impetuosity and chagrin that her thwarted plans might conceivably be now among those emotions - and since the vicinity of those shrieks must be a gathering place to be avoided by him he stole on, down the upper hall, and finding a stair, he went down for two continuous flights.

Aimee's rooms, he knew, had been upon the water, and recalling the general direction of those two lighted windows that he had seen so recently from without, his excavator's instinct led him on. Once he saw the flitting figure of a turbaned woman in time to draw back into a heaven-sent niche and again he flattened into a soundless shadow against the wall as two young serving girls ran by on slippered feet, their anklets tinkling, chattering to each other in delighted excitement.

And then the stealthy opening of a door - it was the very door by which Yussuf had precipitated himself upon the struggle at the supper table some age-long hours ago - gave him a glimpse into the far glooms of the reception room, where its long side of mashrubiyeh windows revealed now between its fretwork tiny chinks of a paling sky.

He could make out the dark-draped marriage throne and the pallor of the disordered cloth upon the abandoned table below, and behind the table the dark draperies of the remaining portieres before the doorway into the boudoir where he had hidden himself and into which he had last seen Aimee thrust.

At the other end of the great room were the entrance stairs to the harem, and there, he imagined, a watchman was stationed, or else stout bolts and bars were guarding the situation. There remained an arched doorway into other formal rooms through which he had seen Aimee and the guests disappear for the wedding supper, and that way led, he surmised, down into the service quarters.

A sorry choice of exits! He could form no plan in advance but trust blindly to the amazing chances of adventure. And first, before he rushed for escape, there was Aimee to find.

Yet for all the mad hazard of the situation he was elated with life. He felt as if he had never fully lived until now, when every breath was informed with the sharp prescience of danger. He was at once cool and exultant, wary yet reckless, with the joyous recklessness of utter desperation.

With cat-like care he surveyed the drawing-room; it appeared deserted but as he watched his tense nerves could see the shadows forming, taking furtive, crouching shape - and then dissolving harmlessly into a rug, a chair, or a stirring drapery. His eyes grown used to the dimness he identified the mantle upon the floor in which he had come and which he had extended to Aimee in that brief moment of fatuous triumph, and beyond it, across a chair, was the portiere which the black had torn down from the doorway to wrap about Ryder's helpless form as he had carried him down to living death.

That mantle, he thought, might yet be useful, and he stole

forward and recovered it, but, as he straightened, another shadow darted out from the boudoir door and silhouetted for an instant against the lighted, room he saw a figure in a long, swinging military cloak.

Discovery was inevitable and Ryder made a swift plunge to take the cloaked figure by surprise, but even as one hand shot out and gripped the throat while the other held his threatening iron aloft, his clutch relaxed, his arm fell nervelessly at his side.

For from the figure had come the broken gasp of a soft voice, and the face upturned to his was a pale oval under dark, disordered hair.

"Aimee!" he breathed in exultant, still half-incredulous joy. "Aimee!... Did I hurt you - ?"

"Oh, no, no!" came Aimee's shaken voice. "Oh, you are safe!"

He felt her trembling in his clasp and he swept her close to him. For one breathless instant they clung together, in a sharp, passionate gladness which blurred every sense of dread or danger. They were safe - they were together - and for the moment it was enough. Every obstacle was surmounted, every terror conquered.

They clung, obliviously, like children, her pale face against his shoulder, her hair brushing his lips, her wild heartbeats throbbing against his own.

Then the girl, remembering, lifted her head.

"Quick - we must go," she whispered. "For there I made a fire - "

He fallowed her frightened, backward glance at the boudoir door and suddenly saw its cracks and key hole strangely radiant with light.

"He left me, to go to those screams," she was saying rapidly. "I tried to run that way - and found that woman coming back. And I told her to wait - in her own room - and I slipped back in there - and suddenly it came to me to thrust the candle about. I thought I would run out and if I met any one I would call, 'Fire', and say the general was burning and perhaps in the confusion - "

The terrible desperation of her both stirred and wrung him. She was so little, so helpless, so trembling in his clasp ... so made for love and tenderness.... And to think of her in such fear and horror that she went thrusting reckless candles into her hangings, setting a palace on fire in the blind fury for escape....

To such work had this night brought her.... This night, and three men - for he and the craven Tewfick and the fanatic bey were all linked in this night's work. Yes, and another man - and he thought swiftly, in a lightning flash of wonder, how little that Paul Delcasse had known when he set his eager face toward the Old World, with his wife and baby with him, that he was setting his feet into such a web ... that his wife would die, languishing in a pasha's harem, and his little daughter would one night be flying in mad terror from the cruel beast the weak pasha had sold her to!

And how little, for that matter, he had known when he had set his own face toward those same sands what secrets he would discover there and what forbidden ways his heart would know.

These thoughts all went through him like one thought, in some clear, remote background of his mind, while he was swiftly drawing on the military cloak she gave him and wrapping her in the black mantle. There was a veil on the mantle's hood that she could fling across her face when she wished, but Ryder had no fez to complete the deceptive outline of his masquerade. He must trust to the dark and to the concealment of the high, military collar of the cloak.

"Do you know a way?" he whispered and at her shaken head, "The water gate," he said, thinking swiftly.

There would be a crowd now about the gate, but if they could only manage to gain those cellars and hide somewhere they could steal out later upon that waterman.

It seemed the most feasible of all the desperate plans. The roofs might be a trap. The harem entrance led into a garden and the garden was guarded by an impassable wall. But if he could only get to the river he knew that he was a strong enough swimmer to save Aimee, or he might even terrorize the watchman into furnishing a boat.

She did not question but guided him swiftly through the arch that led down into the banqueting hall. Twice that day she had gone down those stairs. Once in her bridal state, her eyes shining, her cheeks glowing with the wild joy of Ryder's arrival and dreams of escape, and again, scarcely an hour gone by, she had descended them, tense and desperate, her revolver at the general's head, seeking vainly Ryder's rescue.

And now a third time, a guilty, reckless fugitive in the night, she stole down those stairs into the many-columned hall where she had been feted in state among her guests. Here her only knowledge was of the stone corridor and the locked door through which the bey had led her, but Ryder knew the way that Aziza had brought him and he turned cautiously toward those wide, curving stairs.

Keeping Aimee a few steps behind him, he went down the soft carpet and peered out at the bottom towards the water gate. He saw no bars; the gate was open and against the pale square of the water were the black silhouettes of the general and the gateman, both leaning out at some splashing in the river.

He knew a boy's reckless impulse to shove them both in. It was an unholy thought his better judgment rejected - unless driven to it - yet some  prankish element in his roused recklessness would not have deplored the necessity.

If they looked about - !

But they did not stir as, with Aimee's cold hand in his, he made the tiptoed descent and slipped softly about the corner of the steps. Then, instead of going on down the hall to some hiding place in the ruins, he took a suddenly revealed, sharper turn into a narrow passage just beyond the stairs.

It might lead to another gate, some service entrance, perhaps, it ran so straight and direct between its walls.

Intuitively that excavator's sense of his defined the direction. They were going parallel with the river, although a little way back from the water wall, and in the direction of the men's part of the palace, the selamlik.

He recalled the selamlik vaguely as an irregular mass of buildings, and though the formal entrance was of course through the garden from the avenue, there was a narrow side street or lane leading back to the water's edge between this part of the palace and the nest building, and very likely there was some entrance on that lane.

Bitterly he blamed himself for his lack of complete inspection that morning. To be sure he had told himself, then, as he strolled about the high garden walls and peered down the narrow lane on one side of the Nile backwaters, that he didn't need a map of the place for his arrival at an afternoon reception; he was simply going in and out, and clothes and speech were his only real concern.

He had even said to himself that he might not reveal himself to Aimee - if she did not discover him. He wanted merely to see her again, and be sure that she understood her own history - he had no notion of attempting any further relations with her, any resumption of their forbidden and dangerous acquaintance.

MARY HASTINGS BRADLEY

And it was true that had been the defiant and protesting surface of his thoughts, but deep within himself there had always been that hot, hidden spark, ready to kindle to a flame at her word - and with it the unowned, secret longing that she would speak the word.

And when she had called on him for help, when the trembling appeal had sprung past her stricken pride, and he had seen the terror in her soft, child's eyes, then the spark had struck its conflagration. He had become nothing but a hot, headstrong fury of devotion.

And he said to himself now that he might have known it was going to happen, and that if he had not been so concerned that morning about saving his face and preserving this fiction of indifference he would know a little more about the labyrinth they were poking about in - the little more that tips the scale between safety and destruction.

But he did not know and blind Chance was his only goddess.

The passage had brought him to a wall and a narrow stairs while another passage led off to the right, apparently to the forward regions of the place.

He took the stairs. He had had enough of underground regions when they did not lead to water gates and the stairs promised novelty at least.

He wished he knew more about Turkish palaces. He supposed they had a fairly consistent ground plan, but beyond a few main features of inner courts and halls he was culpably ignorant of their intentions. If it were an early Egyptian tomb or temple now! But then, perhaps the Turks were more indefinite in their building and rebuilding.

At the head of the stairs a door stood half ajar. Through the crack he strained his eyes, but his anxious glance met only the darkness of utter night. Not a gleam of light. And not a sound - except the far, hollow stamping of some stabled horse.

Softly he pushed the door open and he and Aimee slipped within. The place, whatever it was, appeared deserted, a dark, bare, backstairs region - for he stumbled over a bucket - from which to the right he could just discern a hall leading into the forward part of the palace, wanly lighted some distance on, with the pale flicker of an old ceiling lamp.

They seemed to be at the end of the hall and the darker shadows in the walls about them appeared to be a number of doors - closed, so his groping hands informed him.

Oh, for his excavator's steady light, or a pocket flash! Oh, for a light of any kind, even a temporary match! But he dared not risk the scratch, for now he caught the thud of footfalls overhead, heavy footfalls, and there might be stairs unexpectedly close at hand.

He turned to Aimee but the girl shook her head helplessly and hesitant and dashed, for all their young confidence, they wavered a moment hand in hand in the dark, fearful of what a rash move might bring upon them. And in the beating stillness Ryder became conscious that the muffled, monotonous stamping of a horse is a gloomy, disheartening thing in the night, and that footsteps overhead are of all noises the most nervous and unsettling.

What was behind those doors? Not a spark of light came from them, that was one comfort. The rooms, kitchen, service, store rooms or whatever they were, appeared in the same blackness and oblivion.... But any door might open on a roomful of sleeping gardeners and grooms....

Life and more than life hung on the blind goddess.

It was only an instant that they hesitated there, yet it appeared an eternity of indecision, then nearer footsteps sounded, coming down that hall. No more wavering of the scales!

Ryder turned to the door at his left, at the very end of the wall beyond which came that far stamping, and wrenched it open, closing it swiftly behind him. He saw a light now, a mild, yellow ray through an opened door ahead that vaguely illumined the strange old vehicles of the palace, and the stables were beyond.

Some one else was beyond, too, in the stables, for that very instant he saw a black horse backed restively into sight, its tossing head evading the hands that were trying to bridle it.

"The Fortieth Door!" said Ryder to himself with an involuntary thrust of humor.

The door of the horse! The door of forbidden daring! He knew now the vague associations that had stirred in him as he had stared blindly about that place of doors.... But he had opened so many forbidden doors of late that this last was welcome as the supreme test.

And nothing in the world could have been more welcome than a horse - a horse with a way out behind it!

"Stay back," he said under his breath to Aimee, and clasping his bit of iron he moved toward the door.

He could see the attendant now, who was finishing his bridling, and it was Yussuf, the eunuch, so busy gentling and soothing the horse that he cast only one glance in the direction of the sounds he heard and that one glance misled him in its glimpse of the general's cloak.

"By your favor - but an instant," he called out, " and he is ready - "

"Stand aside," said Ryder very clearly, emerging from the shadows at the horse's heels. "Out of the way with you. The horse is for me."

A moment Yussuf gaped. Then he dropped the bridle and his hand went swiftly to the knife hilt in his belt.

"Fool!" said Ryder contemptuously. "Would you tempt fate? Do you think I am such that your knife could harm me? Must I prove to you again that walls are nothings - that I but let myself be taken to prove my powers?"

Ethiopians are superstitious. And Yussuf knew that his brick and mortar had been strong.... Yet they have great trust in a crooked, short-bladed knife, and Yussuf did not relax his hold upon his and for all that Ryder could See there was no hesitation in the grinning ferocity of his black face.

Yet his spring was an instant delayed and in that instant Ryder spoke again.

"Look, now at the wall behind you," he said quickly.

Yussuf looked. And as he turned his bullet head Ryder jumped close and brought his iron down upon it with a sickening force he thought scarcely short of murder.

To his amazement the black did not fall, but staggered only, and Ryder had need to send the knife spinning from his grasp and strike again before the eunuch's knees sagged and his huge bulk sank at Ryder's feet.

This time Ryder took no chance with a shammed unconsciousness. He snatched down bits of leather from the wall and bound the man's hands and feet in tight security and seeing that he was breathing, although heavily, he thrust a gagging handkerchief into his mouth.

Then he dragged the heavy body towards a pile of hay he saw in a vacant stall and concealed it effectively but not too smotheringly - although Yussuf, he felt, would be no grievous loss to society.

Vaguely in the back of his consciousness he had been aware of the excited plunge of the horse and then of a low, soothing murmur of speech, and now he turned to find Aimee holding the bridle and stroking the quivering creature with gentle, fearless hands.

"Is he dead?" she asked quietly of the eunuch.

"Stunned," said Ryder, meaning reassurement and was startled by the passion of her cry, "Oh, I could kill them all - all!"

"I will - if they try to stop us," he promised grimly, forgetful of that oath to Aziza.

Hastily he glanced about the stalls. There was no other horse there, only a pair of mild-eyed donkeys, and though there might conceivably be other horses behind other doors there was no instant to spare in search.

This luck was too prodigious to risk.

The door to the street had already been unbolted and now he threw it back with a quick look into the dark emptiness of the narrow side street, and then, with a tight hold of the reins, he swung himself into the saddle and Aimee up into his arms, her head on his shoulder, her arms clasping him.

It was a huge Bedouin saddle with high-arched back and curved pummel and the slender pair no more than filled it, making apparently no weight at all for the spirited beast which tore out of the stalls at the charging gallop beloved of Eastern horsemen.

For a moment Ryder felt wildly that he might meet the fate of the rash youth in his patron story. He had never ridden a horse like this, which, like all high-mettled Arabs, resented the authority of any but his master, and though a good horseman Ryder had all he could do to keep his seat and Aimee in his arms.

Around the corner of the lane the horse went racing, and down the dark, lebbek-lined avenue his flying feet struck back their sparks of fire. Across an open square he plunged, while irate camels screamed at him and a harsh voice shouted back loud curses. It seemed to Ryder that other voices joined in - that there was a pursuit, an outcry - and then they were out down an open road, wildly galloping, like a mad highwayman under a pale morning sky.

# CHAPTER XXI

## MISS JEFFRIES MAKES A CALL

That morning Miss Jeffries ate two eggs. She ate them successively, with increasing deliberation, and afterwards she lingered interminably over her toast and marmalade.

Still Ryder made no appearance and since the Arab waiter had informed her that he had not yet breakfasted she concluded that he was not at the hotel but had spent the night with some friend of his - probably that Andrew McLean to whom he was always running off.

Nor was he in to luncheon. That was rank extravagance because he was paying at pension rates. His extravagance, however, was no affair of hers. Neither, she informed herself frigidly, was his appearance or his non-appearance. It was only rather dull of Jack to lose so many, well, opportunities.

She was not going to be in Cairo forever. Not much longer, in fact. There were adages about gathering rosebuds while ye may and making hay while the sun shone that Jack Ryder would do well to observe.

Other men did, reflected Jinny Jeffries with a proud lift of her ruddy head. Only somehow, the other men -

Well, Jack *was* provokingly attractive! Only of course, if he was going to rely upon his attraction and not upon his attentions -

Deliberately Miss Jeffries smiled upon a stalwart tourist from

New York and promised her society for a foursome at bridge in the hotel lounge that evening.

Later, when Jack still failed to materialize and behold her inaccessibility, the exhibition seemed hardly to have been worth while.... And there were difficulties getting rid of the New Yorker the next day. He had ideas about excursions.

It was during the forenoon of the next day that the first twinge of genuine worry shot across the sustained resentment which she was pleased to call her complete indifference. She recalled the vigor of Ryder's warnings about mentioning his adventure and the grave dangers of disclosure, and she began to wonder.

She wished, rather, that he had gone safely out of the house before she went away.

Of course nothing could happen. He had done nothing to give himself away. He was simply a veiled shadow, moving humbly as befitted a lowly stranger among the high and hospitable surroundings.

But still, it would have been better if he had gone....

Those turbaned women had looked queerly at them when they were talking so long in the window. Perhaps it was not simply at the intimacy between a young American and a veiled Oriental. Perhaps their voices had been unguarded or Jack's tones had awakened suspicion. Perhaps he had given himself away in his long talk with the bride. She remembered a Frenchwoman who had come to interrupt that talk who had looked rather sharply at Jack.... And that dreadful eunuch was always staring....

She thought of a great many things now, more and more things every minute.

And still she told herself that she was absurd, that Jack would be the first to ridicule her alarm. He was probably enjoying himself, staying on with his friends, forgetting all about herself.... Still his room at the hotel had not been slept in for two nights now nor had he called at the hotel and he certainly didn't have an extensive supply of clothes and linen upon him beneath the mantle.

Particularly she remembered that he had exhibited some funny black tennis shoes which he had thought would go appropriately with a woman's robes. Absurd, to think of him as spending two days in tennis shoes, and absurd to say that he would go to the shops and buy more when he had plenty of footgear in his hotel room.

Unless he wore McLean's.

She had always regarded the unknown McLean as a most unnecessary absorbent of Jack Ryder's time and attention and now that view was deeply reinforced.

By noon she decided to do something. She would telephone that Andrew McLean and see if Jack had been there. The Agricultural Bank, that was the place. An obliging hotel clerk - clerks were always obliging to Miss Jeffries - gave her the number and she slipped into the booth feeling a ridiculous amount of excitement and suspense.

She had never telephoned in Cairo - only been telephoned to - and she was not prepared for the fact that the telephone company was French. At the phone girl's "*Numero? - Quel numero, s'il vous plait?*" Jinny hastily choked back the English response and clutched violently at French numerals.

"*Huit cent - no, quatre vingt - un moment!*" she demanded desperately and hanging up the receiver, sat down to write out her number in French correctly.

And then she got the Bank, and, still clinging to her French, she requested to speak to Monsieur McLean and was informed that it was Monsieur McLean himself.

"*Je suis* - oh, how absurd! Of course you speak English," she exclaimed. "This French telephone upset me.... I wanted to speak to Mr. Ryder if he is there - or else leave a message for him, if you know when he will come in."

"Ryder?" There was a faint intonation of surprise in the voice. "I've no idea really when he'll be in," said McLean, "but you may leave the message if you like."

"Hasn't he - haven't you seen him for some time?" stammered Jinny, feeling that McLean must be taking her for a pursuing adventuress.

"Well - not for some time."

Her heart sank.

"Not - not for two days?"

"It might be that," said the Scotchman cautiously.

Two days. Forty-eight hours, almost, since she had left him in that harem! And McLean had not seen him. Of course there might be other friends who had and McLean might know of them.

"I'm afraid I'll have to see you," she said desperately. "It's rather important about Jack Ryder - and if I could just talk with you a minute - this afternoon - ?"

"I have no appointment for three fifteen," McLean told her concisely.

Evidently he expected her to call at the Bank.... He was used to being called on.... "Shall I come - ?" she began.

"I can see you at three fifteen," McLean reassured her, and she repeated "Three fifteen," with an odd vibration in her voice.

"I wonder," she murmured, "if I came at three ten - or three twenty - ?"

*   *   *   *   *

But she didn't. She was humorously careful to make it exactly a quarter past the hour when she left her cab before McLean's official looking residence and stepped into the tiled entrance.

She had no very clear notion of Andrew McLean except that he was, as Jack had said, Scotch, single, and skeptical, that he was Jack's intimate friend and an official sort of banker - and the word banker had unconsciously prepared her for stout dignity and middle age.

She was not at all prepared for the lean, sandy-haired, rather abrupt young man who came forward from the depths of the gratefully cool reception room, and after a nervous hand clasp waved her to a chair.

He was still holding her card, and as he glanced covertly at it she recalled that she had given him no name over the telephone and that he had known her only by the time of her appointment. Decidedly she must have made an odd impression!

Well, he could see for himself now, she thought, a trifle defiantly. Certainly he was taking stock of her out of those shrewd swift gray eyes of his. He could see that she was, well - certainly a nice girl!

As a matter of fact McLean could see that she was considerably more. Rather disconcertingly more! It was not often that such white-clad apparitions, piquant of face and coppery of hair, teased the eyes in his receiving room.

"You wanted to see me - ?" he offered mechanically.

" Perhaps you have heard Jack Ryder speak of me - of Jinny

Jeffries?" began the girl, determined to put the affair on a sound social footing as soon as possible.

McLean considered and, in honesty, shook his head. "He very seldom mentioned young ladies."

"Oh - !" Jinny tried not to appear dashed. "We are very old friends - in America - and of course I've seen a good deal of him since I've been in Cairo. In fact, he is stopping now at the same hotel with us - with my aunt and uncle and myself."

McLean smiled. "He said it was a tooth," he mentioned dryly.

In Jinny's eyes a little flicker answered him, but her words were ingenuous. "Oh, of course he *has* been having a time with the dentist. That's why he couldn't return to his camp. What I meant was, that at the hotel we have been seeing him every day until - he has just disappeared since day before yesterday and we - that is, I - am very much concerned about it."

"Disappeared? You mean, he - "

"Just disappeared, that's all. He hasn't been at the hotel - he hasn't been anywhere that I know of, and I haven't heard a word from him - so I telephoned you and then when I found he hadn't been here - "

McLean looked off into space. "Eh, well, he'll turn up," he said comfortingly. "Jack's erratic, you may say, in his comings and goings. He means nothing by it.... I've known him do the same to me.... Any time, now; you're likely to hear - "

Miss Jeffries sat up a little straighter and her cheeks burned with brighter warmth.

"It isn't just that I want to see him, Mr. McLean," she took quietly distinct pains to explain. "It's because I am anxious - "

" Not a need, not a need in the world. Jack knows his way

about.... He may have been called back to the diggings, you know - if they dug up a bit porcelain there or a few grains of corn the boy would forget the sun was shining."

Perhaps his caller's burnished hair had shaped that thought. "Jack knows his way about," he repeated encouragingly, as one who demolishes the absurd fears of women and children.

"You don't quite understand." Jinny's tones were silken smooth. "You see, I left him in rather unusual circumstances. It was a place where he had no business in the world to be - "

At McLean's unguardedly startled gaze her humor overtook her wrath.

"Oh, it was quite all right for *me*" she replied mischievously to that look. " Only not for him. You see , he was masquerading - "

"Again?" thought McLean, involuntarily. Lord, what a hand for the lassies that lad was - and he had thought him such an aloof one!

"Masquerading as a woman - so he could take me to a reception."

Jinny began to falter. Just putting that escapade into words portrayed its less commendable features.

"It was a woman's reception," she began again, "at a Turkish house. A marriage reception - "

She had certainly secured McLean's whole-hearted attention.

"A marriage reception - a Turkish marriage reception?" he said very sharply and amazedly as his caller continued to pause. "Do you mean to say that Jack Ryder went into a Turkish house dressed as a woman - ?"

There was a pronounced angularity of feature about the young Scotchman which now took on a chiseled sternness.

Swiftly Jinny interposed. "Oh, you mustn't blame him, Mr. McLean! You see, I wanted very much to go to a Turkish reception and I didn't have the courage to go alone or drag some other tourist as inexperienced as myself, and so Jack - why, there didn't seem any harm in his dressing up. Just for fun, you know. He put on a Turkish mantle and a veil up to his eyes and he was sure he'd never be found out. I ought not to have let him, I know - it was my fault - "

She looked so flushed and innocent and distressed that McLean's chivalry rose swiftly to her need.

"Indeed you mustn't blame yourself Miss - Miss Jeffries. You don't know Egypt - and Jack does. He knew that if he had been discovered there would have been no help for him - and no questions asked afterwards. And it might have been very dangerous for you. The blame is just his now," he said decisively, yet not without a certain weak-kneed sympathy with the culprit.

For if the girl had looked like this ... he could see that she would be a difficult little piece to withstand ... though any man with an ounce of sense in his head would have behaved as a responsible protector and not as a reckless school boy.

"What happened?" he said quickly.

"Oh, nothing happened - nothing that I know of. We got along very well, I thought, although now I remember that some people *did* stare.... But I wasn't worried at the time. I thought it was just because I was an American and he was apparently a Turkish woman, but there was no reason why an American might not get a Turkish woman to act as a guide, was there?... And then Jack told me to go home first - he said it would be simpler that way and that he would slip over to some friend's or to some safe place and take his disguise off. He wore a gray suit beneath it, and the only funny thing was some black tennis shoes.... So I left him. And he hasn't been back since."

She added as McLean was silent, "He told me that he had some engagement for that evening, so I did not begin to worry until the next day."

"Now just how long ago was this?"

"Two days ago. Day before yesterday afternoon."

She looked anxiously at McLean's face and took alarm at his careful absence of expression.

"Oh, Mr. McLean, do you think - "

He brushed that aside. "And where was it - this reception?"

"At an old palace, forever away on the edge of the city. I don't remember the street - we drove and I had the cab wait. But it belonged to a Turkish general. Hamdi Bey," she brought out triumphantly. "General Hamdi Bey."

McLean did not correct her idea of the title. His expression was more carefully non-committal than ever, while behind its quiet guard his thoughts were breaking out like a revolution.

Hamdi Bey.... A wedding reception.... The daughter of Tewfick Pasha....

In the secret depths of his soul he uttered profane and troubled words. That French girl, again.... So Ryder had not forgotten that affair, although he had kept silent about it of late. He had bided his time and taken that rash means of seeing the girl again - and he had involved this unknowing young American in a risk of scandal and deceived her into believing herself responsible for this caprice while all the time she had been a mere cloak and it had been his own diabolical desire....

Miss Jeffries was surprised to see a sudden sorry softness dawn in the young man's look upon her. And she was surprised, too, at his next question.

"I wonder, now, if you were the young lady who took him to a masquerade ball - some time ago?"

Lightly she acknowledged it. "You'll think I'm always taking him to things," she said brightly, but McLean's troubled gaze did not quicken with a smile.

He was experiencing a vast compassion. She was so innocent, so unconscious of the quicksands about her.... Probably she had never heard a breath of that first adventure.

And it was this fair Christian creature whom Jack Ryder had abandoned for a veiled girl from a Turk's harem!

McLean filled with cold, antagonistic wonder. He forgot the lovely image of the French miniature, and remembering Tewfick's rounded eyes and olive features he thought of the veiled girl - most illogically, for he knew that Tewfick was not her father - as some bold-eyed, warm-skinned image of base allure.

Sorrowfully he shook his head over his friend. He determined to protect him and to protect this girl's innocence of his behavior. He would help her to save him.... She could do it yet - if only she did not learn the truth and turn from him. If ever she had been able to make Jack go to a masquerade - that cursed masquerade! - she could work other, more beneficent, miracles.

So now he asked, very cautiously, his mind on divided paths, "Do you say there was nothing to draw suspicion - he did not talk to any one, the guests or the bride - ?"

"Oh, yes, he did talk to the bride," said Miss Jeffries with such utter unconsciousness that McLean's heart hardened against the renegade.

"He talked quite a while to her," she said.

"Did you notice anything - ?"

"Oh, I couldn't hear what was said. He was the last in line and he stayed for some time. He said afterward that it was all right. She was very nice to him," said Jinny earnestly, producing every scrap of incident for McLean's judgment. "She showed him some of her presents - something about her neck."

In mid-speech McLean changed a startled "God!" to "Good!"

"She wasn't suspicious, then?" he said weakly.

"Not as far as I could see. Oh, nothing *seemed* to be wrong. But I did feel uneasy until I got away and then, Jack hasn't come back - "

Again she looked at the young Scotchman for confirmation of her fear and again she saw that careful expressionless calm.

"It's no need for alarm," he told her slowly, "since nothing went wrong. I see no reason why Jack couldn't have walked out of that reception. If we only knew where he was going later - "

"Yes, something might have happened later," Jinny took up. "I thought of that. He might have wanted some more fun and felt more reckless - Oh, I *am* worried," she confessed, her gray eyes very round and childlike.

And if anything had happened she would always blame herself, thought McLean ironically.... The unthinking deviltry of the young scoundrel!... When he found him he'd have a few things to say!

"That's why I came to you," Jinny went on. "I hesitated, for he had warned me so against telling any one, but no one else knows - "

"And no one must know," McLean assured her crisply. "I daresay it's a mare's nest and Jack will be found safe and sound at his diggings or off on a lark with some friend or other, but it's well to make sure and you did quite right in coming to me."

Jinny thought she had done quite right, too.

There was a satisfying strength about McLean. She resented a trifle his masculine way of trying to keep the dark side from her; she was not greatly misled by that untroubled look of his and yet she was unconsciously reassured by it.... And although he refused to be stampeded by alarm he was not incredulous of it, for his manner was frankly grave.

"I'll send out at once," he said decisively, "and see if I can pick up any gossip of that reception. I've a very clever clerk with brothers in the bazaars who is a perfect wireless for information. He has told me the night before a man was to be murdered."

He paused, reflecting that was not a happy suggestion.

"Then I'll send out to Jack's diggings. That express doesn't stop to-night, but I'll find a way. And I'll let you know as soon as I can."

"You're very kind," said Jinny gratefully.

His competent manner brought her a light-hearted sensation of difficulties already solved. Jack was as good as found, she felt in swift reaction. If he was in any trouble this forceful young man would settle it.

But probably he wasn't in any trouble. Probably he was just at his diggings - rushing off from her in the exasperating way he seemed to do whenever they were getting on particularly well.... She remembered how he had bolted from that masquerade which had begun so happily. He had said he was ill, but she had never completely slain the suspicion that his illness sprang from ennui and disinclination.

She rose. " I mustn't take any more of your time, Mr. McLean - and you probably have a four fifteen engagement."

But her light raillery failed of its mark.

"Eh? No, I have not," seriously he assured her. "You are quite the last one I took on - the last before tea."

He paused confused with a strange suggestion.... Tea.... His servant did it rather well.... And it was time -

Usually he had it in the garden. It was a charming garden, full of roses, with a nice view of the Citadel - and his strange suggestion expanded with a rosy vision of Jinny among the roses, beside his wicker table.... Would she possibly care to - ?

He struggled with his idea - and with his shyness. And then the sense that it wasn't quite decent, somehow, to be offering tea to this girl whom anxiety for Ryder's unknown lot had brought to him overcame that unwonted impulse.

He dismissed the idea. And like all shy men he was oddly relieved at the passing of the necessity for initiative, even while he felt his mild hope's expiring pang.

He stepped before her to open the doors to which she was now taking herself.

In the entrance he saw his clerk - the clever one - going out, and excusing himself he went forward to detain the man. For a moment there ensued a low-toned colloquy. Then the clerk, a dark-browned keen-featured fellow in European clothes with a red fez, began to relate something.

When McLean turned back to Jinny Jeffries she saw that his look was sharply altered. There was a transfixed air about him and when he spoke his voice told her that he had had a shock.

"My man tells me," he said, "that Hamdi Bey's bride is dead. He buried her yesterday."

# CHAPTER XXII

## FROM THE BAZAARS

There was a moment's pause.

"What? That lovely girl?" said Jinny in startled pity. She added incredulously, "Yesterday?... And only the day before - why, what *could* have happened?"

That was what McLean was asking himself very grimly.

Aloud he told her slowly. "They say that fire happened. Some accident - a candle overturned in her apartments. And of course the windows were screened - "

"*Fire* - how terrible! That lovely girl," said Jinny again. She was genuinely horrified and pitiful, yet she found a moment to wonder at the evident depths of McLean's consternation. For of course he had never seen the girl.

Yet he looked utterly upset.

"It's one of the most dreadful things I ever heard of," Jinny murmured. "On her wedding night.... And she was so young, Mr. McLean, and so exquisite. She didn't look like a real girl.... She was a fairy creature.... I never dreamed there *really* were rose-leaf skins before but hers was just like flower petals. Jack and I talked about it, I remember. And her face had something so bewitching about it, something so sweet and delicate - "

She broke off revisited with that vision of Aimee's sprite-like beauty.... How little that poor girl had thought, as she stood there in the bright splendor of her robes and diadem, that in a few hours more -

"Oh, I hope that fire - that it was merciful - that she didn't suffer," she said almost inaudibly.

But speech itself was too definitive of horrors.

"It's tragic," she finished simply.

It was tragic, with a complicated tragedy, thought Andrew McLean as he stood there, his eyes narrowing, his lips compressed, his mind invaded with a dark swarm of conjecture, surmise, suspicion, his vision possessed by a flitting rush of pictures.

He saw Jack talking with the girl at the reception.... The girl showing him something about her neck - that accursed locket, he thought acutely.... Jack sending Miss Jeffries home.... Had he arranged that purposely? Was there some mad, improvised scheme of escape in the air?

The pictures became mere flitting wraiths of conjecture, yet touched with horrifying possibility.... Jack lingering, hiding.... Jack making love to the girl, attempting flight.... Jack discovered - and the quick saber thrust - for both.

A fire?... Very likely - to screen the darker tragedy. Hamdi was capable of it to save his pride. And it would dispose so easily of the - evidence.

McLean's thoughts flinched from the grim outcome of his fear. He tried to tell himself that he was inventing horrors, that the fire might be the simple truth, that Ryder's talk with the girl might actually have ended in farewell - at least a temporary farewell - and that his consequent low spirits had taken him off to mope in camp.

That was undoubtedly the thing to believe, at least until there was actual necessity to disbelieve it, and looking at the story in that way, McLean's Scotch sense of Providence was capable of pointing out the stern benefits of the sad visitation.

Whatever mischief might have been afoot between his friend and that unfortunate young girl the fire had prevented. And however hard Jack might take this now, decidedly the poor girl's death was better for him than her life.

No more wasting himself now on sad romance and adventure. No more desire and danger. No more lurking about barred gates and secret doors and forbidden palaces. No more clandestine trysts. No more fury of mind, beating against the bars of fate.

Jack was saved.

Even if he had succeeded in rescuing the girl - what then? McLean was skeptical of felicity from such contrasting lives. Better the finality, the sharp pain, the utter separation. And then -

His eyes returned to the young American before him. She was the unconscious answer to that future. She would save Ryder from regret and retrospection.... In after years, looking back from a happy and well-ordered domesticity, this would all become to him a fantastic, far-off adventure, sad with the remembered but unfelt sadness of youth, yet mercifully dim and softened with young beauty.

Jack must never tell this girl the story. McLean had read somewhere of the mistakes of too-open revelation to women and now he was very sure of it.... She must never receive this hurt, never know that when she had been troubling over Jack's disappearance he had been agonizing over another girl - that the escapade she thought so intimate a lark had been a trick to see the other - that the young creature whose loveliness she so innocently praised had been her rival, drawing Jack from her....

McLean would speak clearly to Ryder about this and seal his lips.... But first he would have to be found.

He became conscious that he had been a long time silent, following these thoughts, while Jinny waited.

"I'll do everything I can to find out about that fire," he told her. "I mean, about any discovery of Jack in the palace," he quickly amended as her face was touched with instant question. "And I'll see if any one in Cairo knows where he is. Then if nothing turns up I'll just pop out to his diggings in the morning and make sure he's all right.... I'll get back that night and telephone you. And until then, not a word about it. Much better not."

"Not a word," Jinny promised. "And if you should happen to find out anything to-night - "

"I'll let you know at once. Well, rather. But don't count on that. The old boy is out in his tombs, dusting off his mummies. You may get a letter, yourself, in the morning," he threw out with heartening inspiration, "And while you are reading it, I'll be tearing along to the infernal desert - "

He had brought the smile to her eyes as well as lips. Bright and reassured and comfortably dependent upon his resourceful strength, she took her leave.

But there was no smile remaining upon Andrew McLean's visage.

Twenty-four hours. Two nights and a day.... And the girl was dead and in her grave - Moslems wasted no time before interment - and Jack was - where?

# CHAPTER XXIII

## IN THE DESERT

Clinging to that plunging horse Ryder made little attempt at first to guide the flight. It was enough to keep himself in the saddle and Aimee in his arms while every galloping moment flung a farther distance between them and that palace of horror.

His heart was beating in a wild, triumphant exultation. Glorious to be out under the free sky, the wind in his face, the open world ahead! He felt one with that dashing creature beneath him.

And Aimee was in his arms, untouched, unhurt, out from the power of that sinister man and the expectation of dread things.

The moment was a supreme and glorious emotion.

They were headed south. And to Ryder's exhilaration this seemed good. Cairo offered no hiding place for that fugitive girl. Even the harbor that McLean could give would not be proof against the legal forces of the Turks. Law and order, power and police were all in the hands of the husband or father. Even now the alarm might be given, the telephones ringing.

Aimee must be hidden until she could be smuggled to France - or until the French authorities could get out their protective documents. The hiding place that occurred to Ryder was a wild and desperate expedient.

The American hospital at Siut. The isolation ward - the pretense of contagious illness. And then later travel north, in the care of nurses -

All this, if he could win over one of the doctors. At that moment winning over a doctor appeared a sane and simple thing to Ryder's mind. The only difficulty he recognized was getting Aimee into that hospital.

But they would not be looking for him in the south. He could manage it, he felt jubilantly. He could smuggle her into his diggings at night and then make his arrangements. Anything, everything was possible, now that the nightmare of a palace was left behind them.

South they went then, at a quieter pace, the Arab's rhythmic footfalls ringing through the still, gray world of before dawn. Across the Nile they made their way, working out on sandbars to the narrow depths, where Ryder swam beside the swimming horse while Aimee clung to the saddle. Then south again along the river road.

The sky was light now. And the river was light. Only the palms and the villages and the flat dhurra fields were dark. And in the east behind the Mokattam hills a thin band of gold began to brighten.

Life was stirring. Small black boys on huge black buffaloes splashed in the river. Veiled girls with water jars on their high-held heads from which the shawls trailed down to the dust filed past from the villages like a Parthenon frieze. On the high banks the naked fellaheen were already stooping to the incessant dipping of the shadouf, while from the fields came the plaintive creaking of the well sweep, as some harnessed camel or bullock began its eternal round.

A flock of sheep came down the river road, driven by their ragged shepherds, and a string of camels, burdened beyond all semblance to themselves, bobbed by like rhythmic haystacks, led by a black-robed, bare-footed child, carrying a live turkey in her arms while before her rode her father, in shining pongee robes on a white donkey strung with beads of blue.

And by these travelers there passed in that brightening dawn two other travelers from the north, a pair on a powerful but tired black horse, a man in a military cloak and a green and gold turban about his bronzed head, and behind him, on a pillion, a black-mantled, black-veiled girl, with bare, dangling feet.

It was Aimee who had evolved the disguise, constructing the turban from the negligee beneath her mantle, and it was Aimee who bargained with the villagers for their breakfast, eggs and goats' milk and bread and rice, while her lord, as befitted his dignity, stayed aloof upon his steed, returning a courteous response of *"Allah salimak* - God bless you" to their greetings.

Then as the day brightened and the last soft veil of mist was burned away before a blood-red sun, that pair of travelers left the highroad and turned west upon a byway that led past fields of corn and yellow water and mud villages where goats and naked babies and ragged women squatted idly in the dust, and on through low, red-granite hills swirled about with yellow sand drift and out into the desert beyond.

Here fresh vigor came to the Arab horse, and tossing his mane and stretching out his nostrils to the dry air he broke into a gallop that sent sand and pebbles flying from his hoofs. To right and left the startled desert hares scattered, and from the clumps of spiky helga the black vultures rose in heavy-winged flight.

Then the breeze dropped, and the swift-coming heat rushed at them like a furnace breath, and slower and slower they made their way, Ryder leading the jaded horse and Aimee nodding in the saddle, mere crawling specks across the immensity of sand.

Then, in the shade of a huge clump of gray-green *mit minan* beside a jutting boulder they stopped at last to rest. The horse sank on his knees; Ryder spread out his cloak and Aimee dropped down upon its folds, lost in exhausted sleep as soon as her head touched the sands. Ryder, his back against the rock, kept watch.

It was not the exultant Ryder of that first hour of flight. The excitement of the night had subsided and withdrawn its wild stimulation. It was a hot and tired and immensely sobered young man who sat there with eyes that burned from lack of sleep and a brow knit into a taut and anxious line.

Realization flooded him with the sun. Responsibility burned in upon him with the heat.

Alone in the Libyan desert he sat there, and at his feet there slept the young girl whose life he had snapped utterly off from its roots.

He was overwhelmingly responsible for her. If she had never met him, if he had never continued to thrust himself upon her, she would have gone on her predestined way, safe, secluded, luxurious - vaguely unhappy and mutinous at times, perhaps, in the secret stirrings of her blood, but still an indulged and wealthy little Moslem.

And now - she lay there, like a sleeping child, the dark tendrils of hair clinging to her moist, sun-flushed cheeks, her long lashes mingling their shadows with the purple underlining of the night's terrors, homeless, exhausted, resourceless but for that anxious-eyed young man.

Desperately he hoped that she would not wake to regret. Even a sardonic tyrant in a palace might be preferable in the merciless daylight to a helpless young man in the Libyan desert.

And she was so slight, so delicate, so made for rich and lovely luxury.... Looking down at her he felt a lump in his throat ... a lump of queer, choking tenderness....

He wanted to protect her, to save her, to spend himself for her.... He felt for her a reverent wonder, a stirring that was at once protective and possessive and denying of all self.

He would die to save her. He tried to tell himself reassuringly that he *had* saved her.... If only he could keep her safe....

He thought of the life before her. He thought of that family in France in whose name he had urged his interference. That unknown Delcasse aunt who had sent out her agents for her lost heirs - would she welcome and endow this lovely girl?

He could not doubt it.... Aimee's youth and beauty would be treasure trove to a jaded lonely woman with money to invest in futures. Aimee would be a belle, an heiress....

He looked down at her with a sudden darkness in his young eyes.... And still she slept, wrapped in the sorry mantle of his masquerade, the torn chiffons of her negligee fluttering over her slim, bare feet.

# CHAPTER XXIV

## THE TOMB OF A KING

There were several approaches to the American excavations. McLean, on that morning after his visit from Jinny Jeffries, chose to borrow a friend's motor and man and break the speed laws of Upper Egypt, and then shift to an agile donkey at the little village from which the gulleys ran west through the red hills into the desert.

It was a still, hot day without cloud or wind and the sun had an air of standing permanently high in the heavens, holding the day at noon. Shimmering heat waves quivered about the base of the farther hills and veiled the desert reaches. It was not conducive to comfort and Andrew McLean was not comfortable. He was hot and sticky and sandy and abominably harassed.

Not a creature, as far as he could discover, had seen Jack Ryder in Cairo since the afternoon of that reception at Hamdi Bey's. He had not been seen at the Museum nor the banks, nor at Cook's, nor the usual restaurants, nor at the clubs with his friends. And the clever clerk - with the two brothers in the bazaar - had unearthed quite a bit of disquieting news about that reception - disquieting, that is, to one with secret fears.

There had been a fire in the apartments of the bride of Hamdi Bey and the bride had been killed instantly - that much was known to all the world. The general had been distracted. He had sat brooding beside his bride's coffin, allowing no one, not even her father, to look upon the poor charred remains that he had placed within. He had been a man out of his mind with grief, gnawing his nails, beating his slaves, - Oh, assuredly, it had been a calamity of a very high order!

One of the brothers in the bazaar had himself talked with an old crone whose sister's child was employed in the general's kitchen, and the fourth-hand story had lost nothing on the route.

The bride's youth and beauty, her jewels, her robes, the general's infatuation, and the general's grief, the reports of these ran through the city like wildfire. And from the particular channel of the kitchen maid and the old aunt and the brother in the bazaars came news of the very especial means that Allah had taken to preserve the general from destruction.

For he had been in the bride's apartments just before the fire. But the power of Allah, the Allseeing, had sent a thief, a prowler, by night, upon the palace roofs, and the screams of a girl in the upper story had called the general to that direction.

And so his preservation had been accomplished.

It was that rumor of the thief upon the roofs which sent the chill of apprehension down McLean's spine. For though the bazaars knew nothing of the thief's identity and it was reported he had escaped by the river yet McLean felt the sinister finger of suspicion. If the thief had not been a thief - unless of brides! - and if he had *not* escaped - ?

Impatiently the young Scotchman clapped his heels against the donkey's sides, enhancing the efforts of the runner with the gesticulating stick.

Suppose, now, that he should not find Jack at the excavations?

It was encouraging, somehow, to hear the monotonous rise and fall of the labor song proceeding as usual, although

McLean immediately told himself that the work would naturally be going on under Thatcher's direction whether Ryder were there or not. The camp knew nothing of Cairo. The camp would be as usual.

And yet, after his first moment's survey, he had an indefinite but uneasy idea that the camp was not as usual.

True, the tatterdemalion frieze of basket bearers still wove its rhythmic way over the mounds to the siftings where Thatcher was presiding as was his wont, but in the native part of the encampment there appeared a sly stir and excitement.

The unoccupied, of all ages and sexes, that usually were squatting interminably about some fire or sleeping like mummies in hermetically wrapped black mantles, now were gathered in little whispering knots whose backward glances betrayed a sense of uneasiness, and as McLean rode past, a young Arab who had been the center of attention drew back with such carefulness to escape observation that McLean's shrewd eyes marked him closely.

It might be that his nerves were deceiving him, but there did seem to be something surreptitious in the air.

Over his shoulder he glimpsed the young Arab hurrying out of the camp.

It might be anything or nothing, he told himself. The man might be going shopping to the village and the others giving him their commissions, or he might be an illicit dealer in curios trying to pick up some dishonest treasure. In native diggings those hangers on were thick as flies.

He dismounted and hurried forward to meet Thatcher's advance. The men had rarely met and Thatcher's air of hesitation and absent-mindedness made McLean proffer his name promptly with a sense of speeding through the preliminaries. Then with a manner he strove to make casual he put his question.

"I say, is Ryder back?"

He knew, in the moment's pause, how tight suspense was gripping him. Then Thatcher glanced toward the black yawning mouth of a tomb entrance.

"Why, yes - he's down there." He added. "Been a bit sick. Complains of the sun."

For a moment his relief was so great that McLean did not believe in it. Jack here - Jack absolutely safe -

Mechanically he put, "When did he come in?"

"When?" Thatcher hesitated, trying to recall. "Oh, night before last - rode in after dark." He added reassuringly, as the other swung about towards the tomb, "He says there's nothing really wrong with him. There's no temperature."

McLean nodded. His relief now was acutely compounded with disgust. He felt no lightning leap of thanksgiving that his friend was safe, but rather that flash of irritated reaction which makes the primitive parent smack a recovered child.

Not a thing in the world the matter! A mare's nest - just as he had prophesied to Miss Jeffries. Why in heaven's name hadn't Jack the decency to send that over-anxious young lady a card when he abandoned town so suddenly?... Not that McLean blamed Miss Jeffries. Given the masquerade and Jack's disappearance and a zealous feminine interest her concern was perfectly natural.

But McLean had left a busy office and taken an anxious and uncomfortable excursion, and his voice had no genial ring as he shouted his friend's name down the dark entrance of the tomb shaft.

In a moment he heard a voice shouting hollowly back, then a wavering spot of light appeared upon the inclined floor and Ryder's figure emerged like an apparition from the gloom.

"I say! That you, Andy?"

Evidently he had been snatched from sleep. His dark hair was rumpled, his face flushed, and he yawned with complete frankness.

McLean knew a sudden yearning to put an arm about him.... Dear old Jack.... Dear, irresponsible scamp.... His reaction of the irritation vanished.... It was so darned good to see the old chap again....

He muttered something about being in the vicinity while Ryder, rousing to hostship, called directions to the cook boy to bring a tray of luncheon.

"It's cool down here," he told McLean, leading the way back.

It was cool indeed, in the Hall of Offerings. It was also, McLean thought, satisfying a recovered appetite, a trifle depressing.

They sat in a small island of light in an ocean of gloom while about them shadowy columns towered to indistinguishable heights and half-seen carvings projected their strange suggestions.

It seemed incongruous to be smoking cigarettes so unconcernedly at the feet of the ancient gods.

But McLean's feeling of depression might have been due to his renewed awareness of catastrophe. For though Jack was here, safe and sound enough, although a bit unlike himself in manner, yet Jack *had* been at that confounded reception in a woman's rig and Jack had seen the girl and talked with her - apparently on terms of understanding.

And if Jack had left Cairo that night, as he said he did - claiming delay on the way due to a tired horse - then Jack knew nothing in the world of the palace fire, and the girl's sudden and tragic death.

And McLean would have to tell him. He would have to tell him that the girl he was probably dreaming of in some fool's paradise of memory and hope was now only a little mound of dust in an Oriental cemetery. That a shaft of temporary wood already marked the grave of Aimee Marie Dejane, daughter of Tewfick Pasha and wife of Hamdi Bey....

And however much McLean's sound senses might disapprove of the whole fantastic affair and his sober judgment commend the workings of Providence, he loved his friend, and he feared that his friend loved this lost girl.

He had to end love and hope and romance and implant a desperate grief....

He thought very steadily of Jinny Jeffries. He cleared his throat.

"Jack, old man - "

He started to tell him that there had been a fire in Cairo, a most shocking fire in a haremlik. It seemed to him that Jack was not listening, that he had a faraway, yet intent look upon his face, as of one attending to other things. And then suddenly Jack seemed to gather resolution and turned to his friend with an air of narration of his own.

"Look here, McLean, there's something I want to tell you - "

"Wait a minute now," said McLean quietly. "I want you to hear this.... It was a fire in the palace of your friend, Hamdi Bey."

He had Jack's attention now - he was fairly conscious of

arrested breath. Not looking about him he went grimly on, "The night of the wedding a fire started in the haremlik.... It was a bad business, a very bad business, Jack. For the girl - the girl Hamdi had just married - "

He was conscious of Jack's look upon him but he did not turn to meet it.

"She died," he said heavily. "He buried her yesterday."

He thought that Jack was never going to speak.

Then, "Died?" said Ryder in an odd voice.

"I expect she breathed in a bit of smoke," said McLean, trying for a merciful suggestion.

"And he buried her - ?"

Jack was like a child, trying to fit bewildering facts together. McLean's sympathy hurt him like a physical pain. He wondered what it could be like to realize that some loved one you had just talked with, in radiant life, was now gone utterly....

And then he heard Jack laugh. Mad, he thought quickly, turning now to look at him.

Ryder's head was tilted back; Ryder's shoulders were shaking. "Oh, my Aunt!" he gasped hysterically. "My Aunt Clarissa - is *that* what Hamdi says!"

He sobered instantly and leaned towards McLean. "That looks as if he's done with her - what? Saving his face that way? You're sure it was Aimee - the girl he had just married? Not some other girl - some co-wife or something?"

And as McLean bewilderedly muttered that he was sure, Ryder began to laugh again. To laugh jubilantly, joyously, triumphantly.

"He's given her up - he's got a saving explanation to thrust in the world's face! Oh, blessed Allah, Veiler of all that should be veiled! The man's through. He's had enough. He isn't going to try to - "

Across the bright oblong of the entrance a shadow appeared.

"Ryder - I say, Ryder," said a hurried voice - Thatcher's voice - and Thatcher came hastily forward in perturbed urgency.

"There's a lot of men outside - police and natives and what not. With warrants. They're searching the place. And they want to see you.... Hang it all, Ryder," said Thatcher explosively but apologetically, "they say you've made off with some sheik's daughter."

He paused, shocked at the monstrosity of the accusation. He was a delicate-minded man - outside of his knowledge of antiquities - and he evidently expected his young associate to fall upon him and slay him for the slander.

"A sheik's daughter - ?" said Ryder in a mildly wondering voice. From his emphasis one might have inferred he was saying, "How odd! I don't remember any sheik's daughter - "

A queer uncomfortable flush spread fanways from Thatcher's thin temples and rayed across his high cheekbones. He did not look at either of the men as he murmured, "It's most peculiar, but that Arab horse - the sheik claims the horse is his, too. He says you rode off on it, with his daughter."

"That's all right," said Ryder absently. "I don't want the horse.... But you say the sheik's there? What does he look like? Thin - with blond mustaches?"

"Oh, no, no, not at all. He is quite heavy and bearded - one-eyed, if I recollect. But there *is* a man with a blond mustache who appears to do the directing - "

"And you mean they are searching?" said Ryder abruptly. "You've let them in - ?"

"They have warrants," Thatcher protested. "And there are proper policemen conducting the search - "

"My good God! Where are they now? Not coming *here*? I don't have any policemen trampling here and meddling with my finds - tell them to clear out, Thatcher, you know there's no sheik's daughter here!"

Ryder gave a quick laugh but the impression of his laughter was not as sharp as the impression of his alarm.

"I did tell them it was preposterous," Thatcher began, "but, you see, after finding the horse - "

"Oh, the horse! I got him for a song - of course the beggar is stolen. Give him back, if they claim him. But as for any sheik's daughter - keep the crowd out, Thatcher, I won't have them here, not in these tombs - "

"I tell you they are policemen - they are armed - you can't resist - "

"How many are they? A lot? But they'll take your word, won't they? Look here, McLean, can't you settle this for me and keep them out?"

"The natives have been talking," murmured Thatcher, reddening still deeper, "and they have said enough about your riding in at night and - and keeping to this tomb all day to make the men very suspicious. They are watching this one now - "

"Then keep them back - long as you can. For God's sake," entreated Ryder with that strange passionate violence.

MARY HASTINGS BRADLEY

"Andy - you do something - hold them back. Give me time. I - I've got to get some things together - I won't have them at my things - hold them back - out here - till I come."

He was gone. Gone tearing back into the gloom and silence of his tomb. And McLean and Thatcher, astounded witnesses of his outburst, turned speedily to the entrance, avoiding each other's eyes.

Agitatedly Thatcher was murmuring that Ryder's finds were valuable, immensely valuable, and it was disturbing to contemplate any invasion, and with equal agitation but more mechanical calm McLean was murmuring back that he understood - he quite understood -

As for understanding he was stunned and dazed. A sheik's daughter! And the father himself claiming her - under the direction of a blond-mustached man.... And a stolen horse.... Jack conceding the horse.... Jack utterly upset at the search party....

But he himself had seen that new-placed shaft with its inscription to Aimee Marie Dejane.... What then in the name of wonders did this mean? There couldn't be *another* girl? McLean's imagination faltered then dashed on at a gallop. Some - some hand-maiden, perhaps, whom Jack had rescued in mistaken chivalry? Perhaps the French girl has sent a maid on ahead?

McLean's head was whirling now. One thing appeared quite as possible as another. Pasha's daughters and sheik's daughters, stolen horses and Djinns and Afrits and palaces and masque-rades at wedding receptions appeared upon the same plane of feasibility.

Outwardly he was extremely calm. Calm and cold and crisp.

At the mouth of the tomb he detained the party of native policemen with their hangers-on of curious natives and examined, with great show of circumspection and authority, the perfectly regular search warrants which had been issued for them at the instigation of an apparently bereft parent.

He conversed with the alleged parent, a stolid, taciturn native dignitary whose accusations were confirmed by eagerly assenting followers. He lived in a small village, not far north of the camp. He had a young daughter, very beautiful. Three nights ago he had surprised her with this young American and they had fled upon his noblest horse.

It was a simple and direct story. And Jack - by his own report - had been out upon the desert that night, had appeared, upon the next night, with this unknown and beautiful horse, and had since kept to the tomb, claiming illness, in a most persistent way.

The camp boys had testified that he had been vividly critical of the food sent in to him, and that he had required extraordinary amounts of heated water.

"All of which," McLean said sternly, in the vernacular, "amounts to nothing - unless you can discover the girl."

"And that, monsieur," said a Turk in the uniform of the Sultan's guards, appearing beside the desert sheik, "that is exactly what we are here to do."

McLean found himself looking into a thin, menacing face, capped with a red fez, a face deeply lined, marked by light, arrogant eyes and embellished with a huge, blond mustache.

"And your interest in this, monsieur?" he questioned.

"I am a friend of Sheik Hassan's," said the Turk loftily. "I shall see that my friend obtains his rights."

And in McLean's other ear a distraught Thatcher was murmuring "That officer chap is Hamdi Bey - a General of the

Guards. You know, Mr. McLean, this really is - you know, it is - "

Hamdi Bey ... Hamdi Bey, two days after his distressing loss, befriending this sheik and trying to involve Jack Ryder in disgrace.

Mystifying. Mystifying and disquieting - yes, disquieting, in the face of Jack's alarm. But for that alarm McLean could have believed the whole thing a farcical attempt of Hamdi's to revenge himself upon Ryder - supposing that Hamdi had discovered Ryder in his masquerade or else as the prowler by night - but Jack's furious anxiety to keep the party out, and his dashing back, ostensibly to preserve his things -

Was it actually possible that he *had* that sheik's daughter concealed in some nook or cranny of the place?

McLean told himself that it was preposterous. It *was* preposterous - but Ryder had been doing preposterous things.... And glancing at Thatcher he perceived that that perturbed and transparent gentleman was also telling himself that *his* suspicions were preposterous.

The search party, tiring of parley, was moving about the hall in businesslike inspection.

And then Ryder reappeared, a distinctly alert but self-contained Ryder, who met the interrogations of the police with scoffing and absolute denial.

But McLean was conscious that there was something tense and nervous in his alertness, something wary and defensive in his readiness, and his own nerves began to tighten apprehensively.

It did not add to his composure to see Ryder salute Hamdi Bey with an ironic and overdone politeness.

" Ah , monsieur le general ! We meet as we parted - in

the depths!"

The general appeared to smile as at some amiable pleasantry, but McLean caught the snarl of his lifted lip, and felt the currents of animosity.

So those two had met! Ryder had been discovered then.... McLean tried, in futile bewilderment, to recall just what amazing thing Ryder had been saying when this party had appeared.

He kept very close at that young man's side as the strange party moved on into the inner chamber. The searchers were scrupulously careful of the excavator's finds; they did not finger a frieze nor disturb a single small box of the tenderly packed potteries and beads and miniature boats, but they scraped every heap of dust to see if it concealed an entrance, they exhausted the resources of each corner, they circled every pillar, shook out every rug of Jack's blankets and required the opening of the large chest in which the wax reproductions of the friezes were placed, awaiting transportation.

"You will perceive, messieurs," declared Ryder in mocking irony, "that no human being is within this last fold of wax - especially a being," he added thoughtfully with a glance at the stolid sheik, "of the proportions of her papa.... This daughter, was she a large young lady?" he inquired politely of the Arab.

The sheik vouchsafed no reply, but from across his ample person the general leaned forward.

"She was small, Monsieur Ryder," he said in silken tones, "but she can raise a man as high as the gallows - or as low as the grave."

"A marvel!" returned young Ryder smoothly. "And was she also of charm - a charm that could kindle fires - ?"

It appeared to McLean that he caught the flaunting

implications of the taunt.

He wished to heaven that Ryder would hold his reckless tongue.

Ryder was turning now to the official in charge of the police.

"If you have satisfied yourselves that this place is empty - "

The man, a rather apologetic, pleasant fellow, shrugged and smiled. "We have examined all - "

There was a moment in which the searchers regarded one another through the gloom in the inquiring embarrassment of the discountenanced and considered departure. But Hamdi Bey had more insistent eyes.

He was circling the place again like a wolf for the scent, flashing his search light over the carved walls, the dancing gleam picking out now a relief of Osiris, now a fishing boat upon the Nile, now the judgment hall of Maat. Suddenly he stopped and began examining a limestone slab.

"These stones - these have been merely piled here," he cried excitedly. "This is a hole - an entrance. Dig them out, men. There is a door there, I tell you."

Hastily Ryder addressed the police. "It is simply the burial vault," he told them. "The sarcophagi are there, ready for transportation. Mr. Thatcher will tell you - "

"I assure you it is merely the actual tomb," said Thatcher nervously. "I have myself assisted my colleague with the preparation."

The slabs had been displaced now, disclosing the small door, with its fine wrought stele. Hamdi flashed a look of triumph upon the man who had obviously tried to conceal that door from them, a look which Ryder ignored as he turned to McLean.

"That is the door which is sealed forever upon the dead, and upon the Ka, the spiritual double," he said in a low conversational tone. "It has some remarkable representations of the jackal Anubis - "

It seemed to McLean a most extraordinary time for a disquisition upon Anubis. If Ryder was attempting to prove himself at his ease he had certainly misjudged his manner.

"Damn Anubis," McLean gave back under his breath. "He's not the only jackal - What the devil's the meaning of this?"

Ryder made no reply. The stone had been pushed back and the searchers were stooping beneath the narrow entrance. Then as McLean's head bent at the door he heard his friend whispering, "I say - you haven't a gun you could slip me - ?"

Mutely he shook his head. And that agitated whisper died away with the last vestige of belief in Ryder's innocence. Apprehensively McLean glanced about that inner chamber he was entering, dreading to encounter instant and damning evidence of a girl.

He found himself in the presence of the dead. The chamber was a small, square, walled-up affair, and at one side stood the three sarcophagi. The other halls had been in total darkness, but the blackness of this place appeared something palpable and weighty. And the air had the dry, acrid tang of dust which has lain waiting for centuries.

It was hot, whereas the other chambers had been cool - or else McLean's disturbed blood was pumping too furiously through his pulses. Instinctively he drew close to Jack, as the party stood flashing their lights over the bare walls and empty corners, and then concentrated the pale illumination upon those caskets of the dead.

"I told you that the place was empty," Ryder said with distinct impatience in his voice. "And now, if you have satisfied yourselves - "

"You are in haste, monsieur," said Hamdi Bey's smooth voice. "If you will permit us to see what is within - "

He approached the first sarcophagus.

The sheik, who appeared to have committed the restoration of his daughter into the other's hands, remained imperturbably beside the entrance while the head of the police came forward to assist Hamdi in raising the painted lid.

"I protest," said Ryder very sharply. He stood upon the other side of the case, eying them combatively. "It is useless to disturb this lid - I tell you that the Persians have been considerably before you."

And indeed the case was empty. Hamdi moved to the next and again Ryder took up his post opposite.

"Again I protest," he insisted. "The least jar or injury - "

But the men raised the lid, and after the briefest look, moved on.

"And now," Ryder spoke very clearly and authoritatively, addressing the head of the police, "I must ask you to stop. Even the dust that you are disturbing is precious. This thing has gone beyond all reason."

The police official looked as if he agreed with him, but Hamdi Bey had moved determinedly to the third sarcophagus. The official hesitated, evidenced discomfort, but moved finally after the bey.

"If there is nothing here," he murmured, "surely you cannot object - "

"There is precious dust here," Ryder repeated. "You must understand - "

"We see for ourselves," said Hamdi Bey, and now his voice had a ring of triumphant steel through its soft smoothness. "Stand aside. This is in the name of the law."

It seemed to McLean that for one mad moment Ryder was tempted to resist. In the flickering light of the torches he stood defiantly above the painted mummy case, his eyes steadily upon the bey, his hands pressing down upon the vivid bloom of the dead woman's pictured face.

Then with a beaten but ironic smile he stood aside.

Slowly the men lifted the lid.... In that moment McLean became aware that his heart was pumping thickly somewhere in his throat and that the rest of him was a hollow, horrible void of suspense.

Hamdi Bey turned his arrogant stare from young Ryder and looked down.... Drawing closer, fearfully McLean's eyes followed him.

He could not believe their evidence. His heart could not stop its idiotic pumping.

But there he saw no terror-stricken girl, no pallid runaway of the harems, but a still, dark-shrouded form, swathed in the tight bandages of the ancient embalmer, a dry, dusty little mummy creature blankly and inscrutably confronting this unforeseen resurrection.

Over their dumbfounded heads he heard young Ryder's mocking laugh.

MARY HASTINGS BRADLEY

# CHAPTER XXV

## IN CAIRO

"It's good news!" said Miss Jeffries with bright positives.

It was her response to Andrew McLean's greeting that evening. He had made rather a tardy appearance at the hotel, for there had been an important dinner with an important bank official passing through Cairo to escape from, but he arrived at last, looking extraordinarily well in his very best dinner clothes.

And Miss Jeffries, for all her harassment of suspense, was no woeful object in a vivacious blue evening frock with silvery gleams.

"He's safe - absolutely safe," McLean confirmed.

He expected radiance. Miss Jeffries' expression was arrested judgment.

"Safe - *where?*"

"At his camp ... I just returned - just in time to dine. I motored out this morning."

"Oh!... It took your whole day. I am so sorry!" For a moment the girl appeared to concentrate her sympathetic interest upon McLean.

"You must simply hate me," she told him repentantly, dropping into one of the chairs in the drawing-room corner she had long been guarding. "Do sit down and tell me all the horrid details.... - Uncle and Aunt are in the Lounge, and I should like you to meet them, but they'll be there forever and I do want to hear first.... Was it fearfully hot?"

"Oh, rather," murmured the young man, confused by this change of interest. "I mean, that's quite the usual thing, isn't it, for deserts? I got up a good breeze going, for I was a bit wrought up, you know - not a soul in Cairo had seen Jack since that day."

"And he was out at his camp," said Jinny thoughtfully. "How - how long had he been there?"

"He says he started that night," said McLean non-committally.

"Oh!... That night.... That was rather sudden, wasn't it?"

"Jack's sudden, you know," mentioned his friend uncom-fortably. "And he had a lot of finds to pack up for transport - they are taking their stuff to the museum and Jack had been away so long, here in the city - "

"No wonder I didn't hear then!" said the girl with a laugh in which it would have taken an acuter ear than McLean's to detect the secret clamor of chagrin and humiliation.

Of course she had *wanted* Jack to be safe.... But he might have been ill - or away on some official summons -

Just back at his diggings. Gone off on an impulse, with no thought to let her know....

And she had rushed to McLean with her silly worries and her anxious concern which he had probably taken for a tender interest....

Heaven knows what disillusionizing thing Jack had said to him that day!... Men were too hateful.

And now McLean had come dutifully to report that the man she was so worried about was quite well and busy, thank you, only he had overlooked any friendship for her, and so had sent no word -

In Jinny's ears was the rush of the furies' wings. But on Jinny's lips was a proud little smile, and her bright look was a shining shield for the wounds of the spirit.

"That *is* a comfort," she said with pleasant, friendly warmth. "You don't know how horridly responsible I felt! Really, Jack ought to have let me know - but that's Jack all over. He's never grown up."

"He's not had much time," returned McLean from the height of his twenty-nine years.

"He never will," said Jinny sagely, "not until - well, not until he meets some girl, you know, who will make him feel really responsible."

It occurred unhappily to McLean that the girl Jack had been meeting so assiduously of late had certainly not added to his claims to responsibility!

Steadily he guarded silence. There are ice fields, on Mont Blanc, where a whisper precipitates an avalanche, and McLean had no intention of starting anything in his friend's slippery field of affairs.

"I have spent more time," Miss Jeffries was confiding brightly, for those imperative reasons of her own so obscure to the bewildered young man, "introducing Jack to nice girls - but it never takes! Not seriously. He's a perfectly dear friend, but he doesn't care anything really about girls - and he does need somebody to get him out of his antiquities and his dusty old diggings ... But of course you think I am a sentimental thing!"

McLean did not tell her what he thought. He was still

fascinatedly engrossed with her revelation of the impeccable Platonic basis of her friendship. His mood of complicated emotion lightened and brightened and at the same time an amazed wonder unfolded its astonishment.

He marveled at his friend. To turn to something fantastic, something bizarre - for so he thought of that veiled girl of the harem - when he had this Miss Jeffries for a friend - but probably the young lady herself had never given him the least encouragement. Women are not easily moved to romance for men they have always regarded as brothers and he could see that her feeling for Jack was the warm, honest, sisterly affection of utter frankness.

The worse for Jack. For now there seemed no ministering angel to mend his troubled future.

It was not only Ryder's troubled future that troubled McLean - it was also Ryder's troubled present. He was very far from easy in his mind about him. After that mystifying performance in the tomb he had not wanted to leave without a frank explanation, but there had been no moment for revelation; Thatcher had hung about them and Hamdi Bey, of all men, had requested a place in McLean's motor for the return to Cairo.

And that dinner engagement had pressed. He could have abandoned it for any real reason, but Jack had assured him that there was none.

"Get the old devil out of here," had been Jack's furious appeal, referring to Hamdi. "Deny everything to him. Only get him out."

And McLean had got him out.

The sheik and his followers after a murmurous conference with the bey had galloped off; the police had turned towards their post and Hamdi had accompanied McLean to the nearest village and his waiting motor.

Clearly he had wanted to talk to McLean and McLean was not sorry for the opportunity to exchange implications. The bey had unfolded his sympathetic friendship for the sheik; McLean had unfolded a cold surprise that anything so disgraceful should be attributed to such a prominent archaeologist. The bey had produced the evidence and McLean had produced a skeptical wonder, and then a thoughtful wonder if the British government had not better take the matter up and sift it, for the benefit of all concerned.

Clearly the thing could not go on. Ryder could not accept such a rumor against his reputation. Yes, he thought he would advise Ryder to take the matter up.

And there he perceived that even the suave and politic Hamdi squirmed. Doubtless to the Turk, McLean represented British prestige and political power and all sorts of unknown influence.... And native testimony, while voluable and unscrupulous, had a way of offering confused discrepancies to the coldly questioning investigators of the law.

And with no real evidence against Ryder -

The matter of the sheik's daughter, McLean perceived, would be dropped. Unless the girl - whatever girl they sought - could be discovered.

If Hamdi wished to pay off some score against the American he would choose other weapons. McLean reflected upon the bey's capacity for assassination or poisoning while he bade him farewell before the dark wall of his palace entrance.

Between them had passed no reference to the bey's recent loss. Since it would not have been etiquette for him to mention the bey's wife, he judged it equally inadvisable to refer to her ashes.

The whole affair was so wrapped in darkness that he could not decide upon any creditable explanation. It would have to wait until he saw Ryder in the next day or two - for Ryder had told him he would try to get in with his finds as soon as possible.

But no matter how he tried to dismiss the matter from his mind he had found himself asking, through the courses of that important dinner and now in the pauses of his conversation with Miss Jeffries - Was there really some girl? Had he only dreamed that tense anxiety of Jack's - had Jack led them on for his own young amusement?

But it was not long possible to maintain an inner communion with Jinny Jeffries for a vis-a-vis.

A divided mind could not companion her swift flights and sudden tangents. Deriding now her silly anxieties and deploring McLean's unnecessary trip, she had branched into the consideration of how busy McLean must be - and McLean found himself somehow embarked in sketchy descriptions of the institution of which Miss Jeffries seemed to think he was the backbone and of its very interesting work throughout the country.

And as he had talked he found himself noticing things that he had never noticed before about girls, the wave of bright hair against a flushed cheek, the dimples in a rounded arm, the slim grace of crossed ankles and silver-slippered feet.

"And you live all alone in that big house?" Jinny was murmuring.

"Not exactly alone." McLean smiled. "There's Mohammed and Hassan and Abdullah and Alewa and Saord-el-Tawahi - "

"What *do* you call him when you are in a hurry?" laughed the girl.

It was a tremendously pleasant evening. He had expected constraint and secret embarrassment and he had discovered this delightful interest and bright vivacity.

And if beneath that interest and vivacity something lay forever stilled and chilled in Miss Jeffries' breast - like a poor hidden corpse beneath bright roses - why at two and twenty expectancies flourish so gayly that one lone bud is not long missed. And chagrin is sometimes a salutary transient shower, and self-confidence is all the more delicate for a dimming cloud.

Moreover McLean's unconscious absorption was balm and blessing.

When in startled realization of time and place he rose at last and she murmured laughing, "And after all you never met Aunt and Uncle!" he felt a queer blush tingle his cheek bones and a daring impulse shape the thought aloud that in that case he must come again.

"We're here five days more," said Jinny, the explicit.

Thoughtfully he repeated, "Five days," and said farewell.

"Now if he decorously waits to the next to the last day - !" murmured Jinny to herself, her opinion of the Scots race hanging in the balance.

He didn't. But it was not the initiative of the Scots race which brought him to her, late that very next afternoon, but a soiled looking note which he held crumpled in his hand.

He found her at tea upon the veranda with her aunt and uncle and while he made conversation with the Pendletons he gave Miss Jeffries the note.

"From our friend Ryder," he said with forced lightness. "It explains itself."

But it certainly did not. It was a hasty scrawl to McLean, saying that Ryder was on his way with the museum finds and sending this ahead by runner, and that McLean must positively be at the Cairo Museum to meet him at five and would he please stop on the way and call at his hotel upon a Miss Jeffries and borrow a woman's cloak and hat and veil, or if she wasn't in, get them elsewhere.

"What is it - another masquerade?" said Jinny blankly.

McLean looked mutely at her and shook his head, but within him horrific suspicion was raging like a forest fire.

He continued his converse with the Pendletons while Jinny went for the things; she returned with a small bag containing coat and hat and veil, and the announcement that she would go right over with him.

"If the things aren't right I'll know what he wants," she declared, and then, smiling, "What *do* you suppose he is up to now?"

McLean felt that he didn't want to know. And most positively he didn't want her to know. But having lacked the instant inspiration to deny her, he could only acquiesce and wonder why he hadn't thought up some brilliant excuse.

He looked helplessly at the Pendletons, but they merely murmured their adieux and their independent niece accompanied McLean to his waiting carriage as if it were the most natural thing in the world.

\*　\*　\*　\*　\*

The caravan was before them. A long line of camels was just turning in the gates and before the steps of a back entrance other camels, kneeling with that profound and squealing resentment with which even the camel's most exhausted moments oppose commands, were being relieved of their huge loads by natives under the very minute and exact direction of Thatcher.

And within the entrance a young man with rumpled dark hair and a thin, bronzed face flushed with impatience was imperiously conveying the Arabs who were bearing the precious sarcophagi.

Over his shoulder he caught sight of the two arrivals.

"I asked for motors - and they furnished these!" he cried disgustedly, gesturing at the enduring camels. "It took us all day though we half killed the brutes.... Hello, Jinny, did you bring the things?"

With light casualness he accepted her appearance on the scene. That glitter in his bright hazel eyes was not for that. "Come in, both of you," he called, plunging after his men.

At the foot of the stairs McLean waited with Miss Jeffries until the men had reached the top and deposited their burdens in the room and in the manner which Ryder was specifying so crisply, and then they came mechanically up.

McLean had the automatic feeling of a mere super in a well rehearsed scene. He had no idea of plot or appearance but his role of dumb subservience was clearly defined.

"You understand," Ryder was calling to the men, "nothing more goes in this room. All else down stairs.... Come in," he said hurriedly to his waiting friends, and shutting the door swiftly behind them, "of course - this doesn't lock!" he muttered. "Jinny, you stand here, do, and if any one tries to come in tell them they can't."

"Tell them you say they can't?" questioned Jinny a little helplessly.

"No - no - not that. Tell them you are using the room; tell them," said Ryder with very brisk and serious inspiration, "tell them your petticoat is coming off!"

"Why Jack Ryder!" said Jinny indignantly.

"Nonsense," said he to her indignation. "Don't you remember when your aunt's petticoat came off on the way to church? It happens."

"But it doesn't run in families!"

Her protest fell apparently upon the back of his head. He had turned to the last sarcophagus and was slipping his fingers beneath the lid. "Here, Andy," he said quickly. "I had it wedged so it wasn't tight shut, but it's been so infernally hot and dusty - "

He was tremendously troubled. It was not the heat which had brought those fine beads of moisture to his brow, white above the line of brown, and drawn such a pale ring about his mouth. McLean saw that the slim, wiry wrists which supported the case's top were shaking.

"Gently now," he murmured and the lid was lifted and laid aside.

The same dark, unstirring form of the tomb scene. The same dry, dusty little mummy.... But with hands strangely reckless for an archaeologist dealing with the priceless stuff of time Ryder tore at those bandages; he unwrapped, he unwound, and in a lightning's flash -

To McLean's tense, expectant nerves it was like a scene at the pantomime. He had divined it; he had foreseen and yet there was the shock and eerie thrill of magic, the appealing unreality of the supernatural in the revelation.

In a wave of an enchanter's wand the mummy was gone. And in its place lay a Sleeping Beauty, the dark hair in sculptured closeness to the head, the long, black lashes sweeping the still cheeks.

# CHAPTER XXVI

## THE PAINTED CASE

"She's fainted," said Ryder in a voice that shook. From his pocket he drew swiftly a thermos bottle but before the top was off those long lashes fluttered, and from under their shadow the soft, dark eyes looked up at him with a smile of very gallant reassurance.

"Not - faint," said the girl, in a breath of a voice. "But it was so long - so hot - "

"Drink this." Ryder slipped an arm about her, offering the filled top of the thermos. "It's over, all over," he murmured as she drank. "You're safe now, safe.... You're at the museum.... Then we'll get you to the hotel - "

"Hotel - ?" the girl echoed with a faint implication of humor in that silver bell of a voice.

She put her hands to her hair and to her face in which the hues of life mingled with the pallor of exhaustion; on her small fingers sparkled the gleam of diamonds and from her slender arms fell back the gold and jade tissues of her chiffon robe.

To McLean she had increasingly the appearance of a creature of enchantments. And to see that young loveliness in its strange gleam of color lying against his friend's supporting tan linen arm -

Sardonically his eyes sought Ryder.

"So that was your mummy!"

"There was nothing else to do." Ryder had withdrawn his arm; the two men faced each other across the girl. "I was in a blue funk - you see, I was hiding her in the inner chamber until I could smuggle her away. And when those wolves came on the scent, and not an instant to lose - I got the bandages off the real mummy and about Aimee.... Lord, it was a close call!"

He drew a long breath. "I hadn't a gun. I hadn't a thing - and I had to grin and play it through ... And I was deathly afraid of Thatcher."

"Thatcher?"

"Yes, Thatcher. You see I'd popped the mummy into a case without its bandages and if Thatcher had glimpsed that he'd have said something - Oh, innocently - that would have given the show away. He knew there was only one mummy and it was wrapped. But the Lord was with me. The men opened the empty case first and at the second they said nothing to show it wasn't empty and Thatcher didn't look in. Then they went on to the third."

"And me - when I heard those voices - I stopped breathing," said the girl. "But I shook so - I thought they would think that mummy was coming to life! And the dust - Oh, it was almost beyond my force not to sneeze - "

"You'd have sneezed us to Kingdom Come," said Ryder, gayly now.

"But I did not," she protested. "I lay there and thought of Hamdi looking down upon me, and my flesh crept.... Oh, it was terrible! And yet it was funny."

Funny.... McLean gazed in sardonic astonishment upon the two young creatures with such misguided humor that they found something funny in this appalling business. Flying from palaces ... hiding in tombs ... taking a mummy's place beneath the dusty bandages of the dead ... Funny....

And yet there was laughter in their young eyes when they looked at each other and a curve of astounding amusement in their lips.

It touched McLean to wonder. It touched him - queerly - to an odd and aching pain. For he saw suddenly that he was looking upon something deathless and imperishable, yet fragile and fleeting as the breath of time....

They were so young, so absorbed, so oblivious....

He had forgotten Jinny Jeffries. So too, - not for the first time, alas! - had Ryder. Now her clear voice from the doorway made them start.

"You might present me, Jack."

Ryder turned, so did the girl in the painted case, and her eyes widened with a startled surprise. The doorway had not been within her vision.

Jinny was leaning back against the door, her hand behind her on the knob she was to guard, her figure still rigid with astonishment.

"I didn't know you - you dug them up - alive," she said with a quiver of uncertain humor.

"My dear Jinny, I had for - Miss Jeffries, let me present you to Mademoiselle Delcasse," said Jack gravely. "I know that you met her the day of her reception - "

Only in that moment did Jinny place the haunting recollection.

"But she was burned - she was killed," she protested, shaken now with excitement.

"She was not burned - although there was a fire. The man who called himself her husband pretended she was killed in order to save his pride. For she escaped from him. And he tried to get her back, setting another man, a false father, after her with lying witnesses - Oh, it's a long story! - so I had to hide her in this case."

"But Jack, you - why were *you* hiding her - ? Did you get her out?" stammered Jinny.

"The night of that reception. You see, I knew she was truly a French girl who had been stolen by Tewfick Pasha and brought up as his daughter - Oh, that's a long story, too! But at McLean's I had happened on the agents who were searching for her from her aunt in France, and so I knew.... And at the reception when I found she hated that marriage I stayed behind and - and managed to get her away," - thus lightly did Ryder indicate the dangers of that night! - "so she could escape to France."

"Oh - France!" said Jinny.

She could be forgiven for the tone. She had been kept shamefully in the dark, misled, ignored.... She had been a catspaw, a bystander.

Not that she cared. Not that she would let them think for a minute that she cared....

But as for this talk of France -

Her eyes met the eyes of the girl in the mummy case. And Jinny found herself looking, not at the interloper, the enchantress, but at a very young, frightened girl, lost in a strange world, but resolved upon courage. She saw more than the men could see. She saw the loveliness, the helplessness, and she saw too the sensitive dignity, the delicate, defensive spirit....

Really, she was a child.

And to have gone through so much, dared such danger.... She remembered that dark, forbidding palace, the guarded doors, the hideous blacks - and that bright, smiling figure in its misty veil.... And now that little figure sat in its strange hiding place, confronting her with a lost child's eyes....

Into Jinny's bright gray eyes came a mist of tears. She was queerly moved. It was a mingled emotion, but if some drops for her own disconcertment were mingled with the warm prompting of pity, her compassion was none the less true.

"I'll be so glad to do anything I can to help," she said impulsively. "If you have no friends to trust in Cairo - "

"I have no friends to trust - beyond this room," said the girl.

"Then I'll take you to the hotel with me. You can register as one of our party and keep your room till we leave - we are going in four days now. And, oh, I know! You can cross on the same steamer with us to Europe, for there's a woman at the hotel who wants to give up her transportation and go on to the Holy Land - she was moaning about it only this noon. It would all fit in beautifully."

It seemed to McLean that an angel from Heaven was revealing her blessed goodness.

Ryder took the revelation delightedly for granted.

"Bully for you, Jinny," he said warmly. "I knew I could count on you."

If for one moment a twinge of wry reminder recalled that she had never been able exactly to count upon him it did not dim his mood. He was alight with triumph.

"I'll see to the transportation, " he said quickly, doing mental arithmetic about present sums in the bank. "And we won't wire your aunt until you're safely out of Egypt - better send a wireless from the ship. I think your aunt is near Paris - "

"We are going to hurry to Paris," said Jinny, "That was our regular plan - "

"And London?" said McLean.

"London, later, of course. Cathedrals, lakes and universities - then London."

"I shall be in London," said McLean thoughtfully, "in June.... If you are not too occupied - "

"With cathedrals?" said Miss Jeffries.

"Where are the things?" demanded Ryder ruthlessly, and thus recalled, Jinny produced the bag.

McLean moved toward the door. "We might go and mount guard in the corridor," he suggested, and he and Jinny stepped outside, back into the everyday world of Egypt where nothing at all had been happening but the arrival of a caravan from the excavations.

Within the room Ryder stooped and lifted the girl from the case and set her lightly on the floor. Ruefully she shook out the torn chiffons of that French audacity of a robe, and with a whimsical smile surveyed the soiled little slippers that she had discarded in her disguise when she had ridden behind the turbaned Ryder upon the Arab horse.

So little time ago, and yet so long away -

Under her long lashes she looked up at the young man, who had set the old life crumbling about her at a touch. Wistfulness edged the brave smile with which she murmured, "And so it is all arranged - so quick. I am safe - I go to the hotel with that nice girl - "

"And I won't be able to see you," he said suddenly.

"But you have seen me, monsieur, these many days - "

"Seen you? I haven't seen you. I've sat outside a tomb on guard, I've marched beside a mummy case - and - and we've said so little - "

It was true. They had said little. The hours had been absorbed in action. Their words had always been of explanation, of reassurance, of anxious planning. Of the future, the future after safety had been achieved, they had said nothing. It had all been uncertain, nebulous, vague....

And now it was upon them.

"And I have never said Thank you," she murmured. "I - I think I began by saying Thank you, monsieur. I remember saying that my education had proceeded to the Ts!"

"If - if only you never want to unsay it," he muttered. "You don't know what's ahead - life's so uncertain - "

"No, I do not know what is ahead," she told him, "but I am free - free for whatever will come."

The brightness of that freedom shone suddenly from her upturned face.

"Anything is better than that man," she vowed. "Even if my aunt, that Madame Delcasse, should not like me - you see, I have thought of everything, and I am not afraid."

"Like you - ? She'll love you," said Ryder bitterly. "She'll go mad over you and give you all she has - she'll marry you to a count - "

"Another marriage?" Aimee raised brows of mockery. "But I am through with the marriages of convenience - "

"You're so lovely, darling, that you'll have the world at your feet," said the young man huskily.

He looked at her with eyes that could not hide their pain. "Oh, I - you - it's not fair - " he muttered incoherently.

He had meant - ever since that sobering moment of guardianship in the desert - to be very fair. He would not bind her with a word, a touch. Not since that impulsive clasp of reunion in the palace had he touched her in caress. With the reverence of his deep tenderness he had served her in the tomb, meaning to deny his heart, to delay its revelation, to wait upon her freedom and her youth....

Nobly he had resolved.... But now parting was upon him.

"It's not fair to you," he said desperately - and drew closer.

For at his blurted words her look had magically changed. The defensive lightness was fled. A breathless wonder shone out at him ... a delicious shyness brushed with dancing expectation like the gleam of a butterfly's wing.

No glamorous moonlight was about them now. No scented shadowy garden.... But the enchantment was there, in the bare and dusty room, with its grim old mummy cases, the enchantment and the very flame of youth.

"Sweet, I'll be on the ship - I'll wait till you are ready," he vowed and at her low murmur, "Ready - ?" he gave back, "Ready - for love," with a boy's stammer over the first sound of that word between them.

"But what is this now," she said wondering, yet with a little elfish gleam of laughter, "but - love?"

His last resolve went to the winds.

And as his arms closed about her, as he held to his heart all that young loveliness that had been his despair and his delight, there was more than joy in the confused tumult of his youth, there was the supreme exultation of triumphant daring.

For he had opened the forbidden door; he had challenged the adventure and overcome the risk.

He had won. And he would hold his winnings.

"Aimee," he whispered. "Aimee - Beloved."

# Choose from Thousands of 1stWorldLibrary Classics By

Adolphus WilliamWard
Aesop
Agatha Christie
Alexander Aaronsohn
Alexander Kielland
Alexandre Dumas
Alfred Gatty
Alfred Ollivant
Alice Duer Miller
Alice Turner Curtis
Alice Dunbar
Ambrose Bierce
Amelia E. Barr
Andrew Lang
Andrew McFarland Davis
Anna Sewell
Annie Besant
Annie Hamilton Donnell
Annie Payson Call
Anton Chekhov
Arnold Bennett
Arthur Conan Doyle
Arthur Ransome
Atticus
B. M. Bower
Basil King
Bayard Taylor
Ben Macomber
Booth Tarkington
Bram Stoker
C. Collodi
C. E. Orr
C. M. Ingleby
Carolyn Wells
Catherine Parr Traill
Charles A. Eastman
Charles Dickens
Charles Dudley Warner
Charles Farrar Browne
Charles Ives
Charles Kingsley
Charles Lathrop Pack
Charles Whibley
Charles Willing Beale
Charlotte M. Braeme
Charlotte M.Yonge
Clair W. Hayes
Clarence Day Jr.
Clarence E. Mulford

Clemence Housman
Confucius
Cornelis DeWitt Wilcox
Cyril Burleigh
D. H. Lawrence
Daniel Defoe
David Garnett
Don Carlos Janes
Donald Keyhole
Dorothy Kilner
Dougan Clark
E. Nesbit
E.P.Roe
E. Phillips Oppenheim
Edgar Allan Poe
Edgar Rice Burroughs
Edith Wharton
Edward J. O'Biren
John Cournos
Edwin L. Arnold
Eleanor Atkins
Elizabeth Cleghorn
Gaskell
Elizabeth Von Arnim
Ellem Key
Emily Dickinson
Erasmus W. Jones
Ernie Howard Pie
Ethel Turner
Ethel Watts Mumford
Eugenie Foa
Eugene Wood
Evelyn Everett-Green
Everard Cotes
F. J. Cross
Federick Austin Ogg
Ferdinand Ossendowski
Francis Bacon
Francis Darwin
Frances Hodgson Burnett
Frank Gee Patchin
Frank Harris
Frank Jewett Mather
Frank L. Packard
Frederick Trevor Hill
Frederick Winslow Taylor
Friedrich Kerst
Friedrich Nietzsche
Fyodor Dostoyevsky

Gabrielle E. Jackson
Garrett P. Serviss
Gaston Leroux
George Ade
Geroge Bernard Shaw
George Ebers
George Eliot
George MacDonald
George Orwell
George Tucker
George W. Cable
George Wharton James
Gertrude Atherton
Grace E. King
Grant Allen
Guillermo A. Sherwell
Gulielma Zollinger
Gustav Flaubert
H. A. Cody
H. B. Irving
H. G. Wells
H. H. Munro
H. Irving Hancock
H. Rider Haggard
H. W. C. Davis
Hamilton Wright Mabie
Hans Christian Andersen
Harold Avery
Harold McGrath
Harriet Beecher Stowe
Harry Houidini
Helent Hunt Jackson
Helen Nicolay
Hendy David Thoreau
Henrik Ibsen
Henry Adams
Henry Ford
Henry Frost
Henry James
Henry Jones Ford
Henry Seton Merriman
Henry Wadsworth
Longfellow
Henry W Longfellow
Herbert A. Giles
Herbert N. Casson
Herman Hesse
Homer
Honore De Balzac

Horace Walpole
Horatio Alger, Jr.
Howard Pyle
Howard R. Garis
Hugh Lofting
Hugh Walpole
Humphry Ward
Ian Maclaren
Israel Abrahams
J.G.Austin
J. Henri Fabre
J. M. Barrie
J. Macdonald Oxley
J. S. Knowles
J. Storer Clouston
Jack London
Jacob Abbott
James Allen
James Lane Allen
James Andrews
James Baldwin
James DeMille
James Joyce
James Oliver Curwood
James Oppenheim
James Otis
Jane Austen
Jens Peter Jacobsen
Jerome K. Jerome
John Burroughs
John F. Kennedy
John Gay
John Glasworthy
John Habberton
John Joy Bell
John Milton
John Philip Sousa
Jonathan Swift
Joseph Carey
Joseph Conrad
Joseph Jacobs
Julian Hawthrone
Julies Vernes
Justin Huntly McCarthy
Kakuzo Okakura
Kenneth Grahame
Kate Langley Bosher
L. A. Abbot
L. T. Meade
L. Frank Baum
Laura Lee Hope

Laurence Housman
Leo Tolstoy
Leonid Andreyev
Lewis Carroll
Lilian Bell
Lloyd Osbourne
Louis Tracy
Louisa May Alcott
Lucy Fitch Perkins
Lucy Maud Montgomery
Lydia Miller Middleton
Lyndon Orr
M. H. Adams
Margaret E. Sangster
Margaret Vandercook
Maria Edgeworth
Maria Thompson Daviess
Mariano Azuela
Marion Polk Angellotti
Mark Overton
Mark Twain
Mary Austin
Mary Cole
Mary Rowlandson
Mary Wollstonecraft
Shelley
Max Beerbohm
Myra Kelly
Nathaniel Hawthrone
O. F. Walton
Oscar Wilde
Owen Johnson
P.G.Wodehouse
Paul and Mable Thorn
Paul G. Tomlinson
Paul Severing
Peter B. Kyne
Plato
R. Derby Holmes
R. L. Stevenson
Rabindranath Tagore
Rahul Alvares
Ralph Waldo Emmerson
Rene Descartes
Rex E. Beach
Richard Harding Davis
Richard Jefferies
Robert Barr
Robert Frost
Robert Gordon Anderson
Robert L. Drake

Robert Lansing
Robert Michael Ballantyne
Robert W. Chambers
Rosa Nouchette Carey
Ross Kay
Rudyard Kipling
Samuel B. Allison
Samuel Hopkins Adams
Sarah Bernhardt
Selma Lagerlof
Sherwood Anderson
Sigmund Freud
Standish O'Grady
Stanley Weyman
Stella Benson
Stephen Crane
Stewart Edward White
Stijn Streuvels
Swami Abhedananda
Swami Parmananda
T. S. Ackland
The Princess Der Ling
Thomas A. Janvier
Thomas A Kempis
Thomas Anderton
Thomas Bailey Aldrich
Thomas Bulfinch
Thomas De Quincey
Thomas H. Huxley
Thomas Hardy
Thomas More
Thornton W. Burgess
U. S. Grant
Valentine Williams
Victor Appleton
Virginia Woolf
Walter Scott
Washington Irving
Wilbur Lawton
Wilkie Collins
Willa Cather
Willard F. Baker
William Makepeace
Thackeray
William W. Walter
Winston Churchill
Yei Theodora Ozaki
Young E. Allison
Zane Grey